ANNIE'S BONES

OTHER BOOKS BY HOWARD OWEN

ANNIE'S BONES

HOWARD OWEN

THE PERMANENT PRESS
Sag Harbor, NY 11963

For information, address:
   The Permanent Press
   4170 Noyac Road
   Sag Harbor, NY 11963
   www.thepermanentpress.com

Library of Congress Cataloging-in-Publication Data

   Owen, Howard, author.
      Annie's bones / Howard Owen.
      Sag Harbor, NY: Permanent Press, [2018]
      ISBN: 978-1-57962-522-1
         1. Mystery fiction.

   PS3565.W552 A815 2018
   813'.54—dc23   2018003373

Printed in the United States of America

To Karen, who sustains me

CHAPTER ONE

May 13, 2016

He doesn't recognize the voice at first. It has been a long time.

"Enjoy your last few days of freedom, asshole," the man says. "They found her. They found Annie."

He sets down the spade and puts both hands on his knees. Squatting like an arthritic catcher in the Virginia mud, he looks out across the backyard fence and wonders what took them so long.

If the town of Portman hadn't evolved so much in forty-eight years that it finally was deemed worthy of a Food Lion, her body might have rested undisturbed until doomsday.

A backhoe operator dug up her bones four days earlier and called the cops. Along with remnants of her skirt and blouse and shoes, the deputy sheriff found the gold necklace. The cursive script, clear as day once the mud was washed off, read A.L.L.

The state police checked in Virginia and then, just across the state line, in North Carolina, where they made a match.

BEFORE GRAYSON Melvin can tuck one last tomato plant into the wet dirt and stand upright, the second call comes.

"Gray?"

He waits for it.

"Somebody from the state police was here just now."

There is a pause, and Betsy's voice seems to crack a little. "What's all this about?"

Maybe, he thinks, full disclosure wouldn't have been such a bad idea.

CHAPTER TWO

1968

He hadn't been in many bars, so there wasn't much basis for comparison. This one, though, had promise. It was mostly empty, and the jukebox was playing "She's a Rainbow" far enough below the threshold of pain to allow for conversation.

After that, the song would always sucker punch him and kick his ass back to 1968.

This was good, he thought. He felt certain that he talked better than he either looked or danced. Getting and holding the attention of a stranger would be easier if he didn't have to scream his best lines into her ear while other strangers, maybe her roommate or some of her friends, judged his performance. Without the second beer, he might not have had the nerve to do what he did.

This time, at least, there was no audience.

If she noticed him, approaching from the right as she sat alone at the bar, she didn't give it away.

He reached into his pocket with his left hand.

When he spoke, she turned toward him, not startled but not letting on that she'd already seen him either.

"I saw you there," he said, trying to modulate his voice, "and I wanted to meet you."

He pushed up his black-rim glasses, Buddy Holly without charisma.

Her smile was thin as a razor blade.

"What if I don't want to meet you?"

She looked like she might be a freshman, too, but he could tell she was out of his league. Hell, she was the majors and he was rookie ball. She was blonde. She was tall and thin, but not too much of either. From what he could see, acceptable butt and nice tits. She had model cheekbones and a perfect little nose. Her eyes, blue as an October Carolina sky, weren't sizing him up, at least not head-on. She was looking into the mirror behind the bar, the one in which she no doubt saw him coming.

Why, he wondered, are you here alone? Why are you ever alone?

Maybe, you dumb-ass, his interior critic whispered, because she wants to be alone.

He took a breath and dove in, all nothing-to-lose mode now.

"I have a proposition for you," he said, taking out the egg timer he'd removed from his pocket.

She smiled. It was an off-center smile, a heard-it-before smile. It was a good smile nonetheless, one that came with dimples. It softened her and maybe gave him courage beyond what the two Budweisers had afforded already.

"You're propositioning me?"

He set his beer on the bar. Then he set the egg timer beside it. An older boy in the dorm had told him about this "smooth move," even gave him the cheap prop.

"Here it is," he said. "We might not have a thing in common, might hate each other's guts, and you're way too pretty to be seen with me, but all I'm asking is three minutes. When I turn this thing over, it'll take three minutes for all the sand to run out. If you're not interested, or I'm not interested, after three minutes, I'll leave you alone."

She lifted her elbow off the bar and took a sip of her own beer. She looked at him, the mischief in her eyes and arched brows promising great reward or great humiliation. He thought she was about to tell him to get lost, but for some reason she didn't.

"OK," she said. "Flip it."

He did. He started talking, trying to win points without looking at the sand slipping away, trying not to be, for three minutes, the geeky eighteen-year-old who would be carded in bars until wars foreign and domestic gave him hard-won maturity. He reminded himself to breathe.

"Where are you from?"

She said she was from the girls' school that adjoined the joint where they were sitting.

"No, where did you come from? Where did you grow up?"

"A little town outside Charlotte. Monroe."

He had been through Monroe. Thinking of her as being from there made her seem less intimidating.

"How about politics?"

She looked at him as if he had asked what color underwear she wore, but she answered.

"Democrat. Liberal. Doesn't make me too popular around here. I think some of my classmates have Klan sheets in their closets."

He told her about his sixth-grade year. He and his cousin were the only boys in their class who were for Kennedy. He couldn't have told her why, really, just an affinity for the underdog, and in the small Coastal Plains town where he grew up, Kennedy was an underdog with fleas and ticks.

"They chased us around the schoolyard every recess for a month, but they never caught us. We were pretty fast."

She laughed, more straightforward than her earlier smile.

"Yeah," she said, "I can see that you're pretty fast."

He went a little deeper.

"Beatles or Stones?"

"Oh, Stones, I guess."

"Yeah," he said. "I think everybody's so hot on the Beatles, it almost makes me not want to like them."

She took another sip and nodded.

"What do you want to do? I mean, what do you plan to major in?"

She shrugged.

"Hell if I know. English maybe. Something that'll get me into law school. Daddy kind of expects that."

That threw him for a couple of seconds, as the sand kept slipping away. His father didn't expect anything that grand. Just being the first college graduate in a long and inauspicious line of Melvins would be more than enough.

She asked her first question.

"How about you?"

"Journalism, I think."

"Huh," she said. "Not business. Seems like all the boys I meet are going into business."

"Yeah," he said, "that'd be the smart move."

"But you're not too smart."

"Yeah. Dumb and ugly. That's me."

He'd already figured that he'd be working for the next forty years or so, doing something. He knew men who were accountants or ran businesses. What they did, he told her, didn't appeal to him.

"And forty years seems like a long time to do something you don't like."

She nodded.

"Good move. As long as you can feed yourself."

"I don't eat much," he said.

"So you want to work for a newspaper?"

"It's worse than that. I want to be a sportswriter."

"Huh," was all she said.

The top half of the egg timer was empty. She looked down, then at her watch.

"Flip it again," she said.

EVERYTHING JAMES Grayson Melvin brought to college fit in the trunk of the very-used Valiant he'd managed to buy with money he saved working for a moving-and-storage company after his junior and senior years of high school, plus a small donation from his grandparents. He wouldn't even have a record player, a suitcase-style stereo that barely fit into the double dorm room, until after Christmas.

His father wasn't busting his buttons over the whole college thing. It was out of Jimmy's comfort zone. He'd dropped out in the eleventh grade, because he broke his leg in a wreck that killed his girlfriend, and because he freely admitted that he didn't care that much for books. School, Gray's father once told him, was for girls. The only books in the house were the Bible, *Gone with the Wind*, a few romance novels from a long-ago fling his mother had with the Book of The Month Club, and the Funk & Wagnalls encyclopedia set, purchased a week and a letter at a time. The set only went through R. Gray's mother left between R and S.

His father would much rather have had a son who was a starting forward or halfback or center fielder instead of one who was class valedictorian and had 20-200 vision. He didn't say it out loud much, though, and Gray appreciated that. When he got a partial scholarship and a loan, Jimmy didn't really fight him over it, although he wondered why he didn't join the army or air force like so many of the other boys. World War II, Jimmy said, had been the making of him.

"Maybe later," Grayson Melvin told his father.

Since his mother went away, the two of them hadn't talked much about anything. His father preferred playing sports to watching them on TV, and they both knew to avoid politics, which had spoiled more than one supper.

When Gray had packed the car, and was getting ready to circle the driveway and head north to Chapel Hill, his father did not give him some overarching, big-picture speech about opportunities and goals, the way Gray came to learn some of his classmates had been lectured by their dads.

"Just remember," Jimmy Melvin said, as Gray started the car and looked out the window at his father, who spoke softly enough that Gray's little sister, standing to one side trying not to cry, probably couldn't hear, "a stiff dick has no conscience."

As if, Gray thought, mine's going to have many chances to be bad.

THE FIRST semester had gone well enough. Gray managed a near-3.0 average, which qualified him as acceptably smart without being over-the-top geeky among the arbiters of cool in his slacker dorm. It was a time and place where white boys with college degrees, not fettered by the troublesome competition of minorities or many female students, could count on cashing in those diplomas for a ticket on the fast track, if not to great riches, at least to a place one or two rungs farther up the dream ladder than their Depression-reared parents could reach.

The "gentlemanly C" was enough.

One junior in Gray's dorm, who'd played freshman football and held the new boys in his thrall, summed it up for
them: "If you give a shit, you ain't worth a shit."

He wrote home once a week, usually to Kaycee, who was
four years younger and left to fend for herself against the
ever-changing weather system circulating around their mer-
curial father. Gray went home for a weekend a month after
classes started and again at Thanksgiving, then spent the
long Christmas holiday back in East Geddie, which already
didn't feel as much like home as it had four months earlier.

Gray hadn't dated much in high school, and the girls
he dated usually were the ones he secretly felt were beneath
him. The girls who were both smart and pretty could do
better, and they did. He had never, on his departure for college, had even his hands, let alone his conscienceless penis,
within the bounds of a girl's panties.

The first semester at Carolina, it was no better. He had
a couple of dates with girls back home, on his infrequent
visits. His new status as college boy, in a town where almost
no one went beyond high school, only seemed to brand him
as different, rather than exotic or sex-worthy.

And there were so few girls on campus that a freshman
like Gray had little chance of success. The knowledge of
that hopelessness made things even more hopeless. Gray was
struck dumb by the girls from such bastions of culture and
taste as Charlotte or Winston-Salem, the best of whom were
claimed by the football team and the more well-heeled fraternity boys anyhow.

Early in the second semester, though, on a Friday night
the first week of February, opportunity knocked, mainly
because Gray had a car. Freshmen weren't supposed to have
them, but he paid a couple who lived a few blocks off campus
to let him park it there.

His roommate, a boy who had acne and chain-smoked, had an idea.

"Let's go to Chatham. I know a guy who says there's gonna be a party there, and the girls are wild. Pussy galore."

Chatham was a private college an hour away, in a town smaller than Chapel Hill. Its main attraction, as everyone at Carolina knew, was the women's college there. It consisted of nine hundred girls and no college-boy competition other than those hardy souls who risked the narrow, twisting road, rich with twenty-mile-per-hour curves, between there and I-85.

The three of them—Gray, the roommate, and the roommate's friend—made the trip, drinking a six-pack on the way up for courage. When they got there, they found out that the friend's information was either accidentally or intentionally bullshit. There was no party, but there was a bar just off campus, and they found to their delight that most of the bar's denizens were coeds from Chatham.

Gray met a girl that night. It was thrilling to go outside to the car and make out with someone he had met only an hour before. He felt liberated, like he could reinvent himself. He and the roommate made another trip back up to Chatham a week later and met two other girls who seemed amenable to spending time in the back seats of strange boys' cars.

The third time, was a Saturday. A girl back home had canceled a date with Gray on the spur of the moment, and his roommate had gone home to New Jersey for a wedding. And so Gray went to Chatham by himself.

That's where he found Annie Lineberger, who changed his life.

HE MET her around five in the afternoon. They talked for the better part of an hour. After a while, he stopped flipping the egg timer.

It was sheer luck, although it would not turn out to be the kind he originally thought. She'd been invited to a dance at the University of Virginia by a guy she knew from somewhere, a junior. He had called and canceled the day before, claiming he had to spend the whole weekend studying.

"Which is complete bullshit," she said. She said it with no hint of anger. "Winston would never spend a weekend studying."

She shrugged.

"His loss."

"I can't even imagine a guy dumb enough to stand you up," Gray said. "Now, me, I'm a veteran at getting the shaft."

And he proceeded to tell her about the girl who'd bagged out on their date back in East Geddie. His instincts told him he was wise not to pretend with this girl, who seemed able to see through him right to his uncool core. He decided to roll the dice and bet that honesty, a reasonable amount of intelligence, and a sense of humor would see him through.

"She was about half as pretty as you though," he added at the end of his sad tale, "so I'm not complaining."

Annie accepted the compliment without false modesty.

"Well," she said, giving Gray a light punch on the arm that somehow seemed intimate, "you're about twice as nice as the guy who stiffed me."

Annie was considerably more attractive and seemed smarter than the two Chatham girls he'd met earlier. He knew, even with his limited experience, that she was something special.

When he asked her what she was doing for dinner, though, she told him she already had plans to eat with a couple of her girlfriends.

"But if you want to come along, if you don't mind spending the evening at a hen party, you're welcome to join us."

Maybe she was just being polite, but Gray accepted. What else did he have to do except drive back to Chapel Hill? Plus, he would have followed her to hell by that time.

Annie had a car and insisted on driving. The evening went as well as such an evening could. They ate at a place that served hot dogs "steeped in beer." ("Whatever in the hell that is," Annie said.) Then they drank some beer without the hot dogs. (These days, Gray wonders what college kids do on dates, since the drinking age has been raised to twenty-one.)

Annie would reach over and squeeze his arm or smile at him from time to time. The other two girls were nice to Gray, and they were kind enough to leave him and Annie alone when they got back to the dorm.

She drove him back to his car. He got out on his side and she got out on hers.

"So," she said, as they stood toe to toe. "Aren't you going to kiss me?"

He leaned down slightly (she was almost as tall as he was) and kissed her, tenderly like a sister, on the forehead. He couldn't have told you then, or even now, why he did it like that.

She looked surprised, but when he asked her what she was doing the next day, a Sunday, she said she wasn't sure. And when he suggested that he drive back up and take her out somewhere, maybe up to the mountains, she agreed.

Gray didn't even know how to get to the mountains from there, but with the aid of a road map and a couple of suggestions from two guys in the dorm who lived in the foothills, he figured it out.

He made his return trip to Chatham the next afternoon. The trip to the mountains was about as ill-planned as possible. There was a threat of snow, and the sun didn't stay up much later than five thirty. They ate a late lunch at a place that served french fries with gravy.

Still Annie seemed to appreciate the effort, and he was shocked to see how easy it was to talk to her. The girls back home never seemed on the same wavelength, and with them he could never get over the idea that it was all a contest. He was supposed to try to get into their pants, and they were supposed to stop him.

Maybe the sisterly kiss the night before helped. For whatever reason, they both seemed at ease with each other, right from the start. They got as far as the Blue Ridge Parkway, only to find out that it was closed because of the approaching snow. They had talked all the way there, and the closure seemed only a minor setback, as if the journey truly was the important thing.

On the way back, with darkness approaching, Annie grabbed his arm and said, "Turn here."

She guided him to a manmade lake at the foot of the mountains, completely deserted on this raw February day. There was a parking lot. When Gray stopped the car, he looked at her and said, "Now what?"

She smiled.

"What do you think?"

CHAPTER THREE

MAY 13, 2016

The Virginia state police arrive at Betsy Fordyce's house in less than half an hour.

Gray thinks about a lot of things in that half hour, among them just turning and running. Then he considers calling an attorney, maybe the one who did his will.

In the end, though, he just gets up, brushes the dirt off his pants, goes inside, and waits for it.

It had been a long time coming, long enough that sometimes he felt the past would bury itself, that he could get away with not mentioning it ever again, even to someone with whom he was spending many of his nights and days. But deep down, he has to admit to himself now, he knew it was coming. He thinks of the one-word sign he once saw beside a small-town mortuary. EVENTUALLY.

He figures the state police must have gone by the place he was renting first, and someone there, maybe his nosy neighbors, told them who he was shacking up with and where she works. "Shacking up." That's the way they would have put it, the judgmental bastards. Too bad they didn't know where Betsy lives. They could have saved her some embarrassment at work.

HE ANSWERS on the first knock. The two troopers ask if he's James Grayson Melvin, and he admits that he is. They ask if they can come in. He hesitates but then opens the door wide.

The older one, with close-cut gray hair now uncovered, seems to be in charge. He lets Gray get comfortable on the leather couch. The two of them perch on the edge of their chairs, facing him.

"We need to ask you about Anne Lawson Lineberger."

Gray nods his head, then thinks that perhaps he should have acted at least a little surprised.

The older one tells him about how they found "remains" outside Portman, down near the state line.

"They matched dental records," he says. "And there was a necklace with her initials."

He looks at the younger one, who is taking notes.

"They tell us you were investigated when she disappeared, back in 1968."

Gray nods again.

"They couldn't find a body. But now they have."

Gray looks the older trooper in the eye.

"Is there something you want to ask me?"

"Just a couple of things," the trooper says, "but I'm sure there are some people who will be asking you a whole bunch of questions pretty soon. We mainly just wanted to make sure you were here."

The other one looks grim and acts like he wants to ask some questions right damn now.

Gray looks at his watch, and as he looks at it, he hears a school bus in the distance, maybe two blocks away.

He stands, and the troopers stand, as if they think he's getting ready to make a dash for freedom.

"My, uh, my girlfriend's grandson. I have to meet him at the bus."

They seem to be contemplating the wisdom of letting him walk out the front door. Maybe they remember that they don't really have the right to detain him, and they step aside.

They walk out with him and watch as he hurries as fast as his bum knee will let him to the bus stop, half a block away. Josh comes bounding off, unhindered by a backpack that's about two-thirds as big as he is. It always amazes Gray how much weight they lay on a nine-year-old these days.

Gray thinks the boy might have back problems later on, but he won't have to worry about being abducted. Betsy is adamant about him meeting Josh the minute he steps off the bus.

As they walk back to the house, with Gray trying to tell the boy as quickly as he can why two men holding pointy hats in their hands are standing at their front door, he looks at the school bus as it passes. Young faces are pressed against the glass. Cop cars and state troopers aren't regular visitors in Betsy Fordyce's leafy west Richmond neighborhood.

They are almost to the house when Betsy gets there. She opens the garage door with the remote and parks the Lexus. When she comes around to the front walk, the look she gives Gray tells him what he already knows: She hates surprises.

"What's this about?" she asks the older trooper. Obviously he didn't share with her when they contacted her at the hospital.

"Can we go back inside?"

"Hell, no," she says. "And you better have a warrant next time you come around here."

Gray puts his arm on her elbow. She tries to pull away, but he hangs on.

"They need to talk to me about something, Betsy," he says. "It's about something that happened a long time ago."

Something in his voice tells her that she should let the two troopers back into her house.

"I'll tell you about it later," he tells her, speaking low.

"It better not be much later," she says. Her mouth is a tight line, a slit from which words come out like bullets.

Gray leads the troopers into Betsy's study and closes the door. They stay for another half hour, asking questions about Annie Lineberger that will surely be asked many more times.

As they leave, the older one states the obvious.

"Don't plan on taking any long trips."

Betsy comes up to him as he stands there, holding on to the just-closed door for support, his eyes closed.

She takes his arm and looks up into his eyes.

"Tell me. Tell me, damn you."

Betsy Fordyce is the best thing to come into Grayson Melvin's life in quite some time.

They met through something Gray never thought he'd be part of: an online dating service. He was getting diminishing returns from a series of girlfriends as age began to tip the scales away from whatever looks and charm he once had. The women in his life tended to leave him before he left them. After the long-ago divorce, he decided that marriage wasn't for him, but single life wasn't exactly lighting up his world either.

On the questionnaire, he didn't lie too much about his pluses and minuses, didn't gild the lilies or polish the turds, and Betsy didn't either. They found that they had more in common with each other than they had with their former spouses. They both liked to travel. They both had a fondness for screened-in porches and college football. They both preferred bourbon, either on the rocks or with just a splash.

They had a few friends in common. They laughed at the same jokes. And they "got along" in the bedroom, and still do, although Gray wonders whether the high PSA numbers he keeps getting will eventually curtail that particularly pleasant part of their relationship.

Betsy was forty-eight and he was sixty-two when they met. She was a nurse practitioner at Richmond's big teaching hospital, widowed and in the process of taking over Josh's upbringing. Gray was estranged from just about everything except his job of trying to inflict English on community college students. The fact that her salary was more than twice Gray's didn't seem to bother her.

Neither does "the age thing." With her hair dyed blonde and her body showing the results of five hard workouts a week, she looks a good twenty years younger than Gray.

"Men," she told him once, "can get away with getting old."

Three years ago, he proposed leaving his apartment and moving in full time. Betsy said she wasn't sure. By then she was committed to raising her six-year-old grandson, and she said that her life was complicated enough, that she thought they shouldn't "rock the boat."

"Things are good," she said. "Why change?"

He wondered if some of it was because Betsy's tony West End neighbors might have disapproved of his moving in, although they surely were aware that his car was parked in her garage more nights than not. He wondered if he should have proposed marriage instead of offering to just move in. He still hadn't taken that step, maybe out of fear of what Betsy would say.

Now it's too late.

GRAY TELLS Betsy what he should have told her years ago. He tells her about how he and Annie Lineberger met, about that spring, and finally about what happened the last Friday night in April of 1968. He tells her about everything that followed, the part of his life he thought he'd left behind.

There are people in Richmond, and many in East Geddie, NC, who know parts of the story. A couple of them know almost all of it. But with years turning into decades, the story had become almost as securely buried as Annie's body. Now, like those sad bones in that soon-to-be Food Lion parking lot, it is about to be disinterred.

"I don't know," Gray says when Betsy asks him for the second time why he didn't tell her before now. "I guess I figured it would be the end of us, if you knew."

She doesn't say anything for a long time.

Out of the corner of his eye, he sees Josh peeking around the corner at the top of the stairs.

"Well," she says when she finally speaks, "I'm speechless. I mean, I thought I knew you."

He gets up and goes to the kitchen to pour some Knob Creek over ice. He comes back and hands one glass to Betsy.

"You do know me. You just didn't know me then. And who was going to believe me? If I'd told you the truth, would you have believed me?"

She takes it as a serious question.

"Yes," she says finally, "I think I would have."

"Well, then you'd have been in a small minority."

Gray has seen so many people, over the years, pretend to believe him when he tells them he's innocent. Some didn't even bother pretending. It has been a great relief to him to see the incident fade from memory, but now it has been revived in spectacular fashion on this damnable day.

They hear a truck pull up outside. Betsy looks through the open curtains. The vehicle has the insignia of one of the local network TV stations on it.

Gray stands up.

"I should leave."

As she watches a well-coiffed female reporter and a cameraman approach the front door, she puts her hand on his.

"No," she says. "Stay."

GRAY FIGURES someone in law enforcement must have told someone at one of the local stations about it. How else would a "news team" be at the front door already, with the chairs where the state police officers sat still warm?

Betsy is less than kind in dispatching the reporter. Gray can see that the camera is live, and he cringes to think of his girlfriend telling the young woman to get the hell off her front porch.

"Well," Betsy says when the front door closes and a temporary peace sets in, "at least I didn't tell her to fuck off."

Josh, eavesdropping, reminds his granny that she owes twenty-five cents to the cursing jar. She rolls her eyes, takes a dollar bill out of her purse, walks over to the retired goldfish bowl in the kitchen, and drops it in.

"The way things are going," she says, "I'll probably say it at least three more times today."

Things calm down until the TV station that got the hot tip leads with the recovered body on the six o'clock news.

"A local man is implicated in a girl's disappearance almost half a century ago," the breathless anchor says before four minutes of commercials.

They devote five minutes to the story, getting almost half the facts right, by Gray's estimation. They make Annie out to have been some kind of teenage runaway rather than the upper-crust, well-grounded girl he remembers. They say Grayson Melvin was a student at Chatham rather than the

University of North Carolina. They insinuate that he was the kind of predator who took advantage of innocent young women.

"Good God," he says, sitting next to Betsy on the couch. "Didn't anybody check this crap before they aired it?"

Betsy reminds him that they could possibly have injected some facts into the story if she hadn't run off the reporter and her sidekick.

"Nah," Gray says. "They still would have gotten it wrong."

They have footage of "Elizabeth Fordyce, a longtime nurse and Grayson Melvin's girlfriend" running the interlopers off her front lawn.

"Nurse practitioner, goddammit," Betsy says to the TV.

"That's another quarter." Josh's voice comes from his room where he's supposed to be doing his homework.

The state police spokesman has no comment on the "ongoing investigation" but promises more developments "soon."

"And so," the anchor says, as Gray's ten-year-old ID photo from the community college where he teaches adorns the screen behind him, "a family in North Carolina wonders if this will finally bring closure to a tragedy. And Richmonders are left to ponder if a killer has been lurking undetected in their midst for more than forty years."

"Well," Gray says, "that just about does it."

He stands and turns to face Betsy.

"It'd be better if I went away for a little while."

She gets up and grabs his arm.

"The hell you will. You're not running."

"Not running, just getting somewhere else so that you won't be in the line of fire. How long is it going to take those other TV idiots to find their way to your door? I don't relish seeing a bunch of fat-ass cameramen stomping down all your azaleas."

"But where can you go?"

"Back to my place. I wouldn't mind seeing some of my neighbors discomfited a bit."

Betsy frowns.

"They'll hound you to death."

"They'd do that wherever I was."

She's quiet for a minute.

"No. You're going to stay right here. You don't need to be alone right now."

They're still debating the issue when Gray's cell phone buzzes.

He answers reluctantly. He listens silently for half a minute.

"I don't know . . . How did you find out?"

After another pause, he says, "I'm not sure. Betsy says I can stay here."

"Will stay here," she says, loud enough for the caller to hear.

"Well," he says to his phone, "maybe that wouldn't be such a bad idea. And it might be a good way to get the facts right."

He puts the phone back in his pocket.

"I'm going to stay at Willie's for a few days."

"Willie who?"

"Oh. Willie Black. You know. The reporter I've told you stories about. I've known him forever. He said he'd keep me at his place for a couple of days."

"And in exchange, he gets to interview you at his leisure."

"Well," Gray says, "I think Willie will get most of the facts right, at least. And maybe we both can avoid having to tell any cameramen to fuck off."

Gray has known Willie Black for thirty-six years, since Willie was a kid still in college working part-time at the paper and Gray was a full-time reporter before his own journalistic career was cut short by the ghost of Annie Lineberger.

It was later, as a bartender, that he became best acquainted with Willie. Gray always said that was because Willie Black spent a lot more time in barrooms than newsrooms.

Because they closed down more than one joint, with Gray either matching Willie drink for drink or bartending, and because Willie was good at teasing stories out of people, he told Willie Black more about Annie Lineberger than he's told anyone else in Richmond, although he didn't tell him everything. Even his wife back then wasn't privy to all the details he gave Willie.

To Gray's knowledge, Willie has not shared any of those details with another soul, either in person or in print, for all these years. Maybe that's why he thinks letting a broken-down night cops reporter pick him up and hide him from the rest of the media hounds isn't such a bad idea.

"I can trust Willie," Gray tells Betsy after she has accepted that he is indeed going.

"Just don't make it look like you're running away," she says.

"Only for a few days. Tell them I left to get my head straight, or some such nonsense."

"Should I get you a lawyer?"

Gray stops at the door and holds her by the shoulders.

"I guess so. I'm going to need one sooner or later. Maybe Willie knows somebody."

Betsy says she'll call Dan Finebaum, an old friend and a partner in one of Richmond's most reliable firms. Gray says that sounds good to him.

The landline phone has rung three times in the last twenty-five minutes. Betsy unplugged it after the third one. While they're talking, Gray's cell phone buzzes again.

"Yeah. OK," he says. "That might be a good idea."

Willie Black has driven by the house and seen what Betsy and Gray haven't noticed yet. Two vans bearing the logos of the two local network TV stations that didn't get the scoop on Annie Lineberger's bones are setting up shop across the street.

"Willie says he'll go around back and pick me up in the alley," he tells Betsy after he explains why the front door wouldn't be such a good idea.

He goes into Josh's room to tell him good-bye.

"Later, Alligator."

"Crocodile," the boy says, not looking up from the video game he's playing.

Then Gray pulls Betsy to him and gives her a kiss he hopes will only have to last a few days.

"Thank you," he says when they come up for air.

"For what?"

"For not asking me if I did it."

CHAPTER FOUR

1968

The two-plus months from the February frosts until the dogwood days of April come back to Gray now in a pastel haze. It is easy enough for a grown man to laugh at the mooniness of puppy love, but there is no time machine to correct the past.

The space between that night in Chatham and the one when it all ended now seems to have been several years long. Even the pain had a pleasure to it.

Gray's grade-point average his first semester wasn't enough to impress his father. Jimmy only said, "It looks like I'm getting my money's worth." Gray chose not to remind him that most of the expense of his UNC education, a laughable pittance by twenty-first-century standards, came from Gray's summer- and part-time jobs, his partial scholarship, or a student loan.

From the moment he met Annie Lineberger, his grades became a plummeting rock, a matter of secondary (if that) concern. His roommate, the one who introduced Gray to the "easy pickings" of the girls' school an hour away, worried aloud about the fact that Gray seemed to treat classes as an option rather than a necessity.

"Man," the zit-scarred roomie told him once when he found him sitting in the windowsill, staring silently out into the quad at two on an early spring afternoon, more or less in the same position in which he had left him at eight thirty that morning, "that girl's really got you by the balls."

Gray sometimes felt like he wasn't able to get enough oxygen. He kept a picture of Annie, the high school senior photograph she gave him when he gave her his East Geddie High School size-twelve class ring, in his wallet. He looked at it so often it was already beginning to fray the way his hopes would.

And he spent so much time on the two-lane road between Chapel Hill and Chatham that the clerk at the Quick Stop outside Mason's Mill where he stopped for cheap gas knew him on sight.

"Chasin' that Chatham pussy again," he would say, every time, grinning with a mouth only half full of teeth. Gray regretted having told the man once that he was headed for a date at the school. He hoped his lack of response to this crude greeting would give the guy a hint, but it never seemed to.

ANNIE LINEBERGER wasn't the only thing getting between Gray and academic competency that spring semester.

In the late fall, he had screwed up his nerve enough to go to the offices of the school newspaper and offer his services. He felt less than inadequate. The people who put out the daily campus paper all seemed incredibly worldly to him in the column photos and in the columns and news stories themselves. They wrote about issues of which Gray Melvin was only barely aware. A strike by university cafeteria and maintenance workers. A speaker who had been barred from appearing on campus because he was a Communist. The war. All Gray knew about the war was that the boys back home who didn't go to college were getting drafted and he wasn't, as long as he stayed in school.

He had been sports editor of his high school paper, literally cranking out the pages on the mimeograph machine, nearly dizzy from its funky sweet smell. He'd taken typing, in a class consisting mostly of girls aiming for secretarial jobs, but he didn't even own a typewriter.

That first November day (it had taken him two months to work up the courage), he walked into the newspaper's offices in the student union after his two o'clock class. He asked an upper-class girl at the front desk, who set down her phone and looked at him with annoyance, whom he should see about applying for a job.

"Go see Corrina," she said.

He gave her a blank look.

She sighed.

"Corrina. Corrina Corrina."

He wondered why she said it three times, but the girl picked the phone back up before he had a chance to ask her anything else and pointed him toward a young woman whose hair seemed to have caught fire. It grew in untamed, asymmetrical curls high above her pale, freckled face. It was the color of a new penny, only brighter. If the lights had all gone out, Gray thought, that hair would have served as illumination.

She was having an animated conversation with a male coworker whose face Gray recognized from the paper's editorial page column logos.

"I don't give a fuck what you think," she said. Gray had not heard many women say "fuck" before that. He deduced from vocabulary and her accent that she must be a Yankee.

She waved her arms as she talked, or rather yelled. "We are not going to run a piece making fun of the people who clean up our shit, who make less per month than your daddy probably gives you for beer money."

Gray was startled. The other fledgling journalists around her, though, must have regarded this as her normal speaking voice. No one even looked up.

The guy she was yelling at was trying to reach her decibel level, but even Gray could see he was getting the short end of it.

"Not so," he said, in a tone that was venturing very close to whiny. "They make more than a lot of people."

Corrina of the three names smiled a ten-watt smile. She looked like a cat about to toy with a small mammal before dispatching it.

"Name some."

"Well . . . sharecroppers. Those people that crop tobacco. And these folks at the cafeteria don't even have to work outdoors."

Corrina shook her head, then launched back into her rant.

She called him a privileged shit who wouldn't last half an hour doing what the janitors, maids, and counter-servers had to do to get by, working two jobs just to pay the bills. She told him he needed to get his head out of his ass and take a look at the real world, not the one his daddy had constructed for him "like a baby's playpen."

She was still reaming him a new one when he backed away, hands up in surrender, smiling.

"OK, Corrina Corrina," he said. "You made your point. Point taken. I'll come up with something else."

"Stop calling me that," she said, then went back to whatever she was composing on her typewriter. The wild mass of hair settled gradually back to Earth. She looked around the room and let go with what Gray could only describe as a cackle.

"The revolution is coming," she said, then cackled again.

The only visible reactions to all this, as far as Gray could see, were a couple of exchanged glances that seemed to be in the general range of "thank God it wasn't me this time."

He was sorely tempted to turn around and walk out. He'd always been a little on the introverted side, and he couldn't imagine how he would have handled being dressed down in front of his peers.

He had promised himself, though, that he would not let the big university cow him, no matter how much it went against his nature to step out of the shadows.

He walked over to Corrina's desk.

He cleared his throat.

"Excuse me."

He said it again, thinking she hadn't heard.

"What?"

"Um, I'm a freshman, and I'd like to work for the paper."

She stopped typing and looked up at him.

"What do you want to do?"

He cleared his throat again. He felt as if the whole room was listening to their conversation, although the clacking of typewriters made that unlikely.

"I'd like to be a sportswriter."

She looked up at him.

"I could've figured that. Every damn guy wants to be a sportswriter. Don't you want to do something more worthwhile?"

Gray thought sports was eminently worthwhile, but he thought it might not be a good time to argue the point.

"Well," he said, "maybe I could start in sports and grow into something worthwhile."

Corrina exploded. Her laugh was so loud and shrill that it hurt Gray's ears

"That's great," she said, wiping a tear from her right eye. "You hear that, Buddy? He's hoping he can grow out of toyland one day."

"Buddy" turned out to be the sports editor, a short-haired frat guy named Buddy Weeks. He squinted his eyes as he looked up at the freshman.

Gray felt that his face must be just about as red as this Corrina person's hair. He started to turn and walk away.

"Hey," she said, calling to him. "Where you going? Can you type? Do you know anything about wrestling?"

He said he could type fifty words a minute and lied about his knowledge of wrestling, which consisted at that time of watching the fake pro matches on Channel 5 in Raleigh when he was a kid and didn't know better.

She walked him over to Buddy Weeks, who didn't seem inclined to warm to a freshman who thought he might grow out of sports but nevertheless needed somebody to do a pre-season piece on the university's wrestling team.

"Three hundred words. Have it to me by tomorrow morning."

He gave him the coach's name and a vague description of where he might find him. Gray was afraid to ask for anything else. Walking back into the sunlight, he wondered where he was going to find a typewriter and somebody who knew shit about wrestling.

He wound up going back to the junior in his dorm who had played freshman football and happened to be in his room that afternoon. Gray figured football was close enough to wrestling that maybe the boy knew something. He had to know more about it than Gray did.

The junior might have been taken by Gray's honesty. ("I don't know anything about wrestling. I need help.") He'd wrestled in high school, and he gave his pupil a crash course, then told him he ought to get in touch with the sports information office, which was in the athletic department building.

"They've got brochures and shit," he said.

Gray got there before the office closed and persuaded the assistant sports information director to give him some basic information—a roster, a schedule, a rundown of who the top returning wrestlers were. The assistant told him the wrestling coach was out but probably would be in his office at eight in the morning.

Gray pumped his junior mentor for more information. In the morning, he was at the coach's door at 7:55, two minutes before the man himself, who had to double as a phys ed teacher to make ends meet.

Gray fell back again on ignorance, which he was finding to be a very useful tool for a journalist.

"I don't know as much as I should about wrestling," he told the coach. "We didn't have wrestling at my high school. They want me to write a story for the student newspaper. Can you please help me out?"

The wrestling coach didn't get interviewed much. His sport was below the radar of any publication other than the student paper on most days.

He gave him thirty uninterrupted minutes. At the end, Gray didn't know a lot about the intricacies of the sport, but he thought he knew enough to fake it.

Just after nine, he was at the student paper's office. Corrina Corrina, who turned out to be Corrine Manzi, was the only other person there. When he asked her if he might use one of the paper's typewriters, she seemed to suppress a smile and told him to take his pick.

"Just don't mess anybody's shit up," she said. Looking at the rat's nest of desk clutter around him, Gray wondered how anyone would know if he messed anybody's shit up.

He found that it wasn't that hard to write three hundred words about a sport of which he knew almost nothing. He quoted the coach (Gray also had taken another girl-centric course in high school, shorthand), mentioned the top return-ees and their records, and noted that the team hoped to use "senior leadership" to improve on its sixth-place finish in the conference the year before.

He counted the words. Two hundred and ninety-seven. He got up to take the two sheets of paper to Buddy Weeks's desk.

"Here," Corrina said. "Let me see that."

He brought it over. She read it, frowned, and made a couple of marks with a red pencil.

She looked up at him.

"Commas go inside the quote marks," she said, "but, not bad. You might do OK. You might even graduate from sports someday."

Gray did several stories for the paper that winter. Corrine Manzi treated him better than he ever thought she might, considering first impressions. She told Gray they started call-ing her "Corrina Corrina" because of a folk song that a would-be boyfriend of hers sang to her one day, arriving in the newsroom unannounced with his guitar.

"I wasn't too hot on him to start with," she told Gray when she surprised him by inviting him to have a cup of coffee with her in the student union one January day. "That kind of sealed the deal."

She was from Pittsburgh and was one of the small minority of out-of-state students. She said she already had a pretty good line on a job at the paper in her home city "but I'm hoping for something bigger."

Gray wondered what could be bigger than Pittsburgh.

BY THE time Annie Lineberger became the sun and moon of Gray Melvin's universe, he was allowed to do a couple of sidebars at basketball games, the plum event for student sportswriters.

As Gray began letting class attendance become more and more optional, he made sure he kept his stock high at the student paper.

Other than the fact that his grade-point average for the semester might be on the shady side of 2.0, it was a magical spring. Or at least it started out that way.

He drove up to Chatham at least once a week. He managed to get Annie a place to stay in Chapel Hill every other weekend, thanks to a high school friend in the nurses' dorm. Other than the back seat of his Valiant, privacy was at a minimum until the weather turned warm enough for outdoor recreation. It was the year before the school allowed "visitation" in boys' dorms for the first time.

And he realized that he did spend far too much time on that two-lane road between Chapel Hill and Chatham. It wasn't just the hours he could have been studying: All those trips made him look needy. Sometimes, he would go up on a Tuesday or Wednesday night, on the spur of the moment. Sometimes, Annie didn't seem as delighted as he might have hoped over his surprise visits.

He wanted her to have his high school senior class ring, and she took it. Sometime in March, though, she told him that she thought they were a little too young to go steady. She told him that she had worn a boy's ring in high school "and it ended kind of bad. He thought he owned me."

She kept the ring, though, and continued to bestow the kind of sexual favors he'd only dreamed of prior to that Sunday night by the lake in the hills of Virginia. When he told her he loved her, she told him right back, although by early April she sometimes dropped the "I" and said, "love you too."

One Wednesday in late March, six weeks after they met, he made one of his impromptu trips and got an unpleasant surprise. He asked for Annie at the front desk and was told she was out. The girl at the desk professed not to know when she would be back. Gray decided to have a beer, at the same bar where they'd met.

He settled in at the bar and looked around. In the back corner, he saw her, or rather the back of her lovely head. Facing him was a tall, blond boy he didn't know. He had just enough self-control not to make his presence known. He finished his beer in two gulps and left. On Friday, though, when he came up for the date they'd arranged the Sunday before, he couldn't help himself.

"Oh, hell," Annie said, when he told her what he'd seen. "Damn. It was bound to happen."

What, he asked, his heart sinking to shoe level.

It turned out that the boy from Charlottesville, the one who had stood her up back in February and opened the door for Gray, was not out of the picture. While not front and center, he definitely was there, sliding into the frame from the side, what Gray supposed the kids now would call photobombing their relationship.

"I'm not sure what's going on," Annie said, shaking her head as if events beyond her control were driving her decisions. "I'm confused right now."

She took his hand and leaned closer to him. They were in a booth, both sitting on the same side.

"I love you, Gray. Really, I do. But this guy, he wanted to come down and see me, and I didn't know you were coming. I just hate this, sneaking around and all."

That's when she suggested that maybe they shouldn't be so "hot and heavy," just see each other as often as they could, but maybe not exclusively.

"You know you're number one," she said, running her hand up his leg.

He said he knew, but it gnawed at him. He wanted to be numbers one through infinity. He tried to stay cool, the way the older boys in his dorm said you had to do, but he didn't have any experience being cool. He only had experience pretending to be cool.

He couldn't help asking her questions about the other boy. He even learned his name, Winston. A couple of times, when they'd had two or three beers, he would mention his name to her, half kidding, hoping she'd say that was all in the past. He even pumped her about the guy whose ring she'd worn in high school, but she told him that was "past history. Nothing you need to know there."

But there was a weekend in mid-April when Annie told Gray she couldn't come down to Chapel Hill that weekend like she had planned.

When he pressed her on it, she told him that "a bunch of us" were going up to Charlottesville. It wasn't going to be a date, really, just a few Chatham girls getting together with some of the frat boys from U.Va. When he asked her if one of the frat boys was going to be Winston, she said he was going to have to stop asking her about Winston.

Anybody with eyes could see what was coming, but Gray kept his closed as tightly as he could, not prepared to bear the unbearable.

"Man," his zit-faced roommate said when Gray told as much as he could bear to tell him about the situation after they had chugged enough cheap Budweiser to get truly drunk, "you need to dump that bitch."

Gray took her side enthusiastically enough to take a swing across the barroom table at the guy. They got tossed out, and the roomie seemed to think it was all kind of funny. Gray didn't tell him anything else about Annie Lineberger after that.

THE FINAL time Gray Melvin saw Annie, he came up the last Friday night in April. By then he had managed to scrape up enough money to rent a room at a motel half a mile from the campus. The Half Moon Inn had seen better days. It was divided into eight separate units, set in a semicircle facing what was once a busy highway before the interstate system made Chatham a backwater. Most of the units seemed to be empty when Gray paid for the one where he hoped to spend the next two nights with Annie. The fat woman behind the desk looked at him through a haze of unfiltered cigarette smoke and warned him that "we don't allow no cohabitation. This is a family establishment."

Gray promised her that he would not be sharing his luxurious room.

"If you do," the woman said, "it'll cost you ten dollars more."

Annie had seemed less than thrilled with Gray's plan. She would check out of her dorm as if going home for the weekend. He would slip her into the room Friday night and Saturday night, maybe go up in the mountains on Saturday.

"I don't know," she'd said, "it seems kind of sleazy to me." Since they had been having sex whenever possible since

the weekend they met, he figured she meant the surround-
ings and not what they would do there.

But Annie said she'd go along with it. By this time, Gray
was getting weaker signals. He figured a good, long weekend
of lovemaking might reverse the ebb tide of their relationship.

He picked her up at six thirty and took her to dinner at
the restaurant connected to the bar where they met. She was
quiet. She told Gray she'd been fighting a cold.

Finally, as he was getting ready to pay the bill, she looked
at him and told him they needed to talk. Inexperienced as
he was, Gray Melvin knew bad tidings when he heard them.
The only other time he could remember someone "needing
to talk" was when his mother broke the news to him, three
years earlier, that she was leaving. She had not told his father
yet, preferring to let her sixteen-year-old son give Jimmy the
news. It also was up to Gray to tell Kaycee, who was twelve
that spring.

"I'd tell her myself," his mother said to Gray, "but I know
she'd just go to pieces."

So Gray followed Annie out to his car. The air was rich
with honeysuckle. He remembers hearing another car peeling out of the parking lot, burnt rubber blending with the
sweet scent.

Inside, he slid his arm over to draw her to him, but she
moved to the far corner of the front seat.

"No," she said. "This isn't going to work."

She sat there, twisting Gray's ring that rolled around on
her thin second finger. He asked her what was the matter.

"I'm just not ready for all this," she said. "You know,
being so serious and all."

Since he already knew she was seeing at least one other
person, the snake-like Winston, he wondered how un-serious
Annie wanted to get.

"Don't you want to spend the weekend with me?" He knew how pathetic it sounded even as the words escaped his mouth.

She looked at him with something that looked depressingly like pity.

"You're sweet," she said. "You deserve better than me."

No, he assured her, he did not. If anything, he felt he deserved less, and he knew that less was what he was about to get.

"I just think we need to have a time-out," Annie said, not looking at him now, staring out the window at the dark parking lot. "You know, maybe we can pick back up again in the fall."

Gray told her that fall was a long way off. He'd planned to take her to Jubilee, the big spring music-and-grain-alcohol bash where even the geekiest of male students at Carolina were able to get acceptable dates, the lure of the event causing girls at surrounding schools to temporarily overlook their partners' obvious shortcomings.

He'd planned to visit Annie in Monroe during the summer. A few weeks earlier, she had told him how thrilled she would be to introduce him to her parents.

"So," Gray said, stating the obvious, "you think we shouldn't see each other until, what, sometime next fall?"

"Something like that."

"And you don't think we ought to spend the night together?"

She nodded.

"That'd probably be a bad idea right now, don't you think?"

And that's when Gray lost it.

"Just get the hell out then," he said, with more force than he'd planned. He'd seen his father lose his temper many times, going from placid to vicious in no time flat. He felt himself helplessly slipping into Jimmy Melvin's skin. "Get out! Now!"

She scrambled out the door, fumbling with the handle. She seemed to be more relieved than scared, as if she'd finally been released from some onerous task. It made Gray almost physically ill to see her walking away, across the parking lot, headed for the dorm half a mile away, out of his life.

He got out of the car. He wondered if he should run after her. He hoped he was dreaming.

CHAPTER FIVE

MAY 13

The smell of cigarette smoke in Willie Black's car makes it hard to breathe.

"Jesus, Willie. I thought you were trying to quit."

"Trying's the key word."

Gray shakes his head and rolls down the window.

Black drives away. As they turn the corner, Gray can see the two TV trucks outside. It looks as if a few of Betsy's neighbors have come out to be entertained. They've probably seen or heard about the discovery by now. Gray can imagine the interviews: "He seemed like a nice fella, but you never know." He wonders how and if he can ever make it up to Betsy.

Willie waits until they are almost to the Prestwould, the twelve-story condo building where he lives, to ask.

"So, did you do it?"

Gray turns to his old acquaintance.

"If you thought I did, would you be offering me a way out of that madhouse back there?"

Willie shrugs.

"Probably. It's a good story, one way or the other."

"Nice to know you have my best interests at the top of your list."

Nobody is in the lobby. Their trip up the elevator to the sixth floor goes unnoticed.

Willie unlocks the front door. Inside, Gray takes a couple of steps and stops.

"How the hell do you afford all this on a reporter's salary?"

"Married well. Or, I guess you'd say, divorced well. Then married well again."

Gray Melvin wasn't invited to Willie Black's fourth wedding, and Betsy's never met him.

"It wasn't that big of a shindig," Willie tells him by way of perhaps apologizing for not including him in the festivities. "Just my mother, my daughter, my grandson, some old friends from the Hill, and a few of Cindy's friends. Oh, yeah. Her son made it down too."

He's introduced to Cindy, and to Abe Custalow, who it turns out was Willie's best man at Wedding No. 4. Custalow, whom Gray has met before, is living with the newlyweds, in the guest bedroom.

"He's been here a lot longer than I have," the former Cindy Peroni says, giving Abe a hug. "No way he's leaving."

Custalow says he's considering moving in with his girlfriend.

"No fucking way," Willie says. "We need your rent money."

Willie Black, and now his new wife, are renting from his third wife, a lawyer who can afford to make the mortgage payments and condo fees on the place where Willie and she both used to live.

Gray supposes he is in no position to cast judgment on the strangeness of other people's lives, all things considered. From what he can see, everybody seems happy with the arrangement, and happy is something Gray Melvin is a bit envious of at present.

Happy, he thinks, might not be in his future.

Custalow and Cindy are watching *Jeopardy*. Cindy seems to know more of the questions than the three contestants.

Willie leads Gray back to the study.

"Now," he says when they're seated, beers in hand, tape recorder on the table in front of them, "tell me what happened. I've heard most of it before, but give me the whole megillah."

"It's a long story."

Willie shakes his head.

"The good ones usually are."

GRAY GIVES Willie the story of Annie Lineberger, up to the night forty-eight years ago when he tells him he saw her for the last time. He pulls his punches a little, not mentioning any of the more prurient details of their sexual experiences, not mentioning just how desperately needy he was, beyond telling Willie that he was "seriously overmatched" when it came to Annie.

"She was the first girl I ever loved," he says, putting it as simply as he can.

Willie brings Gray up to speed on the latest details in the case. All Gray knows, up to this point, is what he's learned from the six o'clock news and the two state troopers, and the two troopers didn't seem interested in telling him any more than they had to.

The worker who dug up the bones while prepping the land for Portman's first Food Lion said he thought at first it was a deer.

"But then I got to thinking," Willie relates the quote from today's Raleigh newspaper, "who the hell buries a deer?"

When they knew they were dealing with human remains, the local authorities, who weren't used to dealing with anything much beyond drunk driving citations, passed the case on up the line.

It took most of four days to determine that they had found Annie Lineberger's bones. It no doubt would have taken a lot longer if she hadn't been wearing a necklace with her initials.

Gray nods his head when he hears this.

"I remember that necklace," he says. "I gave it to her."

It had been a birthday present. He pretty much depleted his beer money for the month buying it. At the time, when the forsythias were just blooming and love was in full flower, he thought it was a very smart move, one that was rewarded amply that long Chapel Hill weekend.

Willie looks at him.

"You seem to have a very dedicated enemy down there. He went to a lot of damn trouble to make sure everybody knew about your old girlfriend's bones being found, and he's pretty much ready to put the hanging before the trial and string your ass up right now."

Gray nods his head.

"Tree. Hayden Tremaine Lineberger the third."

He did meet the guy once before Annie's disappearance. The last time he took her to Chapel Hill, they met her brother and his date at some place in Durham. Tree was a Dookie, well-heeled enemy of the middle-class boys at Carolina. Gray doubts if he would have liked him wherever he went to school.

He was somewhat tree-like, six foot three, wide-shouldered, and thick, the kind of guy who played on the offensive and defensive lines in high school while Gray was running the mile on the track team.

"So," he said after engulfing Gray's hand with one of his ham-sized mitts and squeezing, "are you screwing my sister?"

He laughed as if he'd just told the funniest joke in the world. Gray felt himself blushing. He blushed easily in those days.

"Mind your own business, asshole," Annie advised her brother.

He exhibited a kind of rough humor that sprang from the knowledge that whatever he said, no matter how thoughtless or inappropriate, people usually would laugh out of deference. He belonged to a fraternity that still had a rebel flag hanging in its party room.

Gray didn't see him again until after his last date with Annie. After that, he saw him more than enough, heard from him more than enough. Tree and his father, who went by Deuce and was an attorney and a former city councilman in Monroe, would devote their lives to trying to get justice for Annie, and they saw Gray Melvin's hide as the only appropriate way to achieve that justice. Hayden Tremaine Lineberger II died more than twenty years ago. His son, whose voice Gray heard on the phone earlier today, has carried on the family vendetta with a vengeance though.

"Damn," Willie Black says when he's heard that part of the story, "it sounds like you better not get caught speeding in Monroe, North Carolina."

Gray assures him that this is not a likely occurrence.

"Did you ever try to find out what really happened, since you didn't do it? I mean, I keep getting images of OJ saying he was going to spend the rest of his life trying to find the 'real' killers of his wife and her friend, which was, of course, bullshit."

Gray tells him it wasn't like that.

"She made it clear that we were through. When she walked off from my car that night, I felt like it wasn't my business anymore. Maybe I should have done something, but you've got to understand, I've been playing defense for most of my adult life. Not much time to go on the offensive."

Willie already knows some of the "defense" Gray's talking about, from more than thirty years of trading war stories.

He nods. He's been taking notes, using the tape recorder for backup. He closes the notebook. They've been talking for almost two hours.

"Come on. I need a drink."

Over beers, with Willie, Cindy, and Abe, Gray says he's worried that the police will think he's skipped town. Betsy will tell anyone who has to know that he said he was staying with friends, but he wonders how long that's going to work.

"Well," Willie says, "they're not charging you with anything yet. It might take awhile for it to get to that point, if it ever does. Are you lawyered up?"

Gray tells him that Betsy is contacting Dan Finebaum.

Willie takes a swig.

"Finebaum's OK, but he's used to handling corporate shit. He's mostly trying to keep fat cats fat. You might need somebody a little more used to fighting the establishment instead of sucking up to it."

Cindy nods her head.

"Marcus."

Willie and Marcus Green have had a symbiotic relationship for years, helping each other when they're after the same goal. Sometimes justice and a good story go hand in hand.

The city's foremost high-profile defense attorney now has billboards all over the city proclaiming, "When You Need to Get Mean/You Better Call Green," his bald mahogany pate and fuck-with-me scowl towering over the passing motorists.

"I dunno. Is that guy for real? And do you think he'd take me on?"

Willie laughs.

"If there are TV cameras, Marcus will be there. He can smell air time a mile away. And, yeah, he's for real, despite all the happy bullshit he throws out. You might not need him, but just in case . . ."

BETSY PHONES on her cell shortly after eleven.

"I've been avoiding most of them, but this one was from somebody down in Carolina. I think you might ought to call this one back."

The caller told Betsy he was the district attorney for the two-county area that includes what is now Chatham University.

"He said he needs to talk to you. I guess you know about what. But he didn't sound, I don't know, like he wanted to arrest you or anything. Anyhow I thought maybe it wouldn't hurt to talk."

When Gray fills Willie Black in on the other end of the conversation, Willie advises him against talking with anybody with a badge, especially not from back where the crime occurred.

"Let me bring Marcus into this. He might keep you from stepping on your dick."

Gray is slowly peeling the label off an imported beer that he presumes Cindy bought. He's never seen Willie drink anything fancier than Miller High-Life.

"You're probably right, but I'm probably going to ignore your perfectly good advice."

"Why? Do you have a death wish?"

"I just think I ought to try to clear this mess up. Or at least find out what this district attorney has to say."

Gray can't really put into words what is pushing him to fly headlong into the maw of the storm that has been coming for half a century. He feels like one of those people who live in a high-risk earthquake zone. It was not a matter of if but when. The day of reckoning is here. He doesn't think he ever will get a good night's sleep again until he deals with it.

He could wait and call the DA in the morning, but Betsy said the man promised he would be glad to hear from James Grayson Melvin any time, day or night.

Gray puts down the beer bottle, which is now surrounded by tiny shreds of paper.

"Screw it. Let's get this over with."

"Your funeral. I'll contact Marcus anyhow."

He uses Willie and Cindy's study for privacy and makes the call that Marcus Green or any sane lawyer would advise him not to make.

The district attorney answers on the second ring. He sounds thrilled. Gray figures he didn't really expect to have a sit-down with the prime suspect in this case unless Gray was dragged back there in chains.

They talk about everything except Annie Lineberger for a good five minutes. The DA is a graduate of a Christian law school ("Whatever the fuck that is," Gray thinks) and a marine veteran who has lived in the county seat town five miles from Chatham all of his nonschool and nonmilitary life. He asks about Gray's career and pretends to know where the hell East Geddie is.

"I think we played you all one time in the state basketball tournament. It was 2-A back then, for little-bitty schools like mine and yours."

Could be, Gray says. He knows that the DA, who says he's just turned fifty, would have been about a year old when Gray graduated from East Geddie High.

When they finally get around to Topic A, the DA, whose name is Towson Grimes, expresses his sympathy over something that happened before he was toilet trained.

"It must've been a terrible ('turrible') shock, losing her like that, and not ever knowing what happened until now."

"We had already broken up. We broke up the last night anybody saw her."

"Oh, right. That's right. Sorry. My memory's not so great." Pretending he didn't know this all along. Gray is reminded of the old *Columbo* TV series and wonders if this guy hasn't watched a few reruns.

"Yeah. Yeah," Grimes says. "It's here in the notes. They must have asked you a whole bunch of questions back then."

"Yeah. A whole bunch."

"Well," he stretches it out to three syllables. "We just want to go back over some of this stuff again, if that's OK with you."

Gray feels like the man on the other end of the phone is holding his breath waiting for the answer to that question.

"Sure," Gray says after a few seconds of silence. "I can come down there, if you like."

"Would you?" The DA sounds like someone has just offered to put his kids through college. "I'd be real appreciative if you could do that. When do you think you could come? We could pay your mileage, whatever you think."

Gray wonders if Grimes really thinks he's expecting a parade in his honor when he comes back to North Carolina, but he figures he'll play along for now.

Gray tells him he can be there by noon tomorrow, or he can wait until Monday.

"I don't want to make you work on a Saturday."

"Oh, no problem. No problem at all. I'm a twenty-four-seven kind of guy."

Gray comes back in the living room and tells Willie Black what he's planning to do.

Willie shakes his head.

"You're nuts. You know that?"

"I guess you're going to run the story, like Sunday?"

"Probably. But don't think I'm just going to do a white-wash for you. I'm going to tell your side of the story, but that's not the only side there is. It ain't going to be all uni-corns and rainbows."

"I didn't expect anything less, Willie. Hell, you wouldn't cut your mother any slack if it got in the way of the truth."

"I'd just be sure I spelled her name right."

Gray tells Willie that he might be gone by the time his host gets up in the morning. He figures it's a three-hour drive down to North Carolina, meaning he wants to be on the road well before nine.

"Oh, I'll be up. Cindy doesn't let me sleep late anymore. And if you're nice, she'll even fix you breakfast."

Gray says he'll probably just get up and hit the road, maybe have a cup of coffee first.

"I've known you a long time," Willie says. "I'd thought I'd heard the whole story. But I never knew how deep the crap really was until tonight."

"I was hoping I never had to tell that story to anybody again."

"That's the trouble. Things like this, they don't seem to go away, unless somebody makes them go away."

Gray nods.

"Well, that's why I'm on the road tomorrow. Either it goes away or I do."

He has one last question for his old friend.

"Do you think I did it?"

Willie pauses before answering.

"No, I don't. But I didn't think a bunch of bastards would fly planes into the two biggest skyscrapers in New York City either. I didn't think Donald Trump could make a legitimate run at being president of the United States. The things I didn't think possible but turned out to be true would fill a book."

Gray has to admit that, in Willie Black's place, he might have given the same damn answer.

CHAPTER SIX

MAY 14

Gray stares into the mirror. He's naked, just out of the shower. These days, he has to force himself to look. He figures he's gained an average of a pound each of the forty-eight years since 1968, maybe shedding ten now and then on some half-assed diet or short-lived jogging binge, then gaining back eleven when the thrill was gone.

His hair is mostly an eponym for his first name. The contact lenses his earlier self used out of vanity have long been discarded for glasses that aren't much more stylish than the black-framed beauties he wore as a teenager.

The good things (youth, fitness, hope) were casualties along the way. The things he wanted to shed (the glasses, a mindset dominated by insecurity and introversion) are still there, joined by new issues like stratospheric PSA numbers and the fear that he'll soon be paying for twenty years of smoking.

He thinks about Jimmy, now twenty-three years gone. His father made it almost to seventy. He told Gray once, not six months before he died, "Seventy is enough."

Gray, looking at the wreckage before him, thinks Jimmy might have been right for once.

He HAS a chance to glance at the Saturday paper before
heading south. Cindy has stashed it away under the coffee
table, perhaps thinking it's the last thing he wants to see this
morning.

He fishes it out as she hands him a cup of coffee.

The city's newspaper has become more flashy in recent
years, apparently in a belated attempt to lure millennials who
long ago gave up reading print publications. Where in past
years the Annie Lineberger story might have rated a dry-as-
toast, one-column headline below the fold on A1 (Girl's body/
found; local/man suspect), now the top of the page screams,
in all-cap letters an inch high (JUSTICE AT LAST?) with a
subhead underneath (Local teacher implicated in 48-year-old
murder). Below that are a mug shot of Annie, which Gray
recognizes as her senior high school yearbook picture, and
one of him, apparently obtained from the community college, along with a locator map for readers who don't know
where North Carolina is.

Gray would have been just as happy if the paper had
kept to its sedate, boring, past practices.

"Jesus," Willie says, looking over his shoulder, "they really
spread it on thick, didn't they?"

Willie's dressed, more or less. Last night, before they
went to bed, he and Gray realized that Gray would need
a car to get to North Carolina, and that it wouldn't be the
wisest thing to go back to Betsy's house and get the one reg-
istered to him.

The plan, then, is for Willie to drive Gray down to the
Enterprise place on Main Street and rent a car in his name,
then turn the keys over to Gray as soon as they're out of
sight of the office.

Willie assures his old friend that the story in Sunday's
paper will be a bit more balanced than this.

"They gave this one to somebody else before I got in," he says. "Son of a bitch Baer never lets facts get in the way. This'll be the last he sees of this story if I have anything to do with it."

The reporter seems to have gleaned a lot of his information from the TV news of the night before. In the sidebar that accompanies the (mostly) factual lead story on the front page, he comes rather close to opinion, in Gray's opinion. His time as a full-time reporter and then as a freelancer taught him to keep his own feelings out of the story, but the man assigned to tell readers about Gray Melvin seems to have drifted away from that a bit.

The story wonders a lot. An "unnamed official" wonders why "the alleged perpetrator" never tried harder to find the real murderer "if, indeed, another suspect exists." The same anonymous source wonders why James Grayson Melvin has been so secretive about his past. The source wonders if authorities in North Carolina aren't already preparing to "bring the suspect in" and whether Melvin has gone on the lam.

"No need for a trial here," Willie says. "Start building the gallows. Sorry, Gray. If we couldn't laugh . . ."

"Yeah. We'd all go insane."

He finishes the coffee and thanks Willie and Cindy for keeping him.

"I hope I don't get you in trouble."

"Just about every story I've ever stumbled on that was worth reporting has caused a shit storm. No problem."

On the way out of Willie's building, Gray makes brief eye contact with an old man ensconced in one of the chairs in the condominium building's lobby.

The man looks at Gray, then looks down at the paper he's holding.

"Yeah," Willie says, "that's him. He's killed before, and he'll kill again. Wanna do something about it?"

On the road in the rental car, Gray decides to eschew the interstate and take the perfectly good US highway that runs across Southside Virginia. By nine, he's out of the city, past the declining 1970s suburbs and then the newer ones farther out. It always amazes him how fast you can leave Richmond, something he doesn't do very often anymore.

The local NPR station is asking for money again, and it's starting to fade out anyhow, so Gray turns off the Ford Escort's radio and lets his mind wander as the Virginia woods and dairy and tobacco farms roll by.

He had never been anywhere much when he met Annie. Until the trip to the Virginia foothills that ended his virginity, the only place he'd been outside North Carolina was Myrtle Beach.

His parents would pack him and Kaycee up every year for a week at the beach, back when Myrtle wasn't all country music halls and high-rises shading out the kind of places where Gray and his family used to stay. When he and his friends turned sixteen, they started going there on their own.

He had planned to take Annie, once the weather got warmer, maybe after final exams. She'd been there with her family a few times.

A church message board alongside the four-lane highway reminds motorists to "Remember Your Mother." Mother's Day is six days past, but no one has changed the sign yet.

Gray isn't one to let guilt take up a permanent place in his chest, at least where his mother is concerned. Most of his reservoir of guilt has already been expended elsewhere. But he does have his regrets.

When Cora died four years ago, in the kind of central Pennsylvania town where fracking was seen as a blessing, he came for the funeral. It was the first time he'd been there in seven years. Betsy kept after him to visit her (his mother was long past being able to make the trip down to Virginia), and he kept putting it off. He hasn't visited his mother's grave and can't imagine ever doing so.

As a child, he didn't think the four of them had such a bad life. It was the only life he knew.

If he and Kaycee sometimes heard shouts from the other side of their parents' bedroom door, they never seemed to last long. Cora went to stay with her sister for a few days from time to time, leaving Gray and Kaycee to more or less fend for themselves. Jimmy wasn't much on cooking. But their mother always came back.

She explained to them one time, after their father had taken the baseball bat they'd given Gray on his birthday and smashed it to splinters because Gray had accidentally run over the garden hose with the lawn mower, that his father had had a hard life, and sometimes they just had to give him some room.

Even at fifteen, Gray could see that drinking didn't make things any better, a lesson he fears he unlearned as an adult. His father had been in the Battle of the Bulge. Unlike some fathers, he talked about it, especially when he came home late after happy hour had turned into happy hours.

And so Gray and Kaycee came to view their father as someone heroic rather than a strong contender for town drunk. They had seen their mother forgive him a hundred times and felt they could do no less.

But one day Cora decided she had had enough. Maybe, as their father claimed, she was just "whoring around" with the minister of their little Baptist church. Maybe she just saw that there was nothing ahead for her except more abuse.

What she came to describe as the last straw, in the spring of 1965, was when Jimmy went on a worse bender than Gray had ever seen. He disappeared for three days, greatly imperiling his future as foreman of a roofing crew.

He came back past midnight on a Tuesday night. He kicked the front door in and wanted to know why the fuck it was locked. It was locked, his wife told him, because there was no one there to protect them.

"Well," he'd said, "I'm here now."

He struck her across the face, with his son and daughter watching. Gray tried to intervene, and Jimmy hit him hard enough to drive him into the cheap wallboard, putting a permanent dent there. Cora and her children ran out into the yard in their nightclothes. They walked to a neighbor's house where they were allowed to sleep in the den.

In the morning, when they cautiously returned, Jimmy was in remorse mode, begging their forgiveness.

Cora patted his head as he knelt before her and told him he'd better get dressed or he'd be late for work.

Jimmy was called out of class shortly after eleven that morning. His mother was waiting for him in the school lobby. That's when she told him she was leaving.

"When?" he had asked her.

She looked out across the parking lot through the big plate-glass school front.

"Right now."

She left it to him to tell his little sister, a task that had to wait until they both were at home that afternoon. And then he had to tell Jimmy when he came home from work, not stopping at some bar for once.

Cora told Gray she'd explain it all to him when he was older, but she never did. He never really forgave her for leaving it to him to tell his eleven-year-old sister that her mother had decided to cut her losses, which they came to assume included them.

When it became known that their church's minister had left town the same day as Cora Melvin, Gray remembered where he'd seen the car in which he had watched his mother leave East Geddie for the last time.

Jimmy never talked about it much either. Amazingly he became a better father after his wife left him, maybe because he finally got some of the counseling Cora had begged him to get for years. Even so, the two siblings were uneasy any time he came home later than usual, relaxing only when they saw the demons that had possessed him on more than one occasion were not to be seen that night.

By the time Gray left for college, his father, though no saint, was at least not an apparent physical threat to what was left of his family. Still Gray felt like a deserter that morning, promising his teary-eyed sister that he'd be home soon and that he would always be there for her.

Gray turns off on a state highway just north of the North Carolina line. His route takes him through Portman, a dot on the map that seems to consist of mostly a volunteer fire department, a couple of churches, a Hardee's, a used-car dealership, a shuttered factory building of some kind, two convenience stores, and a smattering of houses in little unpaved streets leading off the two-lane road he's on.

He passes the site where work on the new Food Lion has been halted. He sees the yellow crime-scene tape signifying the gash in the earth where Annie Lineberger's bones were discovered. The enormity of it all is strong enough to cause him to pull off the road at one of the stores, where he leans out the car door and throws up on the pavement. A dark part of him has believed that this day would come, but it still hits him hard. He goes inside to buy a Diet Coke with which to wash away the bile. He imagines that the local people recognize his face. Surely they have daily newspapers delivered even to Portman, Virginia.

It's only twelve miles farther, just over the state line, to Chatham, where the district attorney has agreed to meet him. He drives past the college. He hasn't been there since 1968. He had hoped never to see this town or the school again. He has trouble locating the site of the long-shuttered bar where he first met Annie, and he couldn't tell you for sure which dorm was hers. Somehow all that adds to his sense of loss.

Towson Grimes is waiting for him at their arranged meeting spot, a barbecue joint on the edge of town. He seems surprised when Gray walks into the overcooled building a couple of minutes past noon.

Gray sees a slightly overweight man who waves to him and gets up from the booth he's cornered.

"You must be Grayson Melvin," he says, extending one hand and wiping some coleslaw off his upper lip with the other. "Thank you so much for coming down here."

Gray follows him back to the booth. He orders a pork barbecue sandwich, which comes with hush puppies and french fries. The tea, Gray knows, will be sweetened to diabetic levels whether he asks or not. Betsy calls the area from southern Virginia down and around to Louisiana the stroke belt and says the sweet-tea line starts somewhere around Petersburg. Gray grew up on this food, but at this point in his life, he loves it more than it loves him.

The DA manages, between shoveling in mouthfuls of what the menu calls "The Big Boy Special," to make small talk about everything from ACC basketball to the upcoming elections.

Gray has eaten about half his sandwich when Grimes pushes his plate away, now empty save one french fry, which stands as a lonely and futile testament to self-control.

"Well," he says, "I reckon we've got some things to talk about."

"I guess we do."

He asks Gray if he'll come with him to his office in Colesville, five miles away. He offers to drive them both, but Gray demurs, telling him he'll just follow him over.

"No sense in that," Grimes says. "No need to take both cars over."

Gray says he'd rather drive himself. The DA frowns briefly but gets up and pays for both their lunches.

The county seat is smaller than Chatham, really only a village. Its sole reason to exist seems to be as a government center. Gray follows Grimes into a lot beside the courthouse, not noticing the number of vehicles parked there on a Saturday afternoon.

"It's a one-horse town," the DA says, with what seems to Gray to be forced joviality, "but we like it."

He leads his guest back through a corridor and into his office suite, where the door is unlocked. They walk past the receptionist's desk and into another room, a long expanse with a large conference table in the middle. The district attorney sends his guest in first.

Gray, expecting a one-on-one interview, stops short as he enters the room.

Seated at the table, amply filling one of the chairs, is a figure from Gray Melvin's past. In another chair, across the table, is a well-coiffed woman whom Gray vaguely recognizes from the cable news network whose emblem is on the camera that a fat guy in shorts and T-shirt is holding in the corner of the room.

Despite his considerable girth, Tree Lineberger looks like he might fly out of his chair.

He smiles up at Gray, or at least shows his teeth.

"Been a long time, asshole."

"I'm sorry," Towson Grimes says, hitting himself in the forehead in mock apology. "I forget to tell you that I invited another party that has some interest in Annie Lineberger. You all have already met, I reckon.

"And I didn't think you'd mind if we brought some of the fourth estate here, just to get the whole picture, you know."

Gray can see that the camera is live and knows he's been ambushed.

"Now, we don't want to go making any charges or anything just yet," the DA says. "We thought it'd be better if we just had a chat."

"With the camera on? How about you get me a lawyer."

"Aw, now, Mr. Melvin, this isn't anything official. Just trying to get to the bottom of it all."

The TV reporter cuts in.

"We've just heard so much about this. The whole country's fascinated by it. And we knew you'd want to get your side of the story out there. We've certainly heard enough of the other side."

She looks toward Tree Lineberger when she says this.

"And when Mr. Graves . . ."

The DA clears his throat.

"Grimes."

"Grimes. Sorry. When Mr. Grimes here called and told us you'd be coming in for a chat, we rounded up a cameraman and chartered a flight right down here from Washington."

The woman seems to be trying to sound Southern, without much luck.

The big man looking up at Gray pulls out a chair and pats its seat.

"Yeah," Lineberger says. "Stay a spell. I know we're all dying to hear what you have to say this time."

Gray has been in the same room with Annie's brother on several occasions since her disappearance, none of them pleasant and none of them in the last thirty years. Tree has taken up the cause of his late father: to see that Gray Melvin pays the full price for what happened to his sister. Gray knew that Tree, like Annie herself, would one day, somehow, resurface.

If Gray has gained a pound a year, his nemesis seems to have put on two. Tree Lineberger now must weigh more than three hundred pounds. His face is red enough that Gray can imagine him, like Tree's father, bursting a blood vessel and departing this mortal coil in spectacularly abrupt fashion. He can't believe the man is still alive really. He figures he must be sixty-nine years old with a body that looks like it should have hit its expiration date a good decade ago.

Gray knows through Google that Lineberger is mostly retired now, and that he was himself district attorney for his home county. He supposes that's where he came to know Towson Grimes, and that this surprise party is Grimes's idea of professional courtesy.

Lineberger stands up and points at Gray, who hasn't sat down and steps back a foot.

"They found her bones, you piece of shit. You thought she'd stay buried forever, but you were wrong. Annie's come back from the grave to nail your ass."

Gray can see the camera's still on, catching every delicious moment for the network's viewers to savor later.

"I didn't do it," is all Gray can say.

"Yeah, you said that back then too. They had to take your word for it, with no body and all. Although nobody really believed you then, either, did they?"

No, Gray would have to admit. Mostly they didn't.

He wishes he were smarter, smart enough to have listened to Willie Black and to Betsy and not to have come down here in the naive belief that he could have a face-to-face with Towson Grimes, who stands between him and the door looking rather pleased with himself.

Gray turns toward him.

"You said you and I would talk."

Grimes spreads his arms.

"I just thought you'd want to get it all on the record. Here's your chance to go face-to-face with your accuser. This ain't going to be legally binding or anything."

No, Gray thinks, it's just going to be on everybody's TV from coast to coast. He can't imagine that he looks like anything other than a guilty man caught unawares, facing the righteous wrath of his victim's brother. He wishes he had dressed better.

"You set me up," he says, stating the obvious.

"Well," the DA says, smiling with just his mouth, "maybe just a little. But we've been waiting a long time for this one, you have to understand."

Gray also understands something else. It's an election year, and he's going to be the vehicle to get Towson Grimes reelected. He has always had a fairly respectful attitude toward the forces of law and order. After all, the system worked for him forty-eight years ago. He was not railroaded over Annie's disappearance. He might have been found as guilty as OJ in the court of public opinion, but the law didn't let him down.

He is reminded, now, of something a lawyer acquaintance of his told him years ago. The friend had defended more than his share of criminal cases before going to the "other side" and working for the commonwealth's attorney in Richmond.

They'd had more than a few drinks when the conversation turned to a man who had just recently been exonerated by DNA after serving more than twenty years for a rape he didn't commit.

The lawyer leaned toward Gray and spoke in a low voice.

"Now, if you quote me on this, I'll say you're a damn liar and sue you for slander.

"But," and here he held his right forefinger up, "if you think for one minute that the prosecution is any less willing to bend the rules to win than the defense is, you're sadly mistaken. We are in it to win. Period. Anyhow."

They call them commonwealth's attorneys in Virginia and district attorneys in North Carolina, but Gray can see now just how right his old friend was. His demise will make this overweight elected official who lured him down here a hero to the voters. And he can see for the first time clearly that Towson Grimes is no more interested in hearing his side of the story than Tree Lineberger is.

"Fuck you," he says. "I'm going home. Charge me or get the hell out of my way."

He is knocked forward onto the table by a blow to the back of his head and feels Lineberger's considerable weight on top of him, feels his hot breath. He hears the reporter give a little gasp. He can see the red eye of the camera. He can hear Grimes say, "Come on, now, boys. This is supposed to be a civil conversation."

Lineberger lets him up, shouting his desire to see him executed by the state "so I don't have to do it myself."

Gray feels a little light-headed as he heads toward the door.

"You lied to me," he says to the DA, who seems only mildly shaken by the assault he's just witnessed and appears to have no plans to call in any of the sheriff's deputies whom Gray saw hanging out in the hall on the way in.

Grimes tells the cameraman to turn his camera off.

"Lied? Not really," he says. "We're just interested in justice around here. You know what the good Dr. King said about justice delayed being justice denied. And when it's been denied this long, well, it just makes us all the more eager to see that it gets delivered."

He leans closer to Gray.

"Long and hard."

Gray leaves, with the reporter and cameraman chasing after him, along with Grimes. Lineberger has stayed behind.

"We'll be talking with you real soon," the DA calls after him. "You all have a safe trip back to Richmond. And don't be plannin' any long trips in the near future."

The reporter and her cameraman follow him all the way to his car. He asks them to leave him alone, but she just keeps asking him questions she knows he won't answer. He wonders just how guilty he looks right now.

He rolls the window up, catching the microphone she's stuck inside. As he drives off, she runs a few steps, then lets go. He goes a few yards down the road, stops briefly, and flings the mic into the rose bushes alongside.

"Well," he says to himself as he turns back north toward Virginia, "that went well."

CHAPTER SEVEN

1968

By the time he thought to chase after her, she had disappeared into the darkness.

He figured she was going back to her dorm, but even in the stomach-churning distress following her departure, he knew that he would only make things worse if he went there. He could imagine begging the girl at the front desk to call Annie's room. She probably would know the whole story and would laugh about it as soon as he left. Maybe she would call and then tell him that Miss Lineberger did not wish to see him.

He got back into the Valiant and just sat there, unable to go forward or backward for a few minutes. Years later, he would remember the pain as somehow being worse than what he felt when his mother left. He knew, from the vantage point of thirty years old or forty or fifty, that he had been ridiculously self-absorbed, but he couldn't be nineteen again and change the past.

He had gotten a senior in his dorm to buy a fifth of cheap bourbon, part of the festivities of the weekend that was now reduced to smoldering ruins. He felt the need to do something big, something self-destructive enough to commemorate what he saw as the end of all happiness.

He took the cap off the bottle and threw it out the window. He didn't bother to go by the motel where he'd reserved a room for the weekend, choosing instead to head back to Chapel Hill.

He didn't exactly try to kill himself on the way back, but he took the twenty- and twenty-five-miles-per-hour curves along the steep river valleys as fast as he could. A couple of times, he could feel the car slipping. If he'd been given a lie-detector test, drunk as he was by then, he would have admitted he didn't really want to die. He just wanted to feel like he wanted to die.

By the time he got back to his campus, somehow avoiding both death and the state police, the fifth was two-thirds empty. Grayson Melvin, whose drinking up to that point had been confined mostly to beer, opened the car door at the first major intersection leading back into his college town, and threw up, managing to spew a fair amount of the regurgitated Jim Beam and last night's dinner on himself and the car.

He had no desire to return to his dorm on a Friday night when everyone but the no-date losers was out on the town. He thought there would be some nobility in spending the rest of the evening alone in his car, nursing his hurt feelings. He drove to the back of one of the football stadium parking lots and tried to choke down the rest of the bourbon.

SATURDAY MORNING, the sun woke him. He was lying sprawled across the front seat, the bottle on his chest. The smell of puke was overwhelming, and he had never been so sore. The disaster of the night before came back to him. As soon as he had given up all hope that it was only a bad dream, he cried and beat his head on the steering wheel.

He went to the coffee shop on the main drag next to the campus and found that, despite his grief and the fact that he was still drunk, he was ravenous. He ordered eggs, ham, hash browns, and pancakes and devoured them all.

And then, walking down the street to his car, he stopped and threw up again.

He went back to his dorm room. His roommate was gone for the weekend, which he counted as the only blessing he'd received lately.

He fell into bed and didn't wake up until after dark.

GRAY WOULD call the number he'd memorized in Chatham three times over the weekend from the pay phone down the hall in his dorm. Each time, he was told that Annie Lineberger wasn't in her room.

The third time, after nine on Sunday night, he got her roommate.

The girl seemed confused and a little embarrassed. Her name was Susan Vanhoy. Gray had met her on several occasions and liked her well enough. This time, though, she sounded different.

"I, uh, I don't know. I thought she was with you. Weren't you all supposed to go off somewhere?"

Gray put it as simply as he could.

"I think we broke up."

"Oh. Yeah, I kinda knew that was coming."

Gray asked her how long she knew it was coming.

"We really shouldn't be talking about that," Susan Vanhoy said. "But, well, I thought she was going to stay here. I just got back in, and I don't see any sign she's been here. She said she had a date Satur— . . . Shit. Oops. Sorry."

Gray figured he should have hung up then. Things, which he didn't think could get worse, just did. He supposed that Annie Lineberger, in anticipation of being rid of him at last, had previously lined up her entertainment for the rest of the weekend. He felt sick. He imagined Annie would come stumbling up to her dorm sometime before Sunday night curfew with the well-sated Winston on her arm, having decided to spend Saturday night at whatever the hell place Winston lived in Charlottesville, exchanging fluids with the bastard, maybe having a laugh or two about the poor love-sick sap she'd just dumped.

After a long, awkward silence, Susan said, "I'll tell her you called, when she shows up."

"Don't."

When Gray's own roommate came rolling in, half drunk, after eleven, he asked how the weekend "fuckfest" went. Gray told him it was just great. He wasn't ready yet to deal with I-told-you-sos.

He went out drinking with some of the other guys on his floor and got almost as drunk on beer as he had on bourbon two nights before.

MONDAY WAS a blur. Gray went to two of his classes, including French II, for which he saw no use and which he was in danger of flunking after attending only half the classes that semester so far. The class was at eight in the morning. Gray only went because he couldn't sleep. The intoxicating spring morning, with the sun and the honeysuckle mocking him, only made things worse. He didn't realize, until the girl next to him told him as he was leaving, that he'd left his sunglasses on for the entire hour in the dark classroom.

He went by the student newspaper to see if there were any assignments for him. Corrina Corrina asked him if he was OK as he walked by her desk.

"You look like you've been rode hard and hung up wet," she said.

He just shook his head.

Buddy Weeks assigned him to cover a lacrosse match on Tuesday. Gray nodded his head. The only sport that he knew less about than wrestling was lacrosse.

He was determined never to make a call to that number in Chatham again.

He didn't have long to resist temptation. Before he could call Chatham, Chatham called him.

He was summoned to the pay phone by a boy, two doors down.

"Some chick from Chatham wants your body," the boy said, smirking.

Gray, thinking it was Annie, maybe calling to say she'd had second thoughts, was prepared to be magnanimous. Deep down, though, he knew his jealousy probably would spoil any hopes he had of seizing the high ground in whatever relationship they might still have. Eschewing the advice of the sage upperclassman, he realized that, for better or worse, he did give a shit.

But it wasn't Annie.

"Gray," Susan Vanhoy said, "she's not here."

"What do you mean?"

"I mean she's missing. She didn't come back last night at all, and she didn't come back today. They're looking for her."

The roommate told him that the boy from U.Va. had come to pick her up on Saturday afternoon. According to the girl at the front desk, nobody answered when she called Annie and Susan's room.

"She said the guy sat around for an hour or so, but she just never showed up."

Her parents had been notified, Susan said, and they were on their way up from Monroe.

"They've called the cops too. I think they're going to want to talk to you too."

"What about?"

"What do you think? About when was the last time you saw her? About whether you all had a fight or anything?"

Gray told her that he and Annie had parted on good terms, which was something of a lie, but he supposed that, considering that he had just been dumped by the love of his young life, the terms could have been much worse.

There was something a little hard, almost accusatory, in Susan's voice.

"She told me, when she told me you all were going to break up, that she thought you'd take it hard."

Gray said he supposed he didn't take it any harder than anyone else would have under the circumstances. Susan didn't say anything, for a few seconds.

"Anyhow," she said at last, "you ought to expect to be hearing from somebody sometime soon."

Before she hung up, though, Gray said, "Wait a minute. What about the guy from Charlottesville? Winston what's-his-name?"

"Keppler. Winston Keppler. The girl who was on the desk said he never got past the lobby, and that Annie never came down, that nobody answered the phone in our room. I don't think there's going to be much reason to question Winston Keppler, do you?"

Gray was getting a very bad feeling about it all. The temperature in Susan's voice seemed to be dropping by the second.

"My God," he said, the seriousness of it hitting him, "do you think something happened to her? I mean, should I come up there?"

"No," she said, a little too quickly. "Definitely do not come up here. And, yes, I am afraid something's happened to her. Aren't you?"

Gray knew only one other thing to say.

"I loved her."

Susan jumped on the past tense. She sounded almost hysterical.

"You say it like you know she's gone or something."

"No. Jesus, Susan . . ."

"I've got to get off here," she said, and she hung up before Gray could say anything else.

He skipped his earliest Tuesday class but went to the one at eleven. He hadn't mentioned anything about Annie's disappearance until after Susan's call the night before, when he told his roommate.

"Man, you mean she's been kidnapped or something?"

Gray vaguely remembered shrugging his shoulders and refusing to talk about it anymore. And on Tuesday morning, when the roommate quizzed him again about what he'd said the night before, he told the boy to fuck off.

Coming back from that eleven o'clock class, he was less than surprised to see that his resident adviser was standing with two men sporting crewcuts and wearing police uniforms.

He heard the RA say, "There he is." The two men moved toward him as if they thought he was going to run. The RA shook his head and went back inside the dorm.

"We've got a few questions," the older one said. The younger one nodded. He looked at Gray's hair, which wasn't that long yet but was heading in that direction as the sixties began to finally encroach in North Carolina. He looked as if he'd like to give him a buzz cut or just simply kick his college-boy ass.

The one who was speaking was from Byrd County, where Chatham College was located. The other one was local.

"This is about Annie, right?" Gray said. The two cops exchanged glances.

"We wonder if you'd come with us. We just want to ask you a few questions," the one from Byrd County said.

Gray figured they meant to go to the Chapel Hill police station. He was in the back of the cruiser with the doors locked before he realized that they were going to Chatham.

When Gray said he wanted to go back, the one from Chapel Hill, along for the ride, told him to "shut the fuck up" and reminded him that he had agreed to answer "a few questions."

They got him in a small room with no ventilation, and they tag-teamed him. Miranda rights were still a fairly new proposition, usually honored more or less in the breach where Gray lived. He thinks he might have asked for a lawyer at some point, but when he got a court-appointed one later, he couldn't really be sure, and both the good cop and the bad one swore he had asked for no such thing.

Gray went over his story half a dozen times, and every time he changed some small, meaningless detail, it was duly noted.

"You mean nobody saw you from Friday, when you claim you and Annie Lineberger parted company, until Saturday morning?" the bad cop said. He was about six foot four and looked like he hadn't shaved in a couple of days. He had bad breath, and he was fond of leaning forward, getting in Gray's face and slamming the table between them for emphasis when his answers didn't suit him. "Not one soul? That's pretty damn convenient, don't you think?"

Gray explained again how he had driven back to Chapel Hill but was too upset to go back to his dorm.

The cop smirked.

"I guess you were," he said. "I'd be upset, too, if I'd just killed my girlfriend because she dumped me."

Every time Gray denied it, the cop would slam his fist on the table and tell him to stop lying. Then the good cop, the same one who lured him to Chatham, would come in and tell the other one to chill out.

Then the good cop would start telling him how it was understandable. The girl probably insulted him. They'd had a few drinks. He probably hadn't meant to do her any harm.

And Gray would deny it again. Why, he asked them, would he have phoned asking for her three times if he'd known she was missing?

"Maybe to cover your butt?"

And the good cop would sigh and tell him that they were just trying to get the story straight, and that they were all sure that Gray hadn't meant any harm to the girl. It was just an accident. If he just came clean, they were sure they could clear it all up and get him back to Chapel Hill.

"Just tell us where she is, son," the man said, almost tenderly.

Then, when Gray stuck by his story, the good cop would sigh again and send the bad cop back in to bang on the table some more.

Gray was frighteningly close on a couple of occasions to giving the police what they wanted. But he stayed with his story. He had been upset when she left him and had driven back to Chapel Hill, where he slept in his car on Friday night, then went back to his dorm on Saturday, after eating breakfast and throwing up. He hadn't seen Annie Lineberger after she walked away from his car.

They had nothing on him but the cocksure belief that he did it. They sent him back to Chapel Hill with the warning that he was being watched, and that he had better not be taking any trips anytime soon.

"We're definitely going to be seeing you again real soon," the bad cop told him. "And I guaran-damn-tee you ain't going to be happy to see us."

By the time the Chapel Hill cop dropped him off half a mile from his dorm, it was after ten P.M. He told Gray that it was only a matter of time.

"Soon as they find the body, it's gonna be too late to tell the truth."

They tore the Valiant apart and left it for him to do most of the putting back together. All they found of Annie Lineberger was some of her hair on the front passenger's seat and in the spacious back seat, plus an earring that Gray said belonged to her.

The DA for Chatham at the time made sure that the press was apprised that a UNC student was the prime suspect in the disappearance of a Chatham College girl. Somebody leaked his name to the papers, and by Wednesday morning, Gray Melvin was infamous. The case hit all the hot buttons for selling papers. Beautiful college girl from a well-heeled family missing after dumping her loser boyfriend from the fancy, too-liberal, big state university.

Gray called his father, whose reaction was mostly to be angry at him for "getting yourself in this shit storm in the first place. What the hell are you doing up there anyhow?"

More disturbing to Gray was the realization that his father did not have his back.

"If you did something," he told his son after Gray had related his story for the second time, "you better come clean, boy."

Gray fought back tears as he had this most intimate of conversations on a pay phone that was overheard, he was sure, by a dozen or more dorm mates. He told his father he had nothing to confess.

"Well," Jimmy Melvin said, "I sure hope so."

There was no mention of his father coming up to Chapel Hill to lend moral support, or of Gray coming back home.

Gray thought about returning to East Geddie, but he didn't think that he would fare any better there than he did at school, where he could at least try to salvage his semester, and where at least some of his fellow students seemed to believe him.

It was Corrine Manzi who told him he had to get a lawyer "right damn now." Corrina Corrina would never seem to waver in her belief that he was innocent. When she offered to let him write, in his own words, what happened for the school paper, he turned her down though. He felt unable to make himself any more naked to the world than he already was.

The attorney he got, through the university's legal services, was better than no lawyer at all, but to Gray he seemed more interested in protecting the university than he was in looking out for Gray.

They hauled him back up to Chatham twice more that week. The university's lawyer's most memorable suggestion was that Gray might want to take some time off from school "to get things sorted out." Gray had the distinct impression that his school would be happier if he wasn't walking around the campus anymore. The attorney didn't seem to be interested in hearing his nonpaying client's claims of innocence.

Gray didn't drop out, though, still clinging to the hope that it would all get sorted out, that everyone would shake his hand and tell him how sorry they were for the misunderstanding.

Gray finally told the cops in Byrd County, this time on the record, that he wanted a "real" attorney, one that he felt was looking out for his best interests. They appointed one, a guy just out of one of the state's lesser law schools. The new lawyer seemed mostly interested in getting Gray to confess, "so we can get your sentence reduced, well, as much as we can."

"Does it matter," Gray asked, "that I didn't do it?"

"Well," the lawyer said, looking at his watch, "they don't see it that way."

Gray is amazed now, thinking back, that he was able to hold his own against men who seemed hell-bent on getting him to confess. But he didn't break. And, after a week, they sent him back to Chapel Hill with no set date to return.

"Just be damn sure you stay around, and you let us know where you're at," the district attorney told him. "When we find her, and if it's a body we find, we will be coming for you like the wrath of God."

The university's attorney might have given Gray good advice. A semester already headed for ruin crashed and burned in the distracted aftermath of Annie's disappearance. When he wasn't being taken back to Byrd County for more questioning, he was in no shape to study for final exams. He managed to pass four of his five courses, two of them by the skin of his teeth.

He stopped by the student newspaper on the day of his last final. Corrina Corrina was there, trying to finish one more editorial before she left for her post-graduate internship. She had managed to land one at the *Washington Post*, which she felt was a step or two above Pittsburgh.

He hadn't written anything for the paper in the previous two weeks, in a futile attempt to devote what focus he had left to his studies. Besides it was weird. People avoided him. Strangers would stop and stare as he walked by. He felt everyone was talking about him. Buddy Weeks avoided looking at him when Gray asked him if he had any more assignments. He was seen, he believed, as either a murderer awaiting his inevitable fate or, in the best light, a fuckup who had managed to bring dishonor on himself and his school.

Every newspaper in the state and a few from outside it had given the story major play, although the furor had temporarily died down after several days when neither a live Annie Lineberger nor a dead one showed up.

"Man," his roommate told him as they said their goodbyes, "I knew that girl was trouble."

Gray had lined up a summer job, before his world got shaken up like a kid's snow globe. The previous fall, a boy in his dorm had persuaded him to join him in rushing a couple of the fraternities. Gray decided not to join, mostly because he couldn't afford it.

One seemingly good thing did come out of his rushing though. An older boy in a fraternity was recruiting freshmen to sell "great books." A company would send him and other young men (they were all young men) to some state far away, where they would spend the summer convincing middle-class-or-lower parents that their kids' pursuit of the American Dream would be greatly enhanced by those volumes. It was door-to-door sales, and Gray, on a whim, said yes. He wasn't very good at talking to strangers, and he thought this might help. Plus, the fraternity boy who recruited him said he made $8,000 the previous summer.

Even though Gray was by then persona non grata on fraternity row, the great books purveyor had no qualms. A week after he left Chapel Hill, he would be headed, in his reassembled Valiant, for a town in Wisconsin that he'd never heard of.

He told his lawyer in Byrd County where he would be for the summer. The lawyer didn't think it was such a good idea, but with no charges filed against Gray, he said he guessed he was free to go.

So Grayson Melvin, after a brief and tense visit with his father and his tearful sister, headed north. He thought maybe if he drove far enough, he could go somewhere where nobody knew his name.

CHAPTER EIGHT

May 15

Gray parks on the side street next to the Prestwould. The cathedral's church bells serenade him as he locks the rental.

He stopped on the way back to Richmond for a fast-food breakfast. He saw that the early edition of the Richmond Sunday paper was in the rack outside. He recognized his picture on the front from thirty feet away and decided, after buying a copy with all the change he had in his pocket, to use the drive-through instead of eating inside.

He saw Willie's byline and read the headline ("Who killed Annie Lineberger?") and the first few paragraphs. At least Willie didn't seem to be convicting him before the trial. He set the paper beside on the seat and drove on.

HEADING NORTH yesterday on an unnaturally warm mid-May afternoon, Gray realized he was exhausted, laid low by the previous twenty-four hours. He nearly rear-ended a slow-moving pickup just south of Portman. He pulled over at a convenience store and bought a can of Red Bull, but fifteen miles farther down the road, on the four-lane US highway, he found himself nodding off again.

A motel, sad remnant of the time when the road was a route for Florida-bound tourists, appeared out of the woods on his left. He made a U-turn and pulled into the gravel parking lot, struck by how much it resembled the one where he meant to spend a weekend of lust and love with Annie Lineberger so long ago.

Some construction workers were sitting outside some of the stand-alone cottages in cheap folding chairs. A couple of them had a cooler between them. Three others leaned over a hibachi, grilling hot dogs. A CD player was booming country music.

Inside, the manager might as well have been that woman from forty-eight years ago, the one who warned Gray against indulging in cohabitation, or at least told him he'd have to pay extra if he did.

The room cost $39.20 a night "with tax," her 2016 apparition said. "Weekly rates are on the wall behind you."

Gray gave her two twenties; she said she had to go get the key to unlock the safe.

"Place down the road got held up last week. We don't keep no cash in here."

Gray told her to keep the change.

He planned to nap a couple of hours and then head back to Richmond. Before he lay down, he gave Betsy a call.

"Where the hell have you been?" is how she answered.

He had turned his cell phone off, tired of the endless calls he was getting from friends, strangers, and, mostly, people working for newspapers and TV networks.

He explained that to her.

"I didn't know what to think," she said. "I was worried about you. I am worried about you. How'd it go?"

He brought her up to speed on the day's events, including the ambush prepared by the district attorney.

"Bastards."

"Have the news vultures killed all the grass in your front yard yet?"

She laughed.

"Not quite, but they're working on it."

"I'm sorry. I never meant . . ."

"I know. I know. Don't worry. It's getting better. A couple of the TV trucks have driven off. Looking for you somewhere else, I guess."

He told her that he probably would stay over at Willie Black's at least one more night.

"Willie reminded me about the news media's short attention span. He said they were like a bunch of two-year-old Labrador retrievers. Pretty soon, he said, they'll spot another squirrel and go chasing it."

"Is he calling you a squirrel?"

"Just metaphorically, I guess."

"Well, I want you to get your metaphorical ass back over here as soon as you can. This bed is too big with just one person in it."

"As soon as I can," Gray said. "I hope I don't have bedbugs next time I see you."

Before he drifted off, he called Willie's cell and told him what had happened.

"What the hell did I tell you?" his friend said. "Those guys, they don't mean you anything but harm."

"I know. I know. You'd think I'd be more cynical of human nature by now."

"Get back up here, soon as you can."

Gray said he would, after he took a little nap.

"You OK?"

"Just tired. I gotta go now."

His head was already sinking toward the pillow as he said it. He saw that, while he was talking to Willie, he'd had four other callers. He turned the cell off again.

His own snoring woke him up. The room was dark, and he had a few panicky seconds of disorientation. Was he dead? If so, apparently heaven's harpists were fond of loud, bad, redneck music. He turned on the bedside lamp and looked outside, where it was now pitch dark. The parking lot was littered with people drinking and dancing around the glow of a couple of charcoal grills.

He looked at his watch. Nine thirty.

Betsy answered on the second ring.

"You've got to stop turning that thing off," she said.

He told her that he would reset the alarm for seven A.M. and drive back in the morning.

"But everything's OK?" she asked. "I mean, when you didn't answer . . ."

He realized that she, and probably others as well, could think he might have done something a little more drastic than rent a cheap motel room for the night. It was the kind of fear, he thought, that indicated a certain amount of doubt as to his innocence in Annie's death.

He really couldn't blame them. He had felt it, even in his own family, in the months and years after it happened, the doubt eventually rubbed smooth by time.

He told her to stop worrying. He was just tired was all.

Then he called Willie Black and told him not to wait up. Still groggy, still feeling sleep-deprived but also hungry, he wandered out the door of his unit.

Two men in overalls wearing tattoos instead of shirts greeted him as if he was a long-awaited guest. They pushed a hot dog on him, which he gratefully devoured, along with a couple of cheap beers.

"What the fuck are you doin' here, anyhow?" the one with the ZZ Top beard asked him. It wasn't so much a challenge as bewilderment. Gray saw that he was the only man in the parking lot who was not only wearing a shirt, but one with a collar. The women, from what he could tell, were heavy on makeup and light on teeth.

"I've got some legal issues," he said, sensing that this would be an area in which he and his newfound friends had common ground.

"I hear you there," a heavyset man who'd joined the conversation said. "Man, when the fuckers decide it's you, they got you, no matter what."

He scratched at a tattoo on his bare shoulder. Underneath the skull and crossbones, it read, "Jesus was a pussy."

Gray agreed with the man's assessment of the judicial system. He gradually slipped away, opting not to titillate the crowd by telling them he was a murder suspect. It would just lead to more questions he didn't feel like answering.

Inside, he fell back into a sleep that could not be disturbed by any amount of music, screaming, or free-range fights.

When the alarm woke him, all was quiet in the parking lot. One of the men who'd given him a beer the night before was snoring gently in one of the cheap folding chairs outside the unit two doors down, a bottle cradled on his ample gut. One of the grills was still in the middle of the lot, surrounded by discarded cans and other trash.

He returned the key to the same woman who'd rented him the room the day before.

"I hope the noise didn't bother you none," she said. "The boys get right rowdy sometimes."

She grinned at him, and he realized she was one of the women he'd seen in the lot the night before.

He told her he'd never slept better in his life. He thought she seemed disappointed at that.

Now, as he gets out of his rental, he's thinking about the arc his life has taken. Driving solo does that to him. Normally he can push parts of his past to a place where it only escapes after a four A.M. trip to the bathroom. But this is not a normal time, and he wonders if there ever will be any normal time again.

He hasn't exactly carried a torch for Annie Lineberger for forty-eight years, but there is a tug.

Whatever happened to Annie has damaged his life, diminished it, made him cringe and feel a guilt that has no logical basis. But how can he feel sorry for himself? He is alive, "free, white and twenty-one," as his father had so bluntly put it. Annie, as the weeks and months and years went by with no word, was almost surely dead, it was silently conceded, even by her family. Worse than dead really. Unaccounted for. Neither here nor there. She was like those MIAs from Gray's Vietnam days, a ghost in need of closure. Finding her bones should have been a kind of sad relief. It would have been, even for Gray, if he hadn't been the one suspected of murdering her.

He makes his way up to Willie Black's apartment.

Cindy is the only one stirring. She lets him in and tells him Willie is in the shower. Abe Custalow has spent the night with a girlfriend.

"I see you've already read the paper," she says, pointing to the edition tucked under Gray's right arm.

"Not all of it."

"Well, it's not so bad. And at least the TV crews and the out-of-town papers haven't found out where you are."

He tells her about his ambush in Colesville.

"Yeah, I heard. Willie said somebody told him they'd already played a tape of the interview on that network, the one that sent those people down there. I wouldn't know. It's not one I ever watch."

Gray cringes when he thinks about how he must have come across, about what amusement that cluster-fuck scene must be giving viewers all over the country.

He's had time to read the whole article by the time Willie comes into the living room.

"Late night," he says, then picks up a pack of cigarettes off the coffee table and heads to the study.

"Camel break," Cindy says. "He thinks that if he smokes at the open window, Kate won't notice next time she springs a surprise inspection on us. Fool's errand, but what the hell."

Gray thinks how strange it must be to have an ex-wife as a landlady. He admires his old friend's willingness to jump back into the ring after being floored three times. He definitely admires Cindy's courage for taking him on as a reclamation project.

As if she's reading his mind, she says, "I don't even try to stop him anymore. I find that he makes more of an effort not to get lung cancer if I just let Willie be Willie."

"So," his host says when he comes back, smelling faintly of tobacco. "Did I do you right?"

"As right as was possible, I guess."

"Well, I couldn't get everything about your history in there. The bastards would only give me eighty inches to work with."

Gray grimaces.

There's a lot of his history he'd just as soon didn't see the light of day.

GRAYSON MELVIN got his college degree at last in 1979. He'd spent eleven years first as a soldier and then, on again and off again, as a different kind of college student than the one he briefly was before April of 1968. He also had blown through a marriage.

The school he chose, Virginia Commonwealth University, was full of people like Gray, people who had drifted off the traditional track to higher education, or never got on it. Veterans. Local kids whose families couldn't afford to send them away to college. Former dropouts trying to get a degree one course at a time, showing up for night classes still wearing their work clothes. Middle-aged women indulging a midlife crisis or trying on a new, post-marriage life. A poster in one of the dean's offices said, "If you want ivy, bring your own."

He worked some and took classes when he could, usually a couple at a time. He still wanted to be a journalist, and VCU had what was now called "mass communications." He worked at the student paper. He even managed to get an internship at the city's morning daily newspaper. When he graduated, he was hired full-time. The next year, he met Willie Black. Gray was thirty-one and Willie was twenty-one, but they found that they had things in common. Drinking, mostly.

With his marriage up in smoke, Gray had time on his hands.

HE HAD met Hannah Coble in 1973, two years after moving from his father's house to Richmond. Gray realized that his only chance at anything resembling a normal life would have to take place some distance from East Geddie, where everyone knew who he was and what he allegedly did.

Plus it was obvious to him that one of them wasn't going to make it out of that little house alive if they both stayed there. Gray's father had never been much on self-control and tact, and Gray found that two years in the wartime army had depleted whatever reserve he ever had.

The night the inevitable happened, Jimmy came in drunk and wasn't in bed yet when Gray got back twenty minutes later, drunker.

Jimmy said something about his son's drinking, which had gotten somewhat out of hand. Gray said he came by it naturally. Then Jimmy said, "Well, at least I ain't killed anybody yet."

Kaycee had just left for college, so they had the place to themselves. Gray staggered over to his father, who was sitting at the kitchen table. He had never hit him before, although he'd often wanted to. He punched Jimmy in the nose, knocking him back against the side of the refrigerator.

Jimmy lay on the floor, his legs tangled in the chair.

Gray stood over him.

"You son of a bitch. You never believed me, did you?"

"Well," Jimmy laughed, wiping a trickle of blood off on his sleeve, "I reckon you're a son of a bitch, too, don't you think?"

Gray kicked him. When his father pulled out the switchblade, he backed away.

"Oh, I can see how it happened," Jimmy said. "You get a little nooky and think you're in true love. Then she shits on you. A man's got to do something about that.

"You just let it get out of hand. Didn't know when to stop, did you?"

Gray reached behind him and pulled a butcher knife out of the drawer.

Jimmy laughed and worked his way up, first to his hands and knees and then full upright.

"Yeah, why don't you go ahead and use that thing? Come on. Fuck, I bet you killed plenty of them gooks over there. And we both know what you did to that girl. But you ain't killed a full-grown white man that brought a knife to a knife fight, have you?"

Looking at his father, now standing not three feet away, tossing the knife from one hand to the other and grinning like a maniac, Gray was pretty sure he could take him, and he was pretty sure he wanted to. What the hell. Everyone, including Jimmy, already thought he was a damned murderer. He might as well live up to expectations.

Neither of them moved for a good ten seconds.

Then Jimmy laughed and set down the knife.

"Hell, you ain't worth the damn trouble," he said. "And you ain't got the balls to finish what you started."

Gray just stared at him. He knew Jimmy was drunk, but he knew his father meant what he said about his killing Annie.

He had told Jimmy the whole story, that first weekend after he came back. His father had looked at him for a while, like he was sizing him up for the first time.

"Well," he had told Gray, "just don't say anything if you don't have to."

After that, they had kept away from the subject, until tonight.

"So that's it," Gray said at last as they stared at each other across the small kitchen, the night's dirty dishes piled in the sink behind him. "That's what you think."

Jimmy shook his head and smiled.

"What I think," he said, "is that you need to get your ass out of here. You never know what I might do some night when you're asleep."

He grinned as he picked the knife back off the table.

Gray stayed with an old friend for a week. That's how long it took him to find employment out of state. He knew a guy from Nam who lived in Richmond, and he said he could get Gray a job, working for a roofer.

He had already taken everything he wanted from Jimmy's house. He called his sister at school in Greenville and told her he was leaving, but he didn't tell her why right then. He promised to stop and see her on the way north.

He kept his promise. Kaycee, who had borne the brunt of her father's moods since Gray left for college, hugged him and cried. He promised to get her up to Richmond for a visit as soon as he could get settled. He had thought of himself as her protector all the years they endured first their parents' fights and then Jimmy's anger. Now, looking down on his little sister, feeling the warmth of her head and the dampness of her tears against his chest, he knew he was abandoning her again, no matter what he said about visits.

When he told her what happened in the kitchen, she said she wasn't going back home, ever. She kept that vow for quite a while, even when Jimmy threatened to cut off her tuition money. She dropped out of East Carolina after two years and never lived under Jimmy's roof again. She did spend a couple of summers in the extra bedroom of Gray's cheap apartment in the Fan, but then Hannah came into the picture. Gray's girlfriend and sister never got along well enough to share small living quarters. Soon enough, Kaycee moved back to a place not five miles from where her father still lived. She has never left.

Over the years, Gray sometimes wished he had moved farther away from all the trouble. On a few occasions, Richmond was too close for his comfort. People knew people, and

parts of the story about Annie would come out. What people
heard was often worse than the truth.

BY THE time he met Hannah, he had decided that he did
want a college degree after all. The kind of jobs he got as
a veteran with a high school diploma helped convince him.

She was an incoming freshman that fall, six years younger
than he was. He'd had sex with more than a dozen women
by that time, none of whom made him forget Annie. He still
dreamed about her, although the dreams were seeming less
and less real.

When he showed Kaycee the weather-beaten photo of
Annie he still carried in the deep recesses of his wallet, a
year after he and Hannah were married, Kaycee looked at
it, then looked at Gray. She had seen Annie's picture, years
ago, in various newspapers, but this was the first time Gray
had shown her the now-faded photograph.

"You do know who this looks like, don't you?" she had
said.

Gray had to admit that, yes, he did.

Hannah didn't have Annie's wit, and she didn't have her
pure animal passion, something Gray forced himself to overlook while he convinced himself that he loved Hannah for
Hannah, period.

They dated for two years before they got married.
Hannah, a Richmond girl who was commuting to VCU
when they met, moved in with him six months beforehand.
Her parents weren't that fond of him, even before they heard
the rumors and checked them out.

Three nights before their wedding, her father begged her
not to do it. He took her out to dinner and showed her
the clippings from the Raleigh paper from 1968. Gray later

came to think that she went ahead with the wedding anyhow as much to prove her parents wrong as anything. She told her father she already knew about Annie Lineberger, but she didn't really know everything. Gray hadn't told her as much as he should have. When she confronted him about it later that night, he told her pretty much everything about Annie, except for the ache he still felt sometimes for her. He offered to exit Hannah's life for good.

"No," she'd said, "we've already gone this far. I love you, and that's all I need to know."

Hannah was, as her mother said, "a tad anal." She liked to have things mapped out. Gray would come to wonder, in the four years they were married, if her driving force that night wasn't a refusal to cancel all the wedding plans.

He had to give her credit though. She never gave any indication that she didn't believe what he told her about Annie Lineberger's disappearance, and her parents never mentioned it to him, although there was a certain chill between him and them.

On the day of the wedding, Hannah's father pulled him into the men's room at the little Methodist church.

He put his hands on both Gray's biceps and looked him in the eyes. He seemed to be on the verge of tears. He was a short man who had to look up to Gray.

"You bastard," he whispered, although they were alone, "you better treat my little girl right."

Gray said he would. And, in the sense of not murdering her and burying her in an unmarked grave, he kept his word.

CHAPTER NINE

1968

He was in Wisconsin when the letter was forwarded to him.

"We feel it is in your best interests at this stressful time to take a sabbatical. The university will be glad to entertain an application for readmission at a future date."

It went on a bit longer, but the whole message was contained on one sheet of paper. With the cloud of Annie Lineberger's death hanging over him as the search for what was now presumed to be her lifeless body continued, he was not welcome to return to his college.

He had been outside all that hot, early July day, trying to sell what seemed to him to be the unsellable. The Midwesterners with whom he spoke were almost uniformly polite but also nearly unanimous in their belief that the "great books" Gray was selling were not worth the sizable investment.

He had gotten pretty good at worming his way inside the front door. He took along the same egg timer he had used to woo Annie, and at least some of his potential buyers were charmed enough by his entreaty ("Just give me three minutes; when the sand runs out, you can kick me out.") and his earnestness to let him inside, but mostly they politely sent him on his way. In the first three weeks, he'd had two potential sales.

He'd never been anywhere, so the trip to Wisconsin, a couple of weeks after exams ended, had been an adventure. Mostly, though, it was an escape from the nightmare of the past spring. He and the Valiant made the rounds in places like Oconomowoc and Ashippun. He rented a room with a family and even babysat their kids. He drank cheap beer at night with his fellow student salesmen, all from other schools and all with no knowledge of Gray's recent, unpleasant history.

Until the letter arrived, he'd reached a point where he could go for hours sometimes without thinking about Annie.

He knew his grades were disappointing, but he hadn't flunked out, and he'd made a promise to himself to do better in the fall. The idea that his university might deep-six him without so much as a hearing came as a surprise.

The letter mentioned the possibility of military service in the interim before he was allowed back in the school's good graces. Even Gray, who didn't laugh much that summer, could see the humor in that. The Vietnam War was ramping up. Draft boards eagerly awaited boys who no longer could hide behind student deferments. Military service would be more than an option.

"Man," one of the other boys out selling books told him, when Gray told he'd been kicked out of school—without telling the boy exactly why—"you're gone."

He sleepwalked through his summer job for another week, awaiting the inevitable. Ironically, it was his best week, sales-wise.

The call from his father came eight days after he received the letter.

"Got something here from the draft board," he said. "It's addressed to you. Want me to open it?"

Gray had not yet told his father the bad news, although he did let Kaycee know, calling her one afternoon when he knew she'd be home and his father wouldn't be.

Jimmy did not take the news well, alternating his anger between the university "where I sent my hard-earned money" and his son, who obviously had squandered it.

Gray packed up that night. He said good-bye to his host family, who would never know about Annie Lineberger, had a few beers with the other boys, then got up the next morning to drive back to East Geddie.

His lawyer had been getting in touch with him every week or so to tell him that nothing new had been unearthed, an unfortunate verb. The district attorney really wanted to take it all before a grand jury, but without a body or any evidence of foul play on the part of Gray or anyone else, he knew he was hogtied.

"If you would tell him what you know," the lawyer said, "I'm sure something could be worked out. You know, her family just wants closure." Gray was more sure than ever that his court-appointed lawyer owed more allegiance to the DA than to him, and that he was convinced he was defending a guilty client.

The district attorney and the sheriff of Byrd County assured the news media and the public that the case was far from closed. They had a "solid suspect," the DA said, and were building their case.

Their biggest weapon was what Gray couldn't prove. He could not account for his whereabouts between the time Annie walked away from his car and the next morning.

He had talked to no one, hadn't stopped anywhere on the way back to Chapel Hill. He never returned to the motel

where he had booked a room for two nights. The manager
there told the deputy who talked to her that "the boy" had
seemed kind of strange when he checked in. Gray wished,
for once, that he had made some sort of contact with the
leering, chatty clerk at the country store in Mason's Mill, who
always seemed to remember him.

Nobody recalled seeing the weather-beaten Valiant
parked in the football stadium lot that night. The first time
anyone could vouch for Gray's whereabouts was ten o'clock
Saturday morning, when he stumbled into the coffee shop in
Chapel Hill for breakfast.

The investigators made Gray repeat his story a dozen
times before the case eventually cooled to the point that
the DA wasn't worried about losing his job if he didn't find
somebody to pin Annie Lineberger's murder on. Each time,
Gray told them the same story. If he said he drank two-thirds
of a fifth one time and half a fifth the next, they hopped on
that. They had him show them the exact intersection where
he stopped and threw up on the way back, the precise place
where he parked his car in the stadium lot. There was no
way he could remember the exact spot, and they hounded
him about that.

They tried to get him to admit that he did something out
of rage and despair that "a good boy like you" never would
have ordinarily done, but, "you know, shit happens." Gray
stuck to his story.

And then there was Annie's family. He first encountered
Hayden Lineberger II at one of the seemingly interminable
meetings he had with the investigators before, during, and
after his final exams that spring. Annie's father wasn't supposed to be there, but he had somehow managed to be in
a position to waylay Gray as he left after a ninety-minute
grilling.

Gray, having met the man's son, more or less knew who was bearing down on him in the hallway outside the interrogation room up in Byrd County. Then he saw, bringing up the rear, Annie's brother.

He instinctively took a step back as the big man approached him.

"You did it, you little son of a bitch," the man said. "We're going to barbecue your ass, and then you're going to spend all eternity frying like bacon, in hell."

He spit in Gray's face as Gray was protesting to the man that he was innocent.

"Tell us where she is," he said. By now, Annie's brother and two deputies were holding him back but not taking him away. He was still in spitting distance. "Tell them what you did with her. For God's sake, tell them."

Gray could see that the man was crying, and he knew he was too. Hayden Lineberger looked like he hadn't shaved or slept recently. When Gray told him he was sorry, it only made things worse.

"Sorry? You're sorry? You're gonna be sorry, you piece of shit."

Gray really was sorry for the man's loss—and Hayden Lineberger looked like a man who had accepted the fact that his daughter, by then missing for five weeks, was lost for good—but the Linebergers, father and son, heard it as contrition, even a confession.

The older man lunged. He managed to bloody Gray's lip with a wild swing before they finally ushered him out. Gray knew that he had not seen the last of the Lineberger family.

"Come on," Tree Lineberger said to his father. "The son of a bitch ain't worth it. Let the court take care of him."

Then Tree turned back.

"But if it doesn't," he said, pointing a finger at Gray, "you can bet your ass we will."

In the end, though, neither Annie nor her body appeared, and nothing could definitively tie Gray Melvin to her disappearance. As the summer wore on, the story eventually starved like a forest fire deprived of fuel. Nobody could place Annie Lineberger after she left Gray's car. Nobody could place Gray between the time she slammed the door and the time he staggered into the coffee shop the next morning.

"It's kind of like a tie, like in baseball," the half-assed attorney told Gray. "You know, when the runner and the ball get there at the same time.

"In this case, the tie goes to the defendant."

He was pretty clear in his unspoken opinion that Gray was damn lucky to manage a tie.

Gray had called his lawyer when he got back to East Geddie and told him he was going to be drafted.

"Well," the lawyer said, "that might be for the best, all things considered."

Best for whom, Gray wanted to ask him. If Anne Lineberger's body turned up, they'd yank him out of whatever hellhole the army sent him to. If it didn't, he'd be cannon fodder for the Viet Cong.

He could have enlisted and maybe gotten a better assignment. He could have joined the air force or navy, or tried to get into one of the National Guard units where so many boys who could get in were choosing to sit out the war.

By this time, though, Gray was ready to run up the white flag. If the world wanted his ass, it could have it. After all, Jimmy had been to war, had risked death and seen enough bad shit to mess him up for life. Why should Gray expect any better treatment? The truth, he realized later, was that he wanted punishment, even if he had done nothing to war- rant it. Somehow he should have protected Annie. She was his date, the love of his young life, and he let her run off into the dark. If she never arrived at her destination, whose fault was it?

The last day before he went away to basic training, a letter arrived at his father's house, addressed to Gray. He had gotten a few letters, and more phone calls, until the Mel- vins had to get an unlisted number, from people who wanted Gray and his family to know that justice had not prevailed and that he should rot in prison.

This one had a Monroe postmark.

Gray opened the envelope to find a sheet of notebook paper, folded carefully with six words typed in the center:

"We will never forgive or forget."

It never occurred to Gray that they would do otherwise. The hell of it was, he knew that if he were in the Lineberg- ers' position, he would probably be doing the same thing.

And so, on July 26, 1968, he left for basic training, along- side the farm boys and inner-city kids who knew they were never going to college and the fuckups who were given a choice of war or jail.

"Make me proud," Jimmy had told him when he dropped him off at the bus station for the long trip to Fort Dix, New Jersey.

Gray told him he would. His father hugged him, a unique experience. Until his son got too old to accept beatings, Jim- my's physical contact with Gray had not included hugs.

CHAPTER TEN

THURSDAY, MAY 19

Two days ago, when Gray returned to his one-bedroom apartment, he could feel his neighbors' eyes behind half-drawn shades. And, not unexpectedly, a letter taped to the door by his landlady informed him that he was being evicted.

"They can't do that," Betsy said when he told her. "You haven't even been charged yet or anything."

True enough, but after reading a couple of the notes other residents had stuffed into his mailbox, he had no real desire to continue living there. Only one of his neighbors, a man in his eighties whom Gray had befriended, left him a note that offered at least a scintilla of support. "Hang in there," the old gent offered.

So he spent Tuesday and Wednesday moving his books and modest belongings either to Betsy's house or into a storage locker and abandoning the charms of the Green Valley "luxury apartment" complex, which was neither verdant nor luxurious and sat on the edge of a swamp.

He has been questioned twice by the police, once by those from Virginia, once by North Carolina's finest. He and Betsy take turns trying to keep reporters away. Every trip to the grocery store involves running a gauntlet of photographers and camera crews.

Betsy has taken a week off at the hospital. Gray tried to dissuade her, but she made it clear that she wasn't going to leave him alone "until they get this shit straightened out."

Josh doesn't talk much about what's going on at school, but Betsy knows through one of his teachers that he's being taunted by some of the other kids.

TODAY GRAY gets the call he's been expecting.

He has been working for the past twenty years as an English teacher in one of the area's community colleges. More specifically, he's been bouncing among three campuses, trying to teach young adults how to read and write well enough to transfer to a four-year school and eventually get a college degree. Sometimes, as a bonus, he gets one of them interested in literature.

It doesn't pay that well, but it's the groove or rut he's worn down for himself, one where he thought he could live out his days under the radar, uncoupled from the past.

Now, with his long-buried infamy elevated to national news level, the college that has twice named him teacher of the year has decided, according to the human resources person who called him, "to go in a different direction." That direction, it is made clear, is as far away from Gray Melvin as possible.

There is some small pension coming, when he chooses to activate it. He will get four weeks' severance pay.

"That's it?" is all Gray can summon in way of a response, although he knew this day was coming.

"Well," the voice on the other end says, "you are certainly welcome to reapply as an instructor, as soon as, um, all this has been resolved."

After he hangs up, he thinks of calling his chairman, or even the community college's president, with whom he has been on pleasant professional and social terms. But he knows that everybody has had a chance to weigh in on this one. The dice have been cast, and he's rolling snake-eyes. He's sixty-seven. He's reasonably well-paid as community college instructors go. And he has baggage that has turned up unexpectedly on his doorstep long after he had hoped it was lost forever. His now ex-employers might not believe he's guilty, but they don't believe it enough to go to the wall for him. They do not want his name and theirs to be linked.

He is, in short, screwed.

The legal consequences that are converging on him are so great that he is little fazed by this latest bad news. He has to admit, though, that he did like that damn job. He is going to miss it.

He had figured he could teach kids until he was seventy-five or so, if his health held out, something that is definitely not a given, if his urologist knows what he's talking about.

Gray had never considered himself an extrovert and couldn't have imagined himself standing in front of clusters of kids all day, force-feeding them what passes for knowledge. He only turned to teaching when it became clear that he was not going to be allowed to have a career in journalism that would pay his bills. He had been on track, he thought, for the kind of life he'd imagined for himself as a boy, but the Linebergers took care of that.

Once he tried teaching, though, he came to like it. Maybe not so much the first couple of years, when he was learning how to teach, assigned to instruct high school students in one of the city's more benighted neighborhoods. He would come home drained of adrenaline and generally thinking himself a fool. But he got the hang of it.

Richmond, when he turned to teaching in the 1990s, had promise. Due to benign neglect and tenacious preservationists, many of the old buildings were still there, and even then many of them were starting to be repurposed into restaurants and art studios and housing. The city had character. It had neighborhoods. It did not, like many of the Sun Belt cities to its south, appear to have been built from scratch in the past twenty years. People went into bars their fathers had gone to, attended the same church as their grandparents. They still do. Gray has seen his adopted hometown thrive in many categories.

What it didn't have then, and seems in no threat of having in the foreseeable future, was a school system that worked. Oh, if you were living in the right neighborhood, you could get your kids in good elementary schools, if you couldn't afford the private ones. And, if the offspring were fairly bright, they could get into one of the magnet high schools, where the teachers were first-rate and the fellow students were, for the most part, actually students.

But the middle schools were a nightmare, and so many of the city's residents, of all colors, sold their city homes and moved with regret to the suburbs when their kids reached that age. There, every school seemed new and every child appeared to have two helicopter parents. In a state where cities are not part of counties and rarely can annex parts of them, the Richmond school system has continued its downward spiral. People with school-age children in the city often are there because they have no choice.

Gray taught junior English for three years. He thought he had done some good, a feeling most of his jobs over the years had not given him. But when he had the chance for a post at the community college, where most of the students were at least interested enough in learning to show up for class and not tell their teachers to go fuck themselves, he took it.

He found that he was teaching many of the same students he would have had in his high school classes, except they were the ones who really were trying to get past the cycle of poverty many of their families had been in since their ancestors were slaves. He knew that a better man would have stayed with the high schools, maybe even gone to the dreaded middle schools, where things really went to hell for a lot of the dead-end kids. But he knew what a small percentage of saves he was going to get at that level, and he knew he just wasn't that damn good a person.

He tells the HR employee, before he hangs up, that he will come by sometime in the next few days to collect his few possessions from his tiny office.

"Be sure to call first," the HR person says. Gray knows this means so they can have someone there to watch him while he removes his stuff, for fear that he might commit some act of sabotage or violence. After all, a guy who probably murdered his girlfriend when she dumped him is capable of anything.

He assures his caller that he will give the college plenty of notice.

WILLIE BLACK made good on his promise. He called Gray on Tuesday to tell him that he had a lawyer.

"He's kind of a bullshit artist," Willie told him, "but you might need one. And he's got a good won-lost record."

Gray puts on a clean shirt and a tie this morning for his first meeting with Marcus Green. He isn't sure how he's going to pay him, but he knows he needs a real lawyer this time.

Betsy isn't thrilled that he's decided not to go with Dan Finebaum, but she agrees with Gray that he probably needs a fighter rather than a corporate lawyer.

"That Green guy sure seems to think a lot of himself," she says as she straightens his tie. "Those damn ads of his are on every fifteen minutes, it seems like."

She tells him, not for the first time, not to worry about the money.

"Mike left me plenty," she says. Her late husband died of a heart attack seven years ago, two years before she and Gray met.

Gray says he doubts Mike would have wanted her to spend her inheritance on her boyfriend's lawyer.

"Is that what you are? A boyfriend?"

"I don't know. Do I qualify as a lover?"

She smiles and hugs him.

"Whatever. You'll do."

He knows he should have asked her to marry him years ago. He wonders if the thing that was lurking, that has finally jumped out of the bushes, is what has kept him from doing so. That, and the lousy job he did of being a husband the first time around. He wonders now if he's too late.

There aren't many people in Richmond who believe he had nothing to do with Annie Lineberger's death, if the phone calls and e-mail he's seen are any indication. He is sure, though, that Betsy Fordyce is one of the few.

MARCUS GREEN'S office on Franklin Street does not immediately inspire confidence. The townhouse he's leasing seems a little shopworn on the outside. There is a small sign out front: Green and Ellis. Willie, in the spirit of full disclosure, has told Gray that Kate Ellis, his third ex-wife and landlady, also is Green's partner.

"But don't hold that against him. And she's a damn good lawyer. She just did a shitty job of picking husbands."

Inside, organized chaos seems to be the order of the day. Green is on the phone, talking loudly, and motions Gray to come into his office. Another phone rings unabated. A coffee pot surrounded by Styrofoam cups sits in the anteroom. There is no sign of a secretary, nor of Green's partner. Gray, who is used to substandard apartments, can see that the carpet is somewhat past due date.

Green, his shaved ebony head shining in the afternoon sun slicing through the window behind him, ends his phone conversation. He admonishes the other party to "just keep your damn mouth shut. Don't say anything to anybody. You understand. I'll get by there in a couple of hours."

He shakes his head as he motions Gray to take a seat in a chair that seems to have come with the carpet.

"Kids," the lawyer says. "Damn idiot held up a 7-Eleven wearing some kind of chicken-shit ski mask. Except the clerk and probably everybody in the store knew his voice, and he had on the same T-shirt he'd worn for a week. New York Yankees. Derek Jeter. And when he came back the next day, sans ski mask, he had on the same shirt."

Green sighs.

"He's seventeen years old, and I've got to go down to the city jail and keep him from telling his story to everybody who'll listen. I've got to try to keep him from getting chewed up. He goes to big folks' prison and his life story just gets worse. I don't even know how his momma's gonna pay me."

Green leans back in his chair and looks at his prospective new client.

"So," he says, "what can I do for you?"

Gray tells him everything about that night forty-eight years ago. He tells him about the ambush down in North Carolina.

"Damn, you're as dumb as that young knucklehead I was just talking to. And you're way too old to be that dumb. Why does everybody feel like they've got to talk?"

Gray asks Marcus Green how he might act if he was suddenly recast as the prime suspect for a murder almost half a century old. He's not getting good vibes about the man sitting across the desk.

Green laughs.

"Just be glad you're white. Otherwise they might have lynched your ass back then."

Green seems a little more impressed with Gray when he learns that he taught in the city schools and then in the community college. Green assures him that he is in good hands, and that if anyone can get him out of "this mess," it's him.

"I do have to ask you one question though."

He looks Gray straight in the eye.

"Did you do it? I mean, I'll defend you either way, but I need to know so I don't get surprised down the road. I hate surprises."

"I did not do it. Everything I told you is the truth."

"And you haven't left anything out?"

"Like what?"

"Like, maybe you caught up with that girl after she dumped you, maybe got a little rough. Didn't kill her, nothing like that, but something more than just 'See ya, have a good life.'"

"I never saw her again, after she left my car."

Green scratches his chin.

"OK."

"OK?"

"I'll take the case."

They talk about money. Gray Melvin has, last time he checked, about $100,000 in savings. That, Social Security, and the little pension are it for the long haul, especially now that his teaching career, if not his freedom, seems to be history. What Marcus Green wants, Gray can see, is going to be more than he can afford without breaking and scrambling his paltry nest egg. He knows that he is going to have to accept Betsy's offer.

"I can pay you," he says. "I have a friend. But can we work out some kind of plan?"

Green laughs.

"Yeah, friends are good to have. Don't worry. Nobody pays everything up front. Thing is, I have to have some of it. You'd be amazed how little incentive people have to pay after I've gotten them off. Even less when I don't."

Office carpet and chairs notwithstanding, Gray knows, through Willie, that Marcus Green is not exactly living hand to mouth. He resides in one of the old-money neighborhoods west of town, along River Road.

But he supposes that his new lawyer's financial status indicates that he must have done something right over the years.

They shake hands for the first time.

Green tells him to sit down again.

"I thought we might be able to do business," he says. "So I did some checking around. I know people, even down in Carolina. And that cracker DA down there, Grimes, he seems like he's out to hang his reputation on putting your ass away, from what I hear."

Gray leans closer.

"What did you find out?"

Green holds his thumb and index finger almost together.

"He's about this close," he says, "to bringing charges against you down there. They'll probably be wanting to extradite your ass back down to Byrd County, although the Virginia authorities might want a piece of you, too, since they found the body across the state line."

"What should I do?"

"When it happens, call me. And do what I told that young warrior on the phone to do. Don't say a damn word to anybody."

Green assures him that, if he's telling the truth, there won't be any hard evidence, just the fact that Gray was the last person known to have seen Annie and can't get anybody to account for his presence in the hours after she left.

"They'll have a hard time convicting you on a negative, on what you didn't do. But the girl's family is big down there. I found that out too. They'll definitely be gunning for you."

"What else is new?"

Gray tells his lawyer about the efforts the Linebergers have made over the years to thwart him.

"I thought it might be over," he says, "until this."

Tears suddenly catch up with him. It happens sometimes. Usually it occurs when nobody is around to see it.

"Well," Green says, actually looking concerned, "don't worry. And don't talk to anybody. And that includes that damn Willie Black."

ON THE way back to Betsy's, Gray's cell phone buzzes. He ignores it until he glances at the familiar number. He pulls off the street and answers.

"Kaycee."

"Where the hell have you been? I tried to call your apartment, and it just rang and rang. And then yesterday the recording said it was out of service."

Gray knows he might be the only person in North America without a messaging function on his home phone. He apologizes to his sister and tells her that he's been getting a lot of unwanted calls lately, and that on top of that, he's moved.

"Are you OK?"

He tells her that he's fine, that it's all just a big misunderstanding, that he has obtained the services of a very good lawyer.

He and Kaycee see each other two or three times a year. They talk once every month or so on the phone.

They never fought about anything. They just drifted apart. The only good thing about the four years when Gray returned to East Geddie to help take care of Jimmy toward the end was that he and his sister became temporarily closer, but the gap has gradually widened again. Despite their shared and bruised history, they really don't have much in common anymore, if they ever did. Kaycee was a passable student who never had her brother's zest for knowledge. And she's been more than occupied with her two single-parent children. Little Jimmy, thirty-five now, lives in a group home for special-needs adults in Port Campbell. Doing the math, Gray figures that Krystal would be thirty-three now, wherever she is. It is hard to imagine that his little sister is now sixty-three years old.

"Well, do you want me to come up there?"

Gray knows that Kaycee has a full-time job managing a convenience store and that she has trouble getting away. He was happy to give her his half of Jimmy's house after their father died, so she doesn't have to worry about a mortgage. Still, times are tight, and the way Kaycee asks, he can imagine her crossing her fingers on the other end of the phone, hoping he'll give the right answer.

"I don't think that'll be necessary, Kaycee. I think we've got it under control now."

"It's in the paper down here just about every day. They make it sound like, you know, like you did it."

She lets that last sentence hang, as if she needs some reassurance. When he came back home briefly, between Annie's disappearance and his departure for Fort Dix, there was never any doubt on her part. Even while Jimmy was giving him the fish-eye and asking pointed questions, Kaycee never seemed to doubt. She got into trouble that summer, fighting with another girl who apparently besmirched his already soot-black name.

It hurts that she might not be quite so sure now that her brother isn't a murderer.

He tells her that he's just as innocent as he was forty-eight years ago. Nothing has changed.

"But they found her body and all. And they say you're the last one to see her."

"Well, they knew that in 1968."

"You know what I mean. Anyhow, I haven't said anything to the newspapers, not really. Well, not much."

"The newspapers?"

"I figured you'd seen it. The *News and Observer* sent somebody down here. I guess it wasn't that hard to find me. But I told 'em that there was no way in hell you killed that girl, that you wouldn't hurt a fly."

"Thank you for that."

He asks her about Krystal. The last he heard, she was living in Montana or Idaho or some damn where like that, with two kids and no husband.

"Still out west, I guess," Kaycee says. "I don't know. She'll come back sometime, when she needs help. She always does."

Gray doesn't necessarily think Kaycee should have married either of the fathers of her two children, who both seemed to him to be as common as dung beetles. He does feel bad, though, that he didn't try harder to be some kind of male influence in her life. Little Jimmy was twelve and still unable to tie his shoes when Gray moved back to Richmond after the death of the wasting-away man they were then calling Big Jimmy. Krystal was ten and already, as far as Gray could see, in possession of an interior compass that pointed in the opposite direction of "smart" and "appropriate" whenever possible. He did try to have a talk or two with her, but nothing much came of that except eye-rolling and "you're not my dad." Gray thought the girl should have been happy that anyone was willing to assume that thankless role, even as a surrogate.

When he left, he was guiltily relieved to not be on the go-to list every time trouble inevitably reared its head. He left it all in Kaycee's lap, feeling that his half of their father's one-bath, 1951 house was a cheap price to pay for his freedom.

"You're still my big brother," Kaycee tells him. "And I still love you, no matter what."

Gray thanks her and tells her he will call her soon.

THERE'S ONLY one TV van in the street when he pulls up at Betsy's.

"It's quieted down a little," she tells him when he leaves the lone reporter in his wake and shuts the front door. "There was one call, though, that I thought you might want to return."

The one call, it turns out, is from a town in North Carolina an hour or so southwest of Chapel Hill, about halfway to Charlotte.

"I don't think she even knew about your new-found fame . . ."

"Infamy."

"Whatever. I don't think she even knew who you were. But she said she thought she had something of yours. She said she thought she had your high school senior class ring."

Gray has to stop and think. Then he remembers when he last saw it, glinting in the overhead light as Annie opened the door, after he refused to take it back.

"How the hell does she know that?"

"I don't know. I'm just the messenger. But I thought you might want to call. At least this one wasn't a death threat or some TV buzzard trying to pick your bones."

Gray brings Betsy up to date on his meeting with Marcus Green. He tells her what it's going to cost.

She takes him by the shoulders.

"I already told you once. Don't worry about the cost."

But he does. He wonders if he won't just be wasting Betsy's money.

Josh comes into the room while they're talking.

"They're not going to take you away, are they?" the boy asks.

Josh's father lives on the South Side, not three miles away as the crow flies. Since the boy's mother decided she didn't want to be married, or a mother, anymore, the boy has been the legal responsibility of his father, but Jack Fordyce seems as uninterested in parenting as his former wife. Consequently Josh showed up on his grandmother's doorstep about the same time Gray did. He doesn't call Gray "Dad," but he doesn't refer to his usually absent father that way either.

"Don't worry. I'm here for the long haul."

Gray hopes he isn't giving the boy false hope.

He goes into the bedroom he is sharing with Betsy and calls the number.

The woman's name, on the sticky note, is Dorothea Gaines. The name means nothing to Gray, and he doesn't recall ever being in the town that's on the note.

He identifies himself.

"I know this is kind of crazy," the woman says, "but this thing has just turned into a mystery for me, and you know I love mysteries. Well, you don't know, I reckon, but I do."

"Well, Ms. Gaines . . ."

"Oh, call me Dot. Anyhow, about this ring I found . . ."

She says she was antiquing a couple of months ago at a store in her hometown.

"The place has mostly junk, but it's fun to look, you know."

While she was rummaging through a box of "this and that," she found the ring.

"Man sold it to me for ten dollars. Shoot, the gold in it is worth way more than that.

"But then I got to looking at it. I saw the high school, East Geddie. I'd never heard of it, didn't even know if it was in North Carolina or not. And I saw the initials. JGM, and it had the year on it, 1967. And, like I said, I love a good mystery."

So she started her search.

"My husband says I'm crazy, that I'm wasting my time and money, but I've got a lot of time, and what's money for if you don't spend it?"

She went online and found out that East Geddie High was in the eastern part of the state and had closed in 1969. She joined a website that helped people get back in touch with their old high school classmates, and that led her to a site where she could look at the 1967 East Geddie High yearbook online.

"The Geddie Clan," Gray says. Someone in the past had taken pride in the Scottish heritage of the area and chose that name for the school yearbook. It was a little awkward when the school integrated, but everyone agreed it could have been worse. At least they didn't spell Clan with a K.

"Yes, that's right."

She found one senior whose name might have fit the initials.

"I saw 'James Grayson Melvin,' and I said to myself, 'Dot, that's the one.'"

She said she got in touch with four of his former class-mates before one of them, a man Gray hasn't seen in twenty years, told her he thought Gray Melvin was living in Richmond.

"He said he thought you had gotten in some trouble about something or other."

"You could say that."

"Anyhow, I found out you were a teacher at the commu-nity college there, and somebody at the college gave me the number where they said they thought I could reach you."

Gray had given his former college employer Betsy's number along with the one in the apartment complex where he no longer lives and his cell number.

"And now I've found you!"

Gray congratulates her on her stellar detective work. She says she'll mail him the ring. Although he has no desire to see his class ring again, he thinks such diligence should be rewarded. He offers to pay her for it, along with the shipping. The impact of it all doesn't really hit him until he's about to hang up.

"Wait," he says. "Where did it come from?"

"What? The ring? The antique—well, junk—store, like I told you. Lost Treasures."

"But where did they get it?"

Dot Gaines has no idea.

"I'll tell you what," Gray says. "Just hang on to it, and I'll come down there myself. I've got some business down that way anyhow."

She gives him her phone number and address. He asks her if tomorrow would be a good time for him to come by. They agree on two in the afternoon. She expresses surprise that he's going to be in her part of the state so quickly. Gray tells her that something has just come up that makes it imperative for him to come down.

Betsy is waiting in the den. He tells her about the ring. He explains the circumstances under which he last saw it.

"And now this woman has it? I mean, you're sure it's yours?"

"I'm pretty sure there wasn't anybody else in my class with the same initials."

"So what are you going to do about it?"

He tells her his plan.

"Don't you think it's a little dicey, going back down there again?"

"Well, I'm not going to drive through Byrd County, if I can help it."

"But what are you hoping to find, Gray? I mean, you said she doesn't even know how your ring showed up at some junk shop."

He sighs and looks across the room at the drawn blinds.

"Somebody knows. And, no, I don't feel like passing this off to the police down there. They'll just think I cooked this up to save my butt."

Gray goes back to the bedroom to do some light packing. He'll probably displease his new lawyer and run the risk of looking like he's gone on the lam.

Maybe he's chasing shadows. One thing he knows though. His high school senior ring was still in the possession of Annie Lineberger the last time he saw her. Maybe she threw it in a trash can, and it somehow found its way to Mrs. Dorothea Gaines of Sykes, North Carolina, forty-eight years later.

Maybe, though, it didn't happen that way.

CHAPTER ELEVEN

"Got damn! Why don't you just tie a pork chop around your neck and let 'em throw you to the dogs? The last place in the world you need to be right now is the great state of North Carolina. Make 'em come and get you."

Gray explains to Marcus Green why he thinks he has to find out what he can about his high school ring. His lawyer has to agree that it might not be the best plan to take what he now knows to the authorities.

"But we can hire a private detective. I know one down there that owes me a favor or two. Let the professionals handle it."

Gray thanks him for his advice and silently hopes he isn't going to be charged for it. He explains that he believes he himself has to make this trip. He has been hiding in plain sight for almost half a century, most of his life now, hoping for nothing more than obscurity. He has thought often in the past about finding some way to clear his name, but he always backed down, preferring to let the past fade into forgetfulness.

Except, of course, it hasn't.

"You're an idiot. But keep me posted," Green says. "When, not if, you wind up in some jail down there and you get one call, make sure it's to me."

Gray tells Betsy he'll wait and leave in the morning. It's already nearly dinnertime. When she offers to go with him, he thanks her but declines her offer.

He tells her things might get ugly. In reality, he would just as soon face the ghost of Annie Lineberger by himself.

That night, they make love for the first time since Annie's bones were discovered. Gray still finds it somewhat miraculous that people actually have sex at the tender age of sixty-seven. When he was twenty, he couldn't have imagined it. At forty, even, he assumed that the embers that had always burst into flame at the slightest provocation would eventually turn to dead ashes. That hasn't happened yet. Maybe that's why, according to his urologist, he's in denial about his PSA numbers. Gray knows too many men who have been rendered boner-free as the result of prostate surgery. And he wonders what use he will be to Betsy, whose libido seems to grow more hungry with age, when and if he suffers that small death. She tells him it won't matter, but still . . .

Lying there in the dark, staring at the bathroom nightlight, while she snores softly beside him, he is thankful for what he has. For a few moments, his mind was free of Annie and his dubious future.

Now, though, the relentless carnivores that have been chewing up his recent nights return.

THE SUMMER of 1968 was unlike anything Gray had even imagined he might experience.

No sooner had the initial fruitless investigations into his role in Annie's disappearance gone away than he was kicked out of his university and welcomed against his will into the United States Army.

He wasn't against the war in Vietnam, although he would later come to see it as a monstrous folly. In 1968, the antiwar movement had not yet blossomed in North Carolina. The wakeup call of Kent State was still two years away. Boys whose fathers had fought in World War II were inclined to believe it was only right that they should serve as well. The minority who went to college were glad for the respite and either secretly or openly hoped the whole mess would be over before they had to face the draft board, but if you had asked them, in the spring of 1968, most would have said the war was a necessary evil. The Tet Offensive that January had brought home the reality of Vietnam to some, but the enormity of the war was still in the distance.

There was already talk of a civil suit on the part of the Lineberger family. Nothing would come of it, in the absence of enough evidence to even bring the case to trial in a criminal court. It did, however, add to the load Gray was carrying that summer.

His feeling about Annie seemed to change with the wind. He had never really had a chance to roll in the grief of a nineteen-year-old whose first love has dumped him. It seemed untoward to brood over something that was overshadowed into insignificance by the great cloud that towered over him now. What right did he have to mourn lost love when the girl herself appeared to be lost forever, especially since he was the prime suspect in her disappearance?

He still felt it, though, in his gut. He had lost twenty pounds by the time a bus, a train, and a taxi transported him from Port Campbell to Fort Dix. Kaycee, the only one in his father's house who seemed to notice his anguish, worried about him. She was young enough to appreciate romance. He could pour out his despair to her. In his selfishness, the fact that Annie was lost to him overshadowed the fact that she was lost, period.

Kaycee didn't have much to contribute to the conversation she had with her older brother when she mentioned his weight loss one afternoon and he broke into tears, but Gray was grateful to have a listener. Most of the people who had listened to him lately seemed to be using notepads and tape recorders, and they assured him he would feel better once he confessed.

In the one interview Jimmy gave to the *News & Observer*, he was quoted as saying, "Young people do crazy things, you know." Jimmy said he didn't mean it the way it sounded.

In truth, going away to war didn't seem like the worst thing. What friends he'd had in high school avoided him now, some because they doubted his innocence and some because they were embarrassed by his presence. He went back only once to the Methodist church of his childhood. The unspoken accusations hung like bad air in the sanctuary. When the preacher spoke of "the mercy of Christ to forgive even the most craven sinners," Gray felt the man's eyes were on him alone. Once, on the grounds afterward, he turned suddenly when he heard his name and saw people with whom he had grown up quickly avert their eyes.

He got through basic training and infantry AIT with few bumps along the way. The weight he'd lost actually worked in his favor. He found out that firing an M16 was hardly rocket science, especially since Jimmy had shown him, more or less against Gray's will, a thing or two about guns back when he still thought his son might be the kind of boy who one day would go deer hunting with him.

His company captain called him in, midway through basic training. Somehow he had heard about Annie Lineberger.

"Melvin," he said, "we know about that girl. We don't give a shit what you did, but you damn well better not fuck up again. We don't have room for fuckups here." Since Gray's company was full of young men who had wound up there by dint of fuckups, large and small, he didn't take the captain too seriously.

It seemed like a fool's errand to tell the man, a tall, hollow-eyed African American who seemed especially unkind to white college boys with Southern accents, that he was innocent.

Before he left for Vietnam, he spent his last furlough mostly in New York City with a friend he'd made in AIT. He returned home then, but after a couple of days in East Geddie, he kissed Kaycee good-bye and shook hands with Jimmy, and then he was gone.

Gray was lucky. They all told him that. He wasn't one of the twelve thousand or so Americans who died in Vietnam in 1969. He was given a Purple Heart for being close to a 122mm rocket that killed three of his platoon mates in their shithole bunkers in a place Gray can't and doesn't want to remember, but all he brought home physically was a six-inch scar halfway between his right elbow and shoulder. Today, he can still see the white ghost of that wound, to remind him of other, invisible ones.

For years he would have nightmares centered on that explosion and its aftermath. He emerged from the blast half-deaf, unsure if he was dead or alive. Feeling something wet and warm on his chest, he quickly wiped away matter that recently had been part of a live human being with whom he was playing poker when they heard the scream of "incoming" and the bomb hit. One of the cards, the seven of hearts, also had gotten caught up in the shreds of his fatigues. He kept it for years, a talisman that didn't seem to ward off much of anything. He doesn't know where he lost it.

Kaycee wrote him every week or so when he was in Vietnam. Jimmy even wrote twice. Gray heard from one of his friends from high school. And he got, to his amazement, several letters from Corrine Manzi.

She had talked with him before he left school after exams. She told him he had real talent, and that she believed him and believed in him. He thanked her for that, and they exchanged addresses. On a whim, he wrote her in basic training, and she wrote back. They continued their correspondence throughout his army time. She already was on the fast track in journalism, at a time when many newspapers still consigned female journalists to the society pages.

"Get the hell out of there in one piece and get that damn degree," Corrina Corrina wrote in the last letter before he came back home.

He got back in time for Christmas of 1969. He was out of the army by the middle of 1970. Everybody told him he had his whole life in front of him. It didn't feel that way though.

In the loose-ends days after his discharge, Gray visited Corrine once. She was an assistant editor at a newspaper in Akron, Ohio. She seemed more buttoned-down. She said she had a roommate, another woman who worked in the newsroom. Gray felt awkward, as if she were on some train that was slowly pulling away while he stood at the station waving good-bye.

She wrote him again, and he wrote her. When she wrote again, he didn't reply. By then, he had moved on after falling out with his father, and he didn't give Corrine Manzi his new address in Richmond.

He did get one other letter in Vietnam. It came from Monroe, North Carolina, with no return address.

"We hope you are in hell by now, but if you aren't, we will be waiting when you come back to help you get there."

Like the earlier one, it wasn't signed.

He was visited, upon his brief return to East Geddie, by detectives from Byrd County. They seemed half-hearted in their questioning, as if they had been force-marched there by the district attorney but knew they were pissing in the wind.

They asked the same questions Gray had answered so many times before. He had played that last night over in his mind so often, in sleepless barracks nights and in fortified bunkers, that he had little trouble staying on script. He declined to have a lawyer present.

"When we find that girl's body," one of the men said as they left, "we're going to be back."

But they didn't, and they weren't.

And, in those drifting days, Gray drank.

He had come late to alcohol. He had drunk exactly three beers in his life before he went away to college. At Carolina, he stepped up the pace somewhat. Drinking gave him Dutch courage in social settings, made it easier for a shy kid from a small school to blend in. Without beer, he might never have gotten to know Annie Lineberger.

In the army, and especially in Vietnam, alcohol was how he got through the days and weeks. And marijuana, still an exotic substance on his campus in 1968, was everywhere. "Purple Haze" was more or less an anthem, dark and foreboding like the jungle they were supposed to somehow conquer.

Back home, as the weeks turned into months, he felt almost duty-bound to get shit-faced on nearly a daily basis. That was when Jimmy, no piker himself, expressed concern.

There were other boys back home from Vietnam, and they found each other. Plus the military base next door meant a healthy population of young men either going to war or coming back, guys with "Nothing to Lose" stamped on their foreheads.

They would cruise around Port Campbell, hitting the hangouts, sometimes picking up women, sometimes paying whores. They sat in their cars at the drive-in restaurants and watched the teenage girls, free-range housewives, and hookers drive by in twos and threes, a parade leading nowhere. Sometimes there was eye contact, followed by a slow-speed chase to some less-crowded spot.

He found that he excelled at drinking, in that he could "hold his shit" after his friends were well on the way to wasted. He was progressing toward being what he now thinks of as a functioning alcoholic before he realized that he was drinking for need instead of pleasure.

One night, when he was well beyond what the state of North Carolina defined as drunk, Gray and two other young veterans followed three African American girls back to their cinder-block house. They charged not much more than the men had spent on beer and burgers. Gray's whore was spectacularly unattractive. A combination of her greasy hair and bad teeth and the ten beers he'd already consumed rendered him impotent. He paid her and pretended to his new buddies that all was well.

Their spiral took them next to a tattoo parlor. Gray had eschewed any tats up to that night, but he thought he should have something to show for the evening.

When he woke up the next morning, sore and hung over, he prayed that he had only dreamt what he had done. Looking at his right bicep, though, there it was: the blood-red heart, with "Annie" running through it. The one thing he wanted most to forget was now embedded in his skin.

Jimmy saw it soon enough.

He shook his head.

"You," he said, "are one dumb son of a bitch."

He and Jimmy had their big falling-out not long after that, and Gray was gone to Richmond.

Gray would tell his wife and any other woman who stumbled on the tattoo, no more than two inches square, that it was the name of an old girlfriend. Betsy knew more than anyone what it meant, but she didn't know everything. It had faded over the years, like Gray himself, but when he looked at it now, it shined out like a beacon, demanding to be seen.

If anyone else who had seen him at the beach or in the shower over the years had made the connection since Annie's bones were found, they hadn't said. He wondered how long it would be until the people who wanted to lock him up for the rest of his life found the evidence of his long-ago anguish, and what they will make of it.

CHAPTER TWELVE

1968

It had been oversized, even for Gray's country-boy hands. His knuckles were swollen from jamming them playing football and basketball, and once he squeezed the ring past the second joint, it rolled around with a quarter-inch of air between it and his finger. He had to use moleskin to hold it in place.

On Annie's slim and tapered hands, his senior-class ring was a monstrosity. When she wore it, it reminded him of girls in high school who wore their boyfriends' sweaters, the bottoms of the garments almost reaching their knees.

Still it meant something.

She had never seemed that thrilled to be wearing it, and he knew that it was a gesture more fitting for high school than college. Still she took it when he offered it to her that chilly March day.

Once, when he came up to Chatham on a Friday night, she came down to the dorm lobby for their date, and he saw that it wasn't on her finger.

"Oh, sorry. I forgot," she said. She turned around and went back up. When she returned, she waved her hand with the oversized ring at him. He knew, then, that she probably wasn't wearing it when he wasn't around. He could imagine it sitting there on her dresser. He could imagine her hiding its very existence from the perfidious poacher, Winston.

Still he wanted her to wear it. He wanted to mark her as his, even when he began to see that she wasn't, even if maybe she was his only when he was actually in her sight. Maybe the doubt made him want her to wear it even more.

That late April night she disappeared, she wasn't wearing the ring. For some reason, he didn't notice until they were back in his car, having their "talk."

He would remember later how she retrieved it from her purse, rummaging through the oversized leather bag, when he finally noticed and asked her about it, his heart already full of dread. It was just before she gave him his walking papers.

"Here it is," she said, after searching for a minute or so. She tried to hand it to him. He told her he didn't want it. After she said what she had to say, after he lost his temper and she started to back away from him, reaching for the door handle, she tried again to give it back.

"Keep it," he'd said. "I never want to see it again."

She didn't seem scared of his temper.

He wouldn't remember what she said next for a very long time. In the haze that marked the days and weeks that followed, it somehow slipped his mind. Maybe it was Dot Gaines's sleuth work that brought it back to him.

Annie had sighed.

"This is just like the other time," she'd said. "You boys are all alike. You can't get what you want, and you just throw a little hissy fit.

"This is just like back in high school."

And then she was gone.

He wonders, forty-eight years later, why she didn't just dump the ring in the Valiant. She obviously didn't want it.

He wasn't sure she hadn't done just that. He didn't care. He remembers thinking at the time that maybe the cops would find it wedged behind the seat when they tore the car apart, but they didn't.

CHAPTER THIRTEEN

MAY 20

Betsy finds a cardboard box for Gray to use at the one stop he's making before he heads south again, this time driving his own car.

"Are you sure you won't need more boxes?" she asks. "I mean, damn, twenty years."

He assures her that one box will suffice. He is not in a nostalgic mood.

He pulls into the parking lot at the college where he's earned his salary for most of the past two decades. He called yesterday to make sure someone would be there to "escort" him to and from his desk.

The suburban campus is quiet. In what he considers the only smidgen of good news in the past week, final exams had concluded only four days before he and Annie Lineberger became news again. He was at least able to do right by his last two classes.

Among other items today, he has been told he can pick up the last paycheck he expects to see in quite some time.

The secretary, with whom he is on a first-name basis, comes around the desk and gives him a hug, then calls security.

Five minutes later, a guard who looks like he's all of twenty comes through the door. He looks embarrassed, and familiar.

"Cody?"

The kid, a former high school football player with a thick neck who looks as if he's gained ten pounds since he took the twentieth century American literature overview course Gray taught last fall, nods his head. He was one of the brighter students in the class.

"Gotta pay the bills," Cody says. He explains that he took one course in the spring and "hopes to" get back into something like full-time student status in the fall. He's working another job as well, as a bouncer. He mentions, almost as an afterthought, that he's married now.

It has occurred to Gray more than once in his teaching career, and especially in the last decade or so, that he is not exactly preparing his students for twenty-first century life. Tuition at the community college isn't that steep, but if the people in his classes plan to go on to a four-year school, they'll all be taking out loans and, if they don't major in something more useful than English, they might all be security guards eventually.

Cody apologizes twice while walking Gray back to his former office.

"I mean, I know some dudes who've messed up pretty bad, and it worked out," he says.

Gray pats him on the arm. He appreciates the effort.

He has a hard time deciding what merits space in his cardboard box. There are the awards he got for allegedly being a good teacher. He also scoops up photos of Jimmy and Kaycee, of Kaycee and her kids, one of him and Betsy at the beach, and one of Josh in his Little League uniform. He picks up his *Riverside Shakespeare* and half a dozen other books of which he is particularly fond. He throws in the Rolodex that he still uses, computers be damned, although he wonders how many names on that list will be relevant to him in the future.

He doesn't need more than ten minutes to make his choices. When he looks at the box, now about two-thirds full, he can't help but wonder at how little he's taking away from twenty years of teaching. He's always thought of himself as something of a pack rat, but now he just wants to put it all in the rearview mirror.

Another instructor, a woman he's known for more than a decade, is coming out of her office down the hall as he and Cody walk out. She seems to be on the verge of heading in his direction, but then she does a one eighty and walks away.

The same secretary who summoned the guard has his final paycheck for him. She tells him she will miss him. She and Cody are the only people he's spoken with in his final visit to the college.

"Oh, wait," the secretary says.

He turns around, box in hand.

"I'll need your ID card." She holds out her hand. "Sorry."

THE TRIP back down to North Carolina is uneventful. Near the border, Gray's cell phone buzzes. He recognizes Marcus Green's number.

"You're really gonna do this?" the lawyer asks. "I think I have a fool for a client."

He admonishes Gray again to call him "when, not if" he gets locked up. Gray promises that he will.

"Tell me again about that ring."

Gray goes over the story again.

"Damn, man," Green says, "that ring could have come from anywhere. She might have thrown it away when she was leaving. She could have left it on her dresser and then gone out again. You said she was seeing some other guy, right?"

Gray reminds him that Annie was allegedly a no-show for her Saturday date with the boy from U.Va., and that the cops couldn't find anyone who saw her after she left Gray on Friday night.

"Well, if it was me, I'd go with Occam's razor. The simplest answer probably is the right one. She threw it away or dropped it or left it somewhere."

"Maybe. That's what I'm going to find out."

"You're going into the maw of the beast," Gray's lawyer warns him.

Gray tells him he's been avoiding the beast long enough, and hangs up.

The town of Sykes isn't much. It is in the middle of a region of the state where, despairing of making a living out of the clayey soil, enterprising souls started using the clay itself for sustenance. Pottery signs abound. Sykes itself, on the water tower that hovers above the small downtown, declares, "We Make Clay Pay."

At some time in the past, optimistic town fathers obviously had bigger plans for Sykes. Dirt lanes leading into weeds and stands of pine trees bear street signs: Tenth Avenue. Ninth Avenue. Only when Gray gets to Sixth is there actual pavement and some houses. Dot Gaines's address is on Fifth Avenue, which he follows until it ends less than two blocks later, at the edge of a cornfield. He sees the mailbox with "Gaines" on it in front of a two-story Colonial on his right.

Dot Gaines answers the door herself. It's past noon, and she has prepared a "light lunch" for Gray.

She is a large woman, obviously a fan of her own cooking, but Gray can see that she was quite attractive at one time. A painting of her in slimmer days hangs over the mantel in the living room. He estimates that she is at least as old as he is. He finds it appealing that she has not dyed her hair, or at least if she did, she dyed it an off-white.

"Yeah," she says, when she sees him looking at the painting, "that's me. You know why I didn't ever want to leave Sykes? Because people here remember me when I looked like that."

They sit down to fried chicken, potato salad, field peas, homemade rolls, and sweet tea.

"Save some room for dessert now," she admonishes him.

"I've been reading up on you," she says, looking at him across the table.

He wondered how long it would take her to get up to speed on exactly who Grayson Melvin was. He supposes he's lucky she even answered the door.

"Gordon said I was crazy to see you like this," she says as she passes the potato salad, "and he doesn't even know what I know."

She smooths her napkin and looks him in the eye.

"So tell me what happened. Like I said, I love a good mystery."

Gray supposes he's singing for his supper, or at least for the right to get one step closer to finding out the truth about the ring.

Dot Gaines whistles.

"That's a hell of a yarn," she says. "I can't imagine what you must have gone through. I mean, if you're telling me the truth."

She winks, and he lets it pass.

Finally, after the lemon pie and coffee, she goes to get the ring.

She sets it on the table in front of him. He just stares at it for a moment, then he picks it up. It seems to have been through some hard times the past forty-eight years. It is tarnished and scratched, although Dot has tried to redeem it as much as she could. The stone, once a brilliant blue, is as faded as a midsummer, high-humidity Carolina sky.

But it is, or was, his. He can still make out the initials, JGM, and the year, 1967. He holds it in his right hand, feeling its heft. He holds it close to his face, as if trying to smell some scent of Annie on it.

Dot was right about the ring's provenance. He checked. Nobody else in the graduating class had those initials.

"And you found this at an antique store?"

"Well," she says, "junk store would be more like it. I was just going through a box of this-and-that when I saw it. Somehow it kind of spoke to me, you know? And it's been a wealth of entertainment, finding out who it belonged to and all."

"And the guy that runs the shop, or whoever waited on you, he didn't know where they got it?"

Dot shrugs.

"Not that he told me. And I asked him later, when I started out on my little mission, and he said he couldn't recall."

Gray insists on paying her for it. She resists, insisting that he should consider it a gift "for giving me something to do besides watching old movies and reading mysteries."

"This means a lot," he tells her as she finally takes the ten-dollar bill he offers.

She smiles and takes a sip of her coffee.

"I just hope it helps you," she said. "I don't want to be nosy, but I have a feeling that ring has something to do with all the mess you're in right now."

He tells her that she is very observant.

"Come back anytime," she tells him at the door, pressing his right hand between her two and unexpectedly giving him a buss on the cheek. "I could use the company."

LOST TREASURES is in what passes for Sykes's downtown. The buildings along Main Street all bear mute testimony to earlier, more dignified existences.

What might have been a grocery store has been turned into something called "Come to Jesus Ministries." Two secondhand clothing shops occupy space on one of the town's two commercial blocks. An art gallery and a restaurant front with a "For Lease" sign on the window sit side by side. An insurance agency, a drug store, the town hall, the post office, and a Baptist church look like they could be the only businesses that have been on the strip since Reagan was president. For some reason, none of the downtown storefronts seem to offer pottery. Bradford pears, planted years ago, no doubt by an optimistic garden club, line the street, but many of them have split open, and a few are dead.

Next to the post office sits the business Gray's looking for.

Lost Treasures is advertised not with a permanent sign but with a banner that hangs over the entrance to what once must have been "Bellman's TV and Appliance," according to letters spelled out in stone over the entrance.

Inside Gray is hit with the smell of ancient cloth and wood. It reminds him of the attic in his grandmother's house. Items too new and worthless to be considered antiques litter the place. A young couple who seem to be furniture shopping on the cheap are the only other people in the building other than the man behind the counter.

The proprietor looks to Gray to be in his forties. He is wearing a baseball cap from which his hair is sticking out sideways. The cap says, "Trump the Bitch." He must weigh at least three hundred pounds. His gut more or less rests on the counter as he follows the couple with his eyes, as if they might go running out of the store with a fifteen-dollar easy chair.

Gray walks up and introduces himself. He shows him the ring.

"Dot Gaines says she bought this here," he says.

The fat man looks at it, turning it over in his meaty hands as if he's assessing it.

"Could be," he says, and hands it back. Then, silence.

"Well, do you think you could check and see? I'd like to know."

The fat man squints his eyes, sizing Gray up the way he did the ring.

"Well, who the hell are you?"

Maybe it's the second cup of coffee kicking in. Maybe it's the cumulative effect of all the shit he's gone through in the last week. Maybe he just doesn't like the guy's looks or his cap. At any rate, Gray decides it's no time or place for manners.

He moves close to the proprietor.

"Look, you tub of lard," he says, and watches the man's eyes narrow. "That's my ring. I know Ms. Gaines bought it here, so don't bullshit me about that. It was stolen from me. I'm trying to find out who took it. And if you don't have some kind of damn receipt showing me where you got it, I will have the cops down here to roust this place. Who knows what they'll find."

Gray has no idea where the fat man got the ring. He's taking a stab, though, hoping that he will either produce a receipt or tell him where he got it, just to get Gray out of his hair.

"You can't talk to me like that," the fat man says and starts to come around the counter.

"Sure, I can. And if you lay a hand on me, I'll have you arrested for that too."

The guy stops short. He's two feet away from Gray. The young couple have stopped their rummaging, anticipating some unexpected entertainment.

"I bought that ring fair and square," he says. The way he says it makes Gray think it's not the first time he's been taken to task for his method of buying and selling. He has the look of a man who is on the local cops' short list.

"Then tell me who sold it to you, and I'll be on my way."

The man seems to want to save face.

"Look," Gray says, "I'm sorry. I'm not here to hassle you. But somebody took something from me, and somebody's going to pay. It doesn't have to be you."

The fat man scowls and steps back around the counter.

"Let me see what I can dig up," he says.

"I'm in kind of a hurry. Tell you what, get me a name in an hour and I'll be done with you. Otherwise . . ."

Gray doesn't wait for an answer. He walks out. There's apparently one surviving eatery on the two-block stretch of downtown Sykes. He spends the better part of an hour in the Taqueria Loco, drinking two Dos Equis and keeping a constant eye on Lost Treasures across the street.

Only the young couple come out. One old woman enters. Gray sees no sign that the fat man has left for the day. It occurs to him that the man could have slipped out a back door, but it isn't as if Gray doesn't know where he works. He doubts that whatever nefarious path brought the ring to Lost Treasures is worth skipping town over.

When he comes back into the shop, the proprietor is still behind the counter. He scowls at Gray and hands him a slip of paper.

"Nubby Quick. That's his name?"

"You didn't get that from me," he says. Gray stifles a laugh. Who the hell else would know that the man whose name is on the scrap of paper had sold a 1967 East Geddie High School senior class ring to an "antique shop."

"He live around here?"

The fat man nods.

"About a mile away, that way. Mobile home next to a big farmhouse on the right on Route 16. It's on a hill. Can't miss it."

He points to the right.

Before Gray leaves, the fat man tells him that Nubby Quick, whoever the hell he is, brought in "a whole bunch of shit," most of which he bought.

"Any receipts?"

The fat man just stares at him like he's crazy.

"You won't see me again, if this is right," Gray tells him on the way out the door.

"I hope to hell not," the fat man says.

Gray can't resist a parting shot.

"And by the way," he says as the door closes, "your hat sucks."

It's LATE afternoon by the time Gray leaves Sykes. According to his iPhone, there's a motel fifteen miles away, part of a chain that seems to offer slim odds of bedbugs or long-term drunken residents.

Before he leaves, though, he drives in the opposite direction, wanting to see if the fat man was telling the truth.

He finds the hill, the farmhouse, and the trailer easily enough. He's seen more than a few scenes like this in his two recent sorties through Southside Virginia and into North Carolina.

Somebody maybe two generations ago built a fine, sturdy house overlooking woods and farmland. Maybe the farm played out. Either the soil was crap, or it was turned to crap by years of planting tobacco on it. Maybe the land got subdivided too often through two generations.

Occasionally the old house is gone, burned down or torn down, with only a stand of trees circling a ghost. Sometimes it's empty, abandoned by a family unable to fix it up anymore.

As is the case here, there's often a mobile home sitting next to the big house, mute testimony to the ravages of downward mobility, a tombstone for the American Dream. From eighty acres and growing your own food to a house trailer and a part-time job and health insurance compliments of Obamacare.

Gray is reminded of the old joke: They had a house fire, and it burned all the way down to the axles.

He notes the spot and the name on the mailbox: Quick. Then he turns around at an abandoned gas station a few hundred yards down the road and heads back toward and through Sykes.

He calls Betsy after he checks into the motel and tells her that he thinks he might have a lead on how his class ring wound up in an antique shop. He gives her as few details as possible and tells her he will be home soon.

Then he phones Marcus Green. He fills him in on Dot Gaines, the fat man, and the person who allegedly sold the ring.

"But you haven't confronted the man yet?"

Gray tells him he's had about enough confronting for one day. He gives him more or less the blow-by-blow of his encounter at the antique shop.

He hears Green's booming laugh.

"Jesus Christ. What the hell? You been watching too many 'Law and Order' episodes, man. What if he'd pulled out a big old gun and just shot your ass."

Gray puts it as succinctly as he can.

"I don't have a lot to lose. I'm kind of tired of this crap."

"Well," Green says, "speaking of crap, I have it on pretty good authority that they might be making it official in a day or so, maybe as soon as Monday."

"Official?"

"They're ready to file charges. Which means they're going to be coming for you. You really ought to get your ass back up here so I can be with you when it happens."

Gray tells his lawyer that he's not coming back until he gets what he came for.

It is suggested that he turn the alleged ring seller's name over to the authorities.

"We can use all this if it goes to trial, whether you get to the bottom of it by yourself or not."

"The authorities," Gray tells him, "don't really seem to have my best interests at heart."

"Well, try not to get arrested, or shot."

Gray says he'll do his best and promises to return to Richmond as soon as he can.

"If you can."

Before he hangs up, Green asks him one more question.

"Do you have any kind of protection?"

"Like a gun? No."

"Probably just as well. You'd either shoot him or he'd shoot you. Either way, you lose. But be careful."

There aren't many food options, and Gray doesn't have much of an appetite. He wonders if he shouldn't have just confronted Nubby Quick today. Time seems to be running out.

A pack of Nabs and a Coke from the vending machine in the lobby serve for dinner. He watches a few innings of a baseball game on TV and is starting to drift off when his cell phone goes off.

"Gray?"

"Who is this?"

"A voice out of the past. It's your old editor."

Through the years, he recognizes the voice.

"Corrina Corrina."

"Nobody's called me that since God was a boy."

CHAPTER FOURTEEN

Corrine Manzi and Gray Melvin haven't spoken in more than a decade. They exchange Christmas cards, and she used to call once in a blue moon, usually over the holidays. The last time Gray remembers calling her was in a fruitless effort to get a job. The different arcs their lives have taken since 1968 make him feel awkward around her. He can't stop thinking he's the down-at-the-heels relative being patronized by the family's shining star.

"It sounds like you're in a lot of hurt," she says. Her voice, not as strong and brassy as it once was, reminds Gray that she is even older than he is. "I had a hell of a time tracking you down. You've moved. Finally got in touch with the guy who wrote that story about you in the Richmond paper. Willie Brown?"

"Black."

"Well, I hope you're OK. The vultures are having a field day."

Gray has avoided reading newspapers the last few days. He knows he's still in the media's searchlight, but Betsy says there aren't that many calls, and the local TV crews have stopped camping out in front of her house.

He has to wonder if Corrine Manzi's concern is purely personal. Considering his failure to do anything even close to holding up his end of their friendship, and considering that she was publisher of one of the country's few remaining solvent big-city dailies before she retired two years ago, he thinks his caution is reasonable.

"We are off the record?" he asks.

"Oh, hell, Gray. Yes, we're off the goddamn record. This isn't about getting a story. I'm off the clock permanently."

Gray apologizes, and while he's at it, he apologizes for being a piss-poor friend over the decades.

"Aw, fuck it," she says. "You've got more important things to do than keep up with me."

In retirement, she is living outside Charlotte. She and her longtime partner, the same woman who worked with her in Akron all those years ago, finally got married. She says they live in a neighborhood that seems to tolerate them.

"Some of them are even friendly. Never thought I'd retire down here, but, you know, I'd had about enough of those winters up north. Hell, there are so many of us down here that they don't even call us Yankees anymore.

"Of course, you get outside Charlotte, you're in North Carolina."

So Gray gives her an update on his status, including the fact that his arrest could be imminent.

"It's pretty big news in Charlotte," Corrine says. "That girl, Annie Lineberger, her family is still a pretty big deal in Monroe, and that's in the *Observer's* circulation area. There was an interview with her brother two days ago."

Gray reminds her that he has long been acquainted with Hayden Tremaine Lineberger III.

"Remember the job I had at the Richmond paper, and how I lost it?"

"Good God. That was the jerk? I wasn't much help to you back then, was I?"

"He still believes I murdered his sister. And now that they've found her body . . ."

"Yeah, but forty-eight years?"

"He doesn't seem to have lost a bit of his desire for my head on a pike."

He tells her about the ambush six days ago in Byrd County.

She says that the Charlotte paper even managed to find Annie's old roommate, Susan Vanhoy, who left Chatham after Annie disappeared and moved back to their mutual hometown.

"She still thinks you're guilty, by the way."

Corrine is silent for a few seconds.

"You know," she says finally, "I told you this didn't have anything to do with getting a story, but I might have to retract that statement."

It turns out Corrine Manzi is bored. A couple of years of gardening and being an officer in a national journalism society haven't filled her days as well as she thought they might.

"I mean, everything you've told me so far is off the record. But how would you feel if I did some checking around? I don't need damn freelance money, but it would be fun to do a story. You know, old friend involved in high-profile murder case gets dragged back in half a century later.

"Damn, I don't mean to sound like it's some kind of game. I know it's not. But . . ."

"Yeah. Once a journalist, always a journalist."

"OK, I'm an asshole. But I really didn't track you down to get a story."

"And if I wanted to tell you things now, on the record, you wouldn't hold your hands over your ears."

"I could go over to Monroe, maybe talk to the old room-mate, see if there's anything she remembers that she didn't tell the cops back then. I'm pretty good at getting people to talk. I might even get Tree Lineberger to tell me something he hasn't told those baby reporters at the *Observer*."

Getting people to talk was one of her gifts, even when she was in college. Once, giving Gray an impromptu primer on interviewing, she told him to "let the ears work." Despite her tendency to go on nonstop on subjects about which she was passionate, she had a way of suddenly going mute in an interview. Maybe the quick change of pace made the interviewee even more eager to fill in the conversational gap.

"Let me see what I can find out."

Gray tells her she's welcome to do her best, or worst. He doesn't really have much to lose.

"The thing is," she tells him before she hangs up, "I just don't believe you did it. I didn't then. I don't know why, but there was something about the way you acted back then. You were the most innocent-acting boy I think I ever saw. It didn't seem possible that you would ever hit a girl, much less kill one."

Gray thanks her. He wants to tell her that if he ever had been as innocent as she saw him, everything post-Annie burned away most of whatever was once good and pure.

He doesn't disabuse her, though, and thanks her for caring.

THE JOB in Richmond back in 1971 didn't really pan out. Gray was fit enough to be a roofer after his two years in the army, although he'd gotten a bit beer-soft since his return. The problem was patience, and temper. Gray was not inclined to be berated by the bearded high school dropout who ran his crew. When he managed to burn himself painfully but not seriously with hot tar one winter morning, and the guy seemed to think it was funny, Gray walked off the job and never went back.

He did like Richmond though. He found that the city had enough to keep him entertained without driving him crazy. He liked that it didn't have the rough edges he never liked in his hometown. His roofing boss notwithstanding, Richmonders had at least the veneer of politeness.

He didn't reenter college right away. He never tried to return to the University of North Carolina, which he doubted would take him back anyhow, and he wasn't feeling too kindly toward that institution at any rate. He had been thrown under the bus. Despite the fact that he was asked to leave the college of his choice before the end of his freshman year, he was still getting "alumni" solicitations for years until finally, instead of throwing the enclosed form away, he mailed it back with a nickel and an unkind suggestion inside the envelope.

Among the things that got burned out of him by Annie's death and Vietnam was forgiveness.

When he was a boy, there were times when he wanted to hold a grudge but just couldn't. The bully classmate who knocked his books out of his hands from behind while he was trying to ask some girl for a date could be his best friend again if he made half an effort.

By the time he got out of the army, though, Gray found that it was easy to hold a grudge. He could hold a grudge and squeeze it until it squealed.

He was wandering around Richmond one fall day a few months after he ended his career as a roofer. His old Vietnam friend told him about a job as a bouncer at a place on the Jeff Davis Highway that made the crime report on a regular basis. He was hired, and he made friends with one of the bartenders, who showed him enough about mixing drinks that, when the bartender quit, Gray was hired to take his place.

By the fall of 1972, he'd moved up to bartending at a place that paid a little more and hardly ever made the newspaper's crime report.

His hours were midafternoon to early morning. One day, he took an aimless walk through the Fan District, where he was sharing a two-bedroom apartment. He wound up at the Virginia Commonwealth University library. He walked in unchallenged and wandered around. He was still a voracious reader. In the last couple of years his taste had turned from the classics he'd devoured in happier times and gone darkly in the direction of H. P. Lovecraft.

He was wandering through the fiction stacks when, for no apparent reason, a book fell from the shelf right in front of him.

He jumped when he heard a voice behind him say, "That's a sign. You should read it."

Gray looked at the book: *The Confessions of Nat Turner.* Gray had never heard of William Styron. He picked it up and looked at the speaker.

The man had "college professor" written all over him. He looked to be at least sixty-five, with a thin, wiry frame, long and untamed white hair, and a goofy smile. He had on a tie-dyed T-shirt that urged the questioning of authority.

"He's worth reading," the man said.

Gray nodded his head, holding the book, not knowing what to say.

"You aren't in school here, are you?"

Gray shook his head.

"How can you tell?"

The man laughed.

"The students," he said, putting air quotes around the words, "don't care enough to go browsing through the stacks. At least not the ones I teach."

He asked Gray where he was from, and what he did. Before he knew it, they were sitting at a table, and he was telling much more than he usually did about himself and what brought him to Richmond. The man, who said his name was McDowell, had Corrine Manzi's talent of learning by listening.

He didn't badger Gray about going back to school, like a few of his new acquaintances had. All he said, as he was leaving and they were shaking hands, was, "You belong here."

It was enough. Maybe he was ready anyhow. That October, Gray filled out the paperwork to apply to VCU. By January of 1973, he was taking classes, usually a couple a semester, depending on his salary as a bartender and the GI bill. He never saw Professor McDowell again. Sometime during his first year as a reincarnated college student, he tried to find him. There was no record of anyone named McDowell teaching anything at VCU.

He wasn't sure he still wanted to be a newspaperman, but the more he thought about it, the more he figured it was a good spot for a guy who thought he could write fairly well and needed a steady salary.

About the time he was becoming acquainted with Hannah Coble, he heard from a fellow student in one of his newswriting classes that there was an opening in the composing room at Richmond's daily newspaper.

"It'll get your foot in the door," the guy told him. Gray wasn't sure what a composing room was, but he walked down Grace Street the next day and applied.

He got points for being a vet, and soon he was working in the paper's composing room, where he became adept at cutting copy with an Exacto knife and pasting it on pages while frantic editors hovered over him. He learned how important deadlines were to people who had no greater emergencies in their lives.

The paper had only recently gotten rid of its hot-type operation, weathering a vicious strike by the veteran workers whose jobs were being replaced by relatively cheap cut-and-paste help.

"Hell," the composing room manager told him, "I could train a chimp to do this shit."

It wasn't rocket science. But it did give Gray a chance to get to know many of the editors and some of the reporters who wandered anxiously in and out of the composing room. It gave him, as his tipster had promised, at least a toe in the door.

He still bartended on off nights, and some of the same newsroom denizens who were breathing down his neck five nights a week found their way to whatever establishment was hiring him that night. Sometimes he managed to keep happy hour going for them long after they should have been paying full price.

The editors, in turn, found stories for him to write for the paper. He covered high school and small-college sports. He did the occasional feature or news story emanating from VCU. He took direction well. With rare exceptions, he delivered his stories on time, even after night football and basketball games.

His reporting further slowed his slog toward a degree, but he knew it was worth it. He felt that he was a lock to get a full-time job, at a newspaper with a union-wages newsroom, when he finally graduated.

After he and Hannah were married in 1975, his days got more crowded, but now, looking back through nostalgia's filter, he would do the same thing again, only with a different outcome. Even his deteriorating marriage couldn't kill the buzz he got from seeing his life finally turning into something like he had imagined what seemed like a hundred years before.

Gray sometimes thought of his life in terms of decades. The sixties were a nightmare, taking him from high school nebbish to murder suspect to Vietnam. The seventies were his revival. The eighties he could do without.

In the spring of 1979, he finally got his degree. They were calling it mass communications by then. On June 1, he began working full-time at the newspaper. It wasn't much of a change, except for the fact that his salary more than doubled. He was covering schools in one of the counties, which is where they started a lot of the rookie reporters. It might have been boring to some, but for Gray Melvin, who had started out twelve years before to be a journalist, it was the best job he'd ever had.

His marriage fell apart that August.

He and Hannah had moved into a three-bedroom apartment in the suburbs a month before, after spending most of four years in one student slum rental after another. No more Laundromats. No more on-street parking. No more walls so thin they could hear the neighbors' arguments, and vice versa.

Gray thought a change of scenery might be good for a marriage that had been on the skids for the last two years at least. He was accused by Hannah of "not communicating," an accusation that he thought was ironic considering his major but conceded probably had some truth in it.

After he became a full-fledged member of the newsroom, he spent more and more evenings after work drinking with friends to whom he was not married.

It shouldn't have come as a surprise when she told him one August night that she had "met someone." He couldn't even work up the energy to get upset about it.

He moved back into the city, found another reporter who was glad to have someone share the rent. He and Hannah, when they were dividing up their relatively few possessions, found that there was almost no sentimental value attached to any of them.

"Why the fuck did you ever marry me?" she asked him, in tears.

Before he could come up with a good answer, she was out the door.

He was thriving at the paper. He thought he was on as fast a track as was available at a paper where many reporters and editors stayed until retirement. The older editors liked him because he was that rarity in newsrooms of the era: a Vietnam vet. They felt a link, having been in earlier wars themselves. He usually refrained from remarking on what a God-awful mistake the whole mess had been.

By the next year, he was covering county government, and then he was moved to the night police beat, where he first met Willie Black. The two of them shared night cops until September of 1980, when the past caught up with him.

When his managing editor called him into his office that day, Gray thought he might be in for some kind of commendation. He'd just gotten through covering a sensational triple homicide and had done well with it, he thought. His recent step raise put him in an income bracket that had him looking at condominiums.

When he walked into the room, he saw that the publisher, a small, quiet man in his seventies who always called the people who worked for him "my associates," was sitting in a corner of the small office. The editor, who had championed Gray right from the start, looked like he had indigestion.

"Son," the editor said, "we have a problem."

Which meant, of course, that Gray had a problem.

The problem was Hayden Tremaine Lineberger II.

People in the newsroom knew that there was some dark ghost in Gray Melvin's past, involving some girl he once knew who came to a bad end, but their ranks were full of people whose closets were not skeleton-free. It was why some of them were journalists instead of lawyers or something else more respectable and remunerative. Hell, the managing editor knew about Annie, as much as he wanted to. When he hired Gray full-time, he told him that "we've all had our mishaps over the years, but this is a fresh start." He smiled at Gray, shook his hand, and never mentioned it again.

The publisher spoke quietly.

"When you applied here," he said, "you didn't tell us about your, uh, trouble back in 1968."

There wasn't any reason to tell, as far as Gray was concerned. No charges were ever filed.

But he had not counted on the far-reaching power of the old boy system. Annie's father, like his father before him and his son after him, had prepped at Woodberry Forest. The publisher was a graduate and, like Lineberger, an enthusiastic contributor to the school's coffers. It turned out that he and Lineberger were both on the alumni board.

Gray would never be sure whether Annie's father had known all along that he was living in Richmond and working his way into a full-time job at the paper and was just biding his time, or if he stumbled on the information. In any case, he could imagine the old bastard pulling any kind of secret-handshake strings he could to ensure that Gray lost his job.

So what had been a don't-ask-don't-tell situation became instead a breach of company policy. The awkward conversation hadn't gone on long before Gray knew that his career was over almost before it began.

"I'm sorry," the editor said, and he looked like he really meant it.

The publisher didn't say anything else. He just shook his head as if he had been witness to a terrible accident that he was helpless to avoid.

Gray cleaned out his desk, much as he would thirty-six years later at the community college. His fellow reporters expressed their sorrow and threatened to go to the publisher and demand justice, but Gray was pretty sure nobody was going to go to the wall for him. He didn't really expect them to.

Two days later, while he was putting his meager résumé together, he got a letter with a Monroe, NC, postmark.

"Just try getting a job somewhere else," the brief typed note said. "You can't go far enough to get away from me."

The next day, he called Corrine Manzi, who had progressed to assistant managing editor of the paper in Cleveland and was the most powerful friend he had in the news business. He had sent her some of his clips earlier, and she seemed enthused.

She told him she would get back with him after she did some checking around.

She called back a couple of days later.

"I'm so sorry, Gray," she said, "but we don't have anything right now."

He could hear it in her voice. She was never able to lie convincingly.

"Will there ever be anything?" he asked her.

"I— I don't know. Shit, let me call you right back."

And when she did, presumably on a more private phone, she told him what was what.

Anyone checking with his last employer would be told about Annie Lineberger. Whomever Corrine's boss or human resources department had talked with had related the basics and suggested a call to someone at the Raleigh newspaper or the Byrd County district attorney's office.

Gray had always assumed that his managing editor and the personnel department had been given their marching orders by the publisher.

"I can't help you, Gray," Corrine said. "I wish I could."

He told her he understood and thanked her for trying. When he hung up the phone, he had already decided his so-called career was over. He really had no desire to embark on a personal diaspora in search of a newspaper that had not yet been told of his sordid past.

He was thirty-one years old and felt that his life, up to that time, had been mostly wasted. He was a damn good bartender, and maybe God intended that that was what he was supposed to be.

Eventually he had to call Kaycee and tell her the sad news. He had no desire to speak directly with Jimmy about it. The old man probably would take some kind of perverse glee in his misfortune and admonish him about the wages of sin.

"You ought to sue the bastards," Kaycee said, unable to hide her disappointment. He had no doubt she had told all her friends about her rising-star brother.

He told her he might do that, but it was the last thing in the world he wanted to do. What he wanted to do, same as he had every single day since Annie Lineberger disappeared a dozen years before, was hide from the past.

CHAPTER FIFTEEN

SATURDAY

An all-day rain has set in by the time Gray rouses himself. He's been awake since five and finally surrenders to consciousness at seven.

He knows he is badly out of his element. Whatever awaits him beyond the mailbox bearing the word "Quick" hand-painted in red letters probably will require more from him than he is sure he can deliver. It was one thing to strong-arm the fat man at Lost Treasures into giving him a name. Getting the person who sold him the ring to tell him where and how the hell he got it seems a lot dicier.

For one of the few times in his life, Gray wishes that he was in possession of a firearm.

He avails himself of the motel's indifferent breakfast, which he immediately feels turning into trouble in his digestive tract.

He makes a call to Betsy before he checks out and tells her that he plans to meet with the man who sold his high school class ring.

"By yourself? Does he know you're coming?"

Gray is silent.

"Damn. You're not going to do it yourself? Please, get some help."

He wonders if he needs the kind of assistance people usually refer to when they urge a friend to "get some help," the kind that requires counseling and/or drugs. He is not feeling quite himself today. A more sane person would be going to someone with a badge and a gun right now, but Gray doesn't think he is being paranoid when he distrusts authority at this point.

He tells Betsy not to worry, that he has it under control.

Which he knows damn well he does not. He doesn't even know if he's on a path leading anywhere except a dead end. Maybe the boy, this Nubby Quick, found the ring somewhere. But whatever the answer, Gray knows he has to follow that ring as far as he can.

It's the only path he knows to resolution, which he's more than ready for, whatever the outcome. And it's the only thing left of Annie. He wants to know, once and for all, the size and shape of this ghost that has followed him for more than half a lifetime.

GRAY IS on the road by nine. The windshield wipers on his Camry need replacing. Their efforts to brush away the pelting rain leave large streaks that he tries to see through and around.

He passes through Sykes again, then misses the turn to the farmhouse and mobile home that was so evident to him in yesterday's sunshine. A driver in a pickup so jacked up that the headlights blind him tailgates him and sits down on his horn when Gray slows down and seeks to find a place to turn around.

On the second try, he sees the mailbox. He pulls onto a rut road whose tracks are filled with red, muddy water. Driving by the farmhouse, he sees that it is abandoned. Some of the windows are covered with plywood. Some are open to the elements. An old chimney leans away from the house, defying gravity. As he drives past, he sees that a large sycamore has fallen on the back of the structure and lies there undisturbed, as if it is, like the old place itself, exhausted.

Looking through the streaks on his windshield, Gray can make out a car in the little driveway that encircles the mobile home. The hood is a faded red; the rest of the car is a dull yellow.

There is a light on inside the trailer. He has been wondering if the fat man might have given Norville "Nubby" Quick a heads-up on his coming.

"Last chance," he mutters to himself as he stops the car in front, but he knows he's not going to back away now. Forward seems like the only option.

He didn't think to pack an umbrella, and he gets more or less soaked running from the car to the front door and then waiting for whoever is inside to answer his frantic knock. He can hear heavy metal pounding away inside, so loud that he can feel its vibration on the flimsy door.

The music drops to bearable levels, and the door opens. The man who answers, a boy really, looks like he just woke up. Dope smoke hangs in the air.

"Yeah?" he says, opening wide enough to size up his visitor.

"I'm looking for Norville Quick."

"Who's asking?"

Nubby Quick is a skinny kid. Gray figures he's probably still in his teens. He has sallow yellow hair, black at the roots. His eyebrows and nose are pierced. His pipestem arms are a graffiti wall of tattoos. He looks like he might weigh 140 pounds soaking wet, which is his visitor's condition right now.

Gray can't think of a graceful way to get the conversation started.

"I think you took something of mine," he says to the boy, whom he hopes doesn't have a gun, or at least that whatever firearm he has isn't on him at the moment.

"The hell you talking about?"

"This."

Gray holds up his left hand. He tried on the ring after he bought it from Dot Gaines and saw that it still fit, maybe better than it did when he was eighteen. He figured, what the hell, might as well wear it to the day of reckoning.

The boy tries to close the door, but Gray sticks his foot inside and pushes his way in.

"Get out of my house," Nubby Quick says, and when he takes a swing, Gray understands the nickname. His left sleeve is empty.

A two-armed kid might have been able to take him, but Gray manages to wrestle him down onto a charmless, stained couch after absorbing only a glancing blow. The brief scuffle leaves him sucking wind, but he is in control.

"You're trespassing!" the boy shouts and tries to reach for the phone.

Gray feels like a bully. He was anticipating a confrontation, but he wasn't expecting his adversary to have only one arm.

"I don't want to cause you any trouble," Gray says when the kid finally stops yelling. "I just want to know where you got the damn ring. I lost it a long time ago. I want to know how it wound up with you."

Nubby denies knowing anything about the ring. He seems a little on the dim side, but he appears to figure out eventually that there is no doubt that he is the one who sold the ring and whatever else he brought to Lost Treasures.

"Look," he says, "I just found it, OK? Don't know what the hell you care anyhow. It's just a damn high school ring. Won't worth much, I can tell you that."

"And you found all the other stuff you sold at that store, too, I guess. Listen. I don't care what you did to get the ring. I don't care if you stole it off a blind man. But if you don't tell me where it came from, then I will, as God is my witness, go straight to the sheriff's office, and you can explain to them where you got all that stuff."

If there is a gun in the trailer, Gray doubts that Nubby is fast enough to get it before he can stop him.

The boy seems to be considering his options. Gray isn't interested in telling him the real reason he wants to know where he got the ring. He doesn't want to reveal that he has far more serious legal problems than his young captive does.

The rain hammers the trailer's living room. It seems to have turned from a steady downpour into a monsoon. Nubby starts to get up, but Gray pulls him back down.

"Just you and me," he says. "Tell me where you got it, and I promise you your name won't be mentioned.

"Besides, you don't have a lot of choices, do you? You have to trust me, whether you like it or not."

Finally Nubby starts talking. And when he does, he can't seem to stop. Gray wants to tell him that he probably doesn't have much of a future as a criminal, if a sixty-seven-year-old, out-of-shape ex-teacher can sweat the truth out of him so easily.

It wasn't the first time he had stolen. He says he felt like he was entitled to something, "on account of the arm and all."

He lost it when he was six years old. He and some other boys were out playing. There was a railroad track behind the house. Nubby points backward, indicating that Gray could see where it was, if the trailer had a window that wasn't rendered nearly opaque by dirt and grime.

"Ain't nothing there now. The railroad cut off that line five years ago, even took up the tracks, but there was a train there that day, I can tell you that."

They liked to play chicken with the Lexington and Saluda engine that came by twice a day, once coming and once going. One of the older boys dared Nubby, who was still Norvie then, to stand until he told him to move.

"It was like a initiation. I reckon I was a little too brave."

He tripped when he tried to jump, and the train passed over his left arm.

"I like to of bled to death," he says.

He never finished high school and has been drawing benefits from the government for years.

"And then, last year, Momma passed."

As far as Gray can tell, without getting any further into Nubby Quick's life story, there wasn't any "Daddy" around, so he was on his own.

He knew a woman who had been his teacher in the ninth grade.

"She treated me right, didn't act like I was a retard or something."

The woman had even invited Nubby to her home a couple of times, enough for him to see that she had a lot of nice things lying around.

He further saw that she didn't lock her doors.

"She said it was a good neighborhood, that they looked out for each other. She ought to of been more careful."

So, one day last winter, when Nubby was trying to think where he could lay his hands on some much-needed cash to pay the guy to come and refill his oil tank, he thought of Mrs. Goforth.

"It just come to me," he says. "The way she didn't lock the doors, and how she was gone all day. And I remembered that the house had a bunch of big old trees around it. Made it hard to see from the road. And there weren't no neighbors right beside her place."

Her house was in the next town over, five miles away. Nubby went over there on a rainy December morning "sorta like this," and waited at the 7-Eleven down the road until he saw her car pull out of the driveway. Twenty minutes later, he drove up, walked in, and took what he could carry.

"Couldn't take any big shit," he says, pointing to the empty sleeve, "but there was a lot of stuff that looked like it might be worth something. That ring was in a old box in a closet in her bedroom. There was some stuff in there that looked like it might be worth something. The ring, it just happened to be in there. I didn't get but five dollars for it."

He said he took his haul to the fat man at Lost Treasures because "me and him, we had kind of a business relationship, you might say. I reckon he's the one that told you where he got it."

Gray doesn't say anything about that, but he reassures Nubby that he won't tell anyone how he found out where the ring came from. He doesn't know just yet how he's going to make that happen, but a promise is a promise, even to a thief.

Nubby asks for permission to smoke. Gray tells him to go ahead. He can see the cigarettes and lighter on the counter next to the couch.

Nubby lights up using his one hand. It seems to calm his nerves a little. He turns to Gray, pointing with the lit Camel.

"What I want to know," he says, "is why you give a shit about that ring. I mean, everybody gets one, everybody that gets through twelfth grade anyhow. You must hold a hell of a grudge. That ring must be . . ." Nubby tries to do the math, then adds, ". . . old as shit."

Gray figures he has nothing to lose in putting the fear of God in Nubby.

"It has to do with a murder," he says. "I can't tell you any more than that."

Nubby seems impressed.

"No shit? Man, if it's that important, I should of asked for more for it."

Despite the fact that Nubby Quick is a petty criminal who is inevitably going to wind up as a ward of the state in the near future, Gray feels for him.

"Out of curiosity," he asks, "why are you living in this trailer when there's a house next door?"

Nubby snorts.

"Did you see that fuckin' house? Best thing that could happen to it would be if it was to burn down."

"But couldn't you fix it up?"

"With what? Man, you must live in some world where money grows on trees. I could sell the land here and get a few thousand, maybe, but then where the hell am I goin' to live? This land is all I got."

Gray gets up to leave, keeping an eye on Nubby to make sure he doesn't try to stop him or maybe go for a gun.

The boy laughs.

"Don't worry, man. The gun's in the bedroom, and I ain't ever fired it except to kill snakes."

On the way out, Gray reaches in his wallet and hands the kid a twenty. Nubby acts like he doesn't want to take it, but when Gray assures him it's money well-earned for the information he gave him, he puts it in his jeans pocket.

Gray shuts the door and makes a run for the car, getting soaked again in the process. Before he starts the car, he hears the head-banging music blare out again from the trailer's thin walls.

HE HAS lunch at a fast-food joint and pays for a second night in the motel. The clerk seems surprised that he's back. Gray supposes most travelers don't rent their rooms one night at a time.

He has Nubby Quick's former teacher's address. He is able to find out her full name, Isadora Goforth, by Googling her last name and address. He calls the number listed but only gets an answering machine.

He drives back past Sykes and turns off at a sign that says, "Red Hill, 3 miles." The relentless rain has slacked off somewhat, and he finds the mailbox with "Goforth" on it as he enters the town limits of a place that looks to be no bigger or better-appointed than Sykes.

He turns into the driveway and sees no car. Nubby Quick was correct in his assessment of the house. Despite the fact that it is in the town limits, the lots on both sides are empty, and someone has planted bamboo. It looks as if she is living in a clear spot inside a jungle. It must have been, as Nubby surmised, an easy place to break into.

No one answers when he knocks. When he checks the door, he sees that Isadora Goforth has decided that her neighborhood is not quite as crime-free as she had thought.

Back at the motel, Gray calls Betsy and tells her what he's found out so far.

Then he calls Marcus Green. The lawyer picks up. From the street noise, Gray deduces that the lawyer is in his car.

"Man," Green says, "where have you been? I've been trying to call you and nobody answers."

Gray apologizes and figures he must have accidentally turned his cell off or muted it.

"You need to get back up here," the lawyer says. "They're looking for you. I think you're going to need a lawyer soon."

The last thing he does before he falls asleep is to call his old editor. He tells Corrine Manzi what he found out.

"And you promised this guy you wouldn't drag him into it? How are you going to not drag him into it?"

"It was the only way I could find out what I needed to know. I'll figure some way to keep him out of it."

"Why? He sounds like a scumbag loser."

"I promised."

He can hear Corrine sigh.

"You're not in a position to be doing people favors right now. You need everything you can muster, underhanded, devious, whatever, to get out of this."

"They might be coming for me anytime now."

"Well, let me check around. Red Hill isn't that far from Charlotte. Let me see what I can find out."

"Just make sure you don't tell her about the break-in."

"That's going to be tough. Let me think about it."

Then Gray drops off to what he thinks now might be his last sleep outside captivity.

CHAPTER SIXTEEN

MAY 22

Gray finally wakes enough to know the banging is real and answers the door, still in a fog. Two state policemen are standing there. They ask him if he is James Grayson Melvin. When he nods, they tell him what he's being charged with and read him his rights.

They watch him get dressed, then handcuff him and lead him out into the Sunday dawn. He sees a couple of curtains pulled back as other motel guests take in the show.

He asks one of the troopers, both of them up front while he sits behind a grille in the back, if he gets to call his lawyer.

"We'll let you do that when you get to Colesville," the one in the passenger's seat tells him.

So he's going back to Byrd County. He knows he should have taken Marcus Green's advice and returned to Richmond to await his fate, although he isn't sure how much good that would have done. Screwed is screwed. He wonders if he shouldn't have used a rental car again for this trip south, but he figures they'd have found him soon enough anyhow.

When he clears his head enough to think, he realizes that the charge they cited wasn't homicide.

"Did you say, 'obstruction of justice'?"

But the two troopers aren't in the mood to answer any more questions.

He realizes his cell phone is in his pocket. If he weren't handcuffed, he could call his lawyer on the way to jail. His pleas to be allowed to use the phone are met with silence until the same cop who answered him earlier turns around and speaks.

"You'll be getting to Colesville soon enough. Now shut the fuck up. And don't worry about that 'obstruction' bullshit. We all know what you did to that girl. Conspiracy is going to be the least of your worries."

The drive takes an hour and a half. When they get to the courthouse in Colesville, Gray sees that Towson Grimes has been busy. Three TV crews have assembled, along with several print journalists, ready to record his perp walk to the jail facility that is connected to the courthouse.

Grimes himself, looking somber but satisfied, is waiting when the troopers' car pulls up. He repeats the charges. When Gray asks to make a phone call, the district attorney leads him through the gauntlet of reporters and cameramen to a side door that connects to the jail itself. As he passes the reporters, one of them calls out to him, "Hey, Gray, did you do it? Did you do it?"

Others join in, a cacophony of vultures, Gray thinks, knowing that he could have been one of them if fate hadn't intervened.

Finally they're inside the building. Gray is led to a small room where his handcuffs are taken off and he's allowed to make his call.

He catches Marcus Green in his car.

"My source down there told me they'd arrested you," he says. He sounds like he's eating. "I just pulled out of the McDonald's. I'll be there in two hours. Don't say anything."

"Can you do something for me?"

"Other than get your ass out of jail, you mean?"

Gray asks the lawyer to call Betsy. Then he gives him the number for Corrine Manzi in Charlotte.

"Who? What for?"

"She's a journalist. Or she was. She's checking on some things for me. Tell her I've been arrested. If she can do something, she needs to do it."

BEFORE GRAY is led away to a cell, Towson Grimes confirms what the state trooper told him earlier.

"We know you did it," he says. He smiles as if he's having a very good day. "This was all we could get a warrant for right now, but we'll get there. Justice will be served."

Gray tells the DA about the ring.

Grimes listens. When Gray is done, he just shakes his head.

"So you found your old high school ring, and you claim she had it in her possession when you killed her—excuse me, when she mysteriously disappeared. You're going to have to do a lot better than that."

When Gray is led away, cuffed, his accuser calls out to him.

"You're not getting away this time," Grimes says, then turns to go back out the door for a press conference he's been anticipating for some time.

THE CELL is damp and lit by only a sixty-watt bulb, but at least he's alone. He doesn't suppose the Byrd County jail has many occupants at any one time.

Marcus Green arrives sometime after three in the afternoon.

"Man," he says to his client, "I told you to get your ass back to Richmond."

"You think they wouldn't have arrested me just because I was in Virginia?"

"Might have had a little more time to prepare."

Gray looks at his attorney, sitting in the room's only chair across from his bed.

"Prepare for what?"

"The inevitable. You could have told your lady friend in person that you're going to be OK. To maybe give me time to stall them a little bit."

Green tells him that he's learned the arraignment will be on Tuesday when he believes he can get the judge to set bail, although the figure might be "a tad on the high side."

"Now I've got to get a lawyer down here to work with me. Can't have some incompetent Virginia attorney like me screwing up the fine North Carolina justice system. That's the way it works. So you get to pay two of us now. Know why sharks won't bite lawyers?"

"Professional courtesy."

"OK, you've heard that one. Look, don't worry. They don't have shit on you really. Nothing on those bones points to you."

He reaches across the space between them and puts his hands on his client's shoulders.

"We're going to get you out of here. You've got the Green monster working for you. Now tell me again about that ring."

Gray fills him in on what's happened so far.

"Well," Green says, "I hope that woman, that Manzi person, is a good reporter. Sounds like you ought to get Willie Black down here. Son of a bitch is good at digging up dirt."

"I don't think I can afford to pay two lawyers and a reporter."

Green laughs.

"Willie won't cost you anything. Especially since he's an old drinking buddy of yours. Reporters ain't like lawyers. They don't need much to live on, and they hardly ever charge for their services. I don't think they like money."

Marcus Green leaves in half an hour, promising to show up Tuesday loaded for bear, with a North Carolina lawyer "to make it legal and all."

He also promises that he will be giving his own press conference "as soon as I can gather a crowd. These crackers don't know what a press conference is. Wait until they get a load of the Marcus Green show. I could've taught Johnnie Cochran a few tricks."

The cell grows quiet again. Gray can hear talk and laughter in an office somewhere in the distance. He sighs and sits back, realizing that he is very tired.

He hasn't been in jail in a long time.

THE YEARS after Gray Melvin lost his job at Richmond's morning newspaper run together in his mind. He often thinks that most of his past that is worth remembering occurred between 1968 and 1980. In the years after that, he thinks now that he was trying to lose himself rather than find himself. Time flew, and he didn't mourn its passing.

A few inquiries, after Corrine Manzi told him what the score was, confirmed that he was a journalistic leper, at least among papers that paid enough to cover rent and food. He did some freelancing at a couple of local weeklies, but his main source of income came from bartending. The Lineberger family's vengeance or perseverance didn't extend far enough to keep him from earning a living mixing drinks.

He never worked at one restaurant much more than a year. He always seemed to be in demand. He saw a lot of his old friends from the newspaper, none of whom quit because of his dismissal, but none of whom seemed to hold his troubled past against him. Almost nobody ever mentioned that past, and Willie Black was the only one of his one-time peers with whom he shared most of the whole story of Annie.

He did it one night when he got off work and joined Willie at a nip joint on Meadow Street, where they tried to drink the place dry.

The story spilled out. Gray realized that he was on the verge of choking up.

"Good Lord," Willie said. "You've got some heavy shit to carry around. I guess it would ease your mind if they found her."

Gray just shook his head and asked Willie to keep it to himself. To Gray's knowledge, he did.

Gray Melvin's only night in jail prior to 2016 came in 1983.

As was often the case, he had been drinking. He was good at separating work and play; he never drank when he was behind the bar. In front of it, that was a different matter.

He was just getting off work at the place in the Fan where he had been tending for five months. Somebody told him about a party a few blocks away, on Floyd. The place was being rented by a bunch of VCU students, and Gray realized that at thirty-four he was one of the oldest people there.

He started trying to catch up with the crowd, most of which had at least a three-hour head start on him, alcohol-wise.

He didn't know where the guy came from. Out of nowhere, one of the few people there who was as old as Gray was standing beside him.

"I know what you did," the man said, right in his ear. He said it in a kind of singsong voice, like a little kid teasing a classmate.

Gray looked around. The guy didn't look familiar. He was pudgy and short with reddish-blond hair. He was glassy-eyed drunk. Gray knew the look too well. If he'd been behind the bar, he'd have given the bouncer a sign.

But there was no bouncer there. When Gray moved away from his tormentor, the man followed him.

"I know what you did," he repeated. "I know what you did to that girl."

Gray asked him what girl, although he had a sick feeling.

"You know what girl," the guy slurred. "The one down there in North Carolina. You're a bad man." He giggled when he said it.

Gray had inherited some of Jimmy's temper, and like his father, he didn't control it very well when he'd been drinking.

When he told the guy to leave him the fuck alone, it just seemed to incite him.

"Oh, what're you goin' to do? Goin' to kill me too?"

Gray saw that they were drawing a crowd. He wanted to throttle the little bastard, but he still had enough self-control to leave, or try to.

His tormentor followed him out the door. Gray was half a block down the street, and the man was right behind him, still hurling insults.

Gray stopped short, and the little drunk bumped into him. The collision caused the man to fall. The beer bottle in his hand broke as he hit the pavement. When he held his hand up, with half the bottle still in it, Gray could see the blood.

"You hit me!" he said. He advanced on Gray, still holding the jagged remnants of the bottle.

There wasn't much time to reason, and Gray was out of patience by then. It was a one-punch fight, and he would have just left the drunk there on a Fan front yard, but somebody had called the cops. When he saw the blue lights reflecting in the window of the townhouse in front of him and heard the beep of the siren, he just stood there and waited for it.

The man he punched turned out to be a real-estate agent who had grown up in Monroe, North Carolina, where the sad story of Annie Lineberger had never faded. He had lived in Richmond for five years and knew Gray Melvin lived there, too, though he had made no effort to interfere with his life. But he was a belligerent drunk who just happened to be thrown together with Gray at the same after-hours party. When someone said his name across the room, alcohol and coincidence converged.

The punch sobered up the drunk enough to put together what he thought was a plausible story, of how he had just happened to mention something that happened fifteen years ago, and "the guy just went nuts." He said he cut his hand when Gray hit him and knocked him down, causing the bottle to break.

Gray's protests went unheeded, and he spent the night in the city lockup. By the next day, numerous witnesses had come to Gray's defense, and he was out by two in the afternoon. His tormentor didn't press charges, and Gray heard later that the man moved away from Richmond.

If he ever thought that the past could stay buried, though, that night disabused him of the notion.

THROUGH HIS freelancing, he had made friends with an editor at the weekly. The editor, perhaps seeing the sad future of print journalism or maybe just eager to make a real salary, left to take a job in media relations at one of the tobacco companies that were then one of Richmond's financial foundations.

In 1986, he told Gray about a job there. It did involve some writing, and Gray thought he had done just about all there was to do in the profession of bartending. So he applied, and they hired him. He didn't mention 1968, and the people who interviewed him seemed mostly amused by the story of his night in jail.

He lasted for three years, during which time he joked with friends that he was thinking about taking down all the mirrors in his apartment. He really did feel bad about what he was doing. He was making a better salary than the reporters at daily newspapers, but he soon came to understand that it was his job to defend the indefensible without hesitating or blushing.

The former editor who had lured him to the job defending tobacco left before he did.

"You can only sell this shit for so long," the man told Gray when they had a few drinks the day he left. "It's a young man's game. You can only do this with a straight face for so long."

Gray was looking around at other possibilities but already was discovering that flacking for a tobacco company was not the way to burnish a résumé when he got a call from his sister.

Jimmy had had a stroke. He was an old sixty-six, long past giving a damn about his health. He smoked, he drank like a fish, and he had not, to anyone's knowledge, been to a doctor since Cora left him.

"I need some help down here," Kaycee said. Gray's initial reaction was to say to hell with the old man, whom he had seen about twice a year since he left for Richmond.

But in the end, he knew he couldn't say no. Somehow Kaycee and Jimmy had made up, and she assured Gray that his father was a kinder, gentler version of the man Gray remembered. Plus she had her hands full with the kids.

And so he quit the best-paying job he'd ever have and moved back to East Geddie.

He stayed there for three years, until Jimmy died in 1992. They were not easy years. Gray managed to get numerous jobs bartending. There were always openings in the joints around Port Campbell, the nearest town of any size. They catered principally to the military base next door. Those three years were mostly work and looking after Jimmy. He and the old man would sit in the living room and watch baseball or old war movies and drink. Jimmy wasn't supposed to drink, but Gray figured, what the hell. His father was never going to have anything like full use of the left side of his body again, and he could barely be understood. The doctors at the VA hospital in Port Campbell said they'd done all they could.

The last time Gray could understand what his father said, they were watching a Braves game one Monday night. Jimmy motioned for him to come over to where he was half lying on the couch.

"You ain' be' sush bad shun," the old man managed to get out. Then he closed his eyes. Later that night, he had another stroke. This one sent him to the hospital where he died two days later.

Gray took heart in the fact that his father's last words to him were the kindest ones he'd received from the old man in his memory. "Not such a bad son" was high praise. They were as close to a benediction as Jimmy Melvin could manage.

They called Cora, up in Pennsylvania, but she didn't come down for the funeral. Gray had forgiven his mother for everything up to that point (unlike Kaycee, who always referred to her afterward as "that bitch"), but not coming down for the funeral was not pardonable. If he could give up three years of his life he figured Cora could spare a couple of days.

Kaycee wanted him to stay for good, but he had had as much of East Geddie as he could stand. He had nothing in common with the occasional classmate he'd bump into. The only mercy in those three years was that the people in his hometown seemed to have mostly forgotten about his tainted past.

When he got the chance to move back to Richmond and teach in the beleaguered public schools in 1993, he didn't think twice.

Now, ALL that, all those years of tending bar and flacking for Big Tobacco and teaching kids and wiping his father's butt just kind of run together. Lying on the bed in his cell, amazed that the sleep he so desperately wants refuses to come, he wonders what the hell it was all for.

CHAPTER SEVENTEEN

MAY 24

Gray is led into the small, musty courtroom at ten A.M. There are only a dozen rows of seats on each side of a center aisle, with two more rows to the right side for jurors. Marcus Green is with him, along with a tall, thin North Carolina lawyer by the name of Flint Massey. Green, Massey, and a deputy accompanied him from his cell, Marcus complaining about the crappy night he spent in the nearest chain motel he could find.

Betsy is seated two rows back, surrounded by a crowd that seems to be mostly news media. Two rows behind her, he spies the grim countenance of Tree Lineberger, along with a couple of other men who appear to be relatives of his.

Betsy is able to come up, squeeze his shoulder, and wish him luck before she goes back to her seat.

"You're a lucky SOB, to have a lady like that covering your back," Green told him.

"I can't believe she came all the way down here for this," Gray says.

The lawyer laughs.

"You don't know the half of it."

The judge comes in. He appears to be in his forties, young enough that his robes seem like a party costume, a send-up of serious jurisprudence. The fact that he is no more than five feet four adds to the effect. Gray figures he wasn't even born when Annie Lineberger disappeared.

Gray has assumed that pretty much everyone in the Byrd County judicial system is on the same page, the one that has him convicted already. It becomes apparent very quickly, though, that the judge and Towson Grimes are not on friendly terms.

When the district attorney asks that Marcus Green's request for bail be denied, the judge ignores him and sets bail at three hundred thousand dollars.

This causes the kind of uproar that no doubt gladdens the hearts of the reporters who are present. Their only sorrow is that no cameras were allowed at the proceedings. Tree Lineberger and his cronies stand and begin shouting profanities, causing the judge to have them hauled out of the room.

"Your honor," Grimes says, in a way that hints at air-quotes around "honor," "surely you can't let this suspected murderer walk out of here."

"I can," the judge replies, "if he can come up with bail. And, unless I'm missing something, he hasn't been charged with murder, at least not yet."

"But he could flee the country."

The judge sighs.

"Well, Towson, I guess we just confiscate his passport then, if he has one. Do you have a passport, Mr. Melvin?"

Gray shakes his head.

"No, your honor."

The judge turns back to the district attorney, whose skin tone indicates he is either flustered or furious.

"Tell you what, Towson. We'll forbid him to leave the state of North Carolina until the trial. How's that?"

Grimes mutters, loudly enough that Gray can hear him but the judge can't, "Better than nothing."

"What's that, Mr. Grimes?" the judge asks. The way he says the DA's last name seems to indicate that Grimes is on thin ice.

"That's fine, your honor," he says. "But I still say that he is a risk for flight . . ."

The judge shakes his head and interrupts.

"Towson, you don't exactly have this one nailed down. Now I'm not going to have this man, who might or might not have committed a heinous crime here forty-eight years ago, sit in our clean, modern, but somewhat cramped jail for nine months, which is how long it's going to be until I can clear off the two weeks this trial is going to take."

Towson Grimes looks back at Gray, shakes his head, and lifts his arms in resignation.

Marcus Green stands and addresses the judge.

"Your honor, we will be able to post bond at the nearest convenience."

He winks at Gray, whose life savings are a tiny fraction of the bond.

"What I was saying," Green tells his client later, "about her having your back."

And so Gray learns that Betsy Fordyce has put up the home she's almost paid for to post the bond that will free him.

The judge calls for Gray to stand.

"Mr. Melvin, you heard what I said, about not leaving North Carolina. Now, that might be an inconvenience, having to live down here in such a wild and uncultured place after enjoying the urbane comforts of Richmond, but you've got a whole state to pick from. Surely you can find somewhere to get comfortable until we try you."

Gray nods his head.

After the judge dismisses them, Gray retrieves his valuables, and Marcus Green leads his client out into the sunlight, where the cameras await.

The reporters start throwing questions at him.

Green puts a hand on his shoulder.

"Let me handle this," he says.

Marcus is in his element. There are camera crews there from three states, plus a Fox News team.

The lawyer runs a hand over the nonexistent hair on his shiny ebony head and assumes what Willie Black calls his "fuck with me" look, a scowl that screams Angry Black Man.

"Ladies and gentlemen," he says, "you are witnesses today. You are witnesses to a gross miscarriage of justice, or at least to an attempted miscarriage. Nine months from now, if not sooner, you will see that the state's attempts to abort justice will have failed. Our client, who has done nothing more egregious than be the unfortunate last person to see his beloved Annie Lineberger alive, will be exonerated."

The North Carolina lawyer, a younger man who appears to be recently out of law school, stands at his side and nods.

Green answers a few questions before the Lineberger contingent shows up.

Tree walks up to Gray, who is happy that the camera crews and reporters are still there as witnesses.

"You think you're gonna get away with this, don't you?" Lineberger says, moving in close and saying it low enough that it can't be heard by anyone more than five feet away. He and his accomplices close around Gray as a couple of sheriff's deputies move in on them.

"Well, you won't get away with this. Nothing you or your nigger lawyer does is going to change that."

One of the camera crews picks up Lineberger's use of the "n" word, and it will make him temporarily infamous on various TV networks and the Internet. The nightly news also will be treated to Marcus Green telling the world that "we all see now what kind of people we are dealing with down here."

Tree turns on one of the cameramen and shoves him before the deputies intervene. When he realizes the extent to which he's stepped in it, he and his posse turn and leave. He gives Gray the finger, and the cameras record that too.

Betsy catches up with Gray and his lawyers. She kisses him.

"You didn't have to do that," he tells her. "It's your house, for God's sake. But thank you."

"I know I didn't have to do it. I did it because I wanted to."

Marcus Green, seeming more pleased than daunted by being the recipient of a racial slur, asks Gray what he's going to do for the next nine months.

Gray tells him that he doesn't intend for it to take that long. When his lawyer asks him what he means, he tells him that he'll keep him abreast.

"Well," Marcus says, "tread lightly. And if I were you, I'd wait until those goons leave before you set off to wherever the hell you're going."

BETSY HAS taken two days of leave. She drives Gray back to Sykes, where his car still sits in the motel parking lot. He is amazed to find it there, not towed or otherwise violated.

On the way down, he filled her in on his recent adventures.

"Jeez, you think this woman, this Manzi person, can help you out? I mean, why is she doing this?"

Gray shrugs his shoulders. He doesn't know himself, but he suspects that Corrina Corrina's old reporter instincts made an old friend's dilemma irresistible.

Betsy cuts to the chase.

"She doesn't have the hots for you, does she?"

Gray shakes his head.

"I'm pretty sure she's playing for the other team."

"Well, good. Just so she doesn't go switching sides."

Gray manages a smile, a rare one these days.

"Thank you for having so much faith in my animal magnetism. Seriously, though, what lust I can muster these days, I'm saving it all for you."

"You're too hard on yourself," Betsy says. "Speaking of hard, do you think this damn place might have a room with a nice king-size bed."

She reaches down and strokes him.

"I'll see what I can do," Gray says.

Two hours later, his cell phone buzzes. He rolls over, trying not to wake Betsy, lying in the tangled sheets beside him.

"Gray? I didn't wake you up, did I? Where the hell are you?"

Corrine Manzi has been busy.

"That lawyer of yours said you might need some help. I gather you're not in jail, unless you smuggled a cell phone in."

Gray brings her up to speed, and then she does the same for him.

As soon as Marcus Green called and told her Gray had been arrested, she went to work. On Sunday afternoon, she drove over from Charlotte to Red Hill and found the residence of Isadora Goforth.

The teacher had returned home from a weekend with her sister in Durham just a couple of hours before Corrine knocked on her door.

"I didn't exactly lie to her, but maybe I bent the truth a little."

Corrine told Isadora that she was investigating a criminal case involving a stolen ring. The ring, she said, had turned up in a pawn shop, and there was reason to believe that it was a clue in a crime.

Isadora, a stately woman with gray hair and the kind of demeanor and piercing eyes that struck fear in many a past student, asked what that could possibly have to do with her.

Corrine told her that the ring was in a batch of property, some of which seemed to have belonged to her.

The teacher, who had not had much hope of recovering the items stolen from her home, expressed shock.

"We can't tell you anything else right now," Corrine said, "but we have located some of the items, and they will be returned to you. Right now, though, we just need to know a couple of things about the ring."

"I was talking out my ass," Corrine tells Gray, "but I figure you can find a way to get whatever hasn't been sold already back to her."

Gray isn't sure at all that he can do that and keep his promise to the hapless Nubby Quick, but as Corrine talks, he thinks of something.

"So what did you find out?"

"I found out where the damn ring came from, if that's what you want to know."

Gray Melvin's high school ring, it turns out, was the property of Isadora Goforth's former husband. He was a serial hoarder, and when he up and left one day, running off with the real-estate saleswoman who'd sold them their home, he left a bunch of crap behind.

Isadora threw a lot of it away, but there were boxes of things she just never got around to pitching.

"He didn't have a lot that was worth saving," she told Corrine, and Corrine tells Gray that she doesn't think she was just talking about material possessions.

"But why . . . ?"

Corrine cuts him off.

"I'm getting to that. Don't interrupt."

ISADORA GOFORTH was, for a rather long time, Isadora Hill. She married Bobby Wayne Hill in 1977. She thought she had found the love of her life, but Bobby Wayne was a much better suitor than he was a husband. According to Isadora, he had a tendency to want what he didn't have and disrespect what he did have.

He begged her to marry him. She was a teacher, making a decent salary working at the same school from which she later would retire. He was a salesman who yearned to be his own boss. He was, by Isadora's account, handsome.

"She said that the first two years weren't so bad, but then she found out secondhand that he had been seen with one of his female coworkers, at a time when he was supposed to be out of town, shilling for whatever the hell company he was with then."

He begged her forgiveness, but a blind woman could have seen that Bobby Wayne was not the type to get all obsessive about the marriage vows.

He went into business for himself three times and failed three times. Isadora told Corrine that he would be excited and energized every time he took off on his own, but as soon as he got his new business off the ground, he lost interest.

"She said he was about as unfaithful in his business life as he was at home."

He had a temper too. Isadora said he never struck her, but he would "blow a gasket" over small things, and he did get in a couple of bar fights over the years.

Still she put up with Bobby Wayne. She would have been just as happy never to have married at all, but she told Corrine she was a creature of habit, and marriage had become a habit.

Plus Bobby Wayne always came back to her.

Until 2009.

That spring, not long before their thirty-second wedding anniversary, she came home from school one day to find a note on the dining-room table.

She saw Bobby Wayne Hill only twice after that. She managed to usually be somewhere else when he came around to collect what items he considered worth having. She had been wise enough to have her own savings account and investments through most of their marriage. She said she figured she was better off than her ex-husband after they split. "And better off than I was before he left too," she added.

When the divorce was final, she was more than happy to revert to her birth name. Other than a few things that he didn't bother to put in the U-Haul he rented for his last trip to Red Hill, she was rid of just about anything to remind her of those thirty-two years.

"The weird thing is, she said she still loved him, in a way. She said he just couldn't help himself. You men are such dogs."

Corrine said Isadora couldn't shed any light on why Gray's high school ring was in the box that got stolen.

"She said she didn't know why he didn't take the ring, but she guessed it was down there with a lot of other junk in the box that got stolen. She said she never even knew it was there until she went through everything after he left."

Gray has been listening, trying not to butt in. Now, though, he can't restrain himself any longer.

"But why the hell did he have my ring? What was he doing with it?"

Corrine Manzi seems to be relishing the tale she's spinning. He can imagine her getting the same kind of buzz she used to get when she would break a story for publication.

"Well," she says, "I did a little more digging."

Isadora told her that Bobby Wayne had moved back to Lexington after he left her. And, as far as she knew, he was still living there.

"So I checked some records. I haven't lost all my journalistic skills in my dotage. And I found out that he was indeed still a resident of Lexington, North Carolina. I found out he was divorced from the woman he left Isadora for. He's on Social Security, retired, and living in some neighborhood that looks like it might be what you'd call lower-middle class."

Gray tells her how impressed he is.

"And I assume you have his address."

"Of course. But wait; there's more."

Gray waits.

Bobby Wayne Hill moved to Lexington right after a stint in Vietnam. But he wasn't from that town originally.

"I found out where he's from," Corrine says. "And I even found out what high school he went to."

More silence.

"Don't you want to know where Bobby Wayne Hill went to high school?"

"I want to know just about every damn thing about Bobby Wayne Hill."

And so she tells him. To Gray, she seems sad to have to finally let go of the nugget she's been hanging on to all through the conversation.

Gray is silent for a few seconds.

"Son of a bitch," he says when he can speak again.

CHAPTER EIGHTEEN

MAY 25

Betsy stays over for breakfast. Gray buys a Greensboro paper, which has an article about his bail hearing on the top of B1, along with a picture of Tree Lineberger and the two acquaintances who turned out to be cousins being led away from the courthouse. "Outburst follows alleged killer's release," reads the headline. They have a shot of Gray leaving the court building as well, looking old and tired rather than relieved.

Betsy wants to go with him "whatever comes next," but he tells her he has to do this part alone.

"You want to do everything alone," she says as she picks at her eggs and toast. "That's kind of the problem, isn't it?"

He reaches across the Formica tabletop and puts his hand atop hers.

"There is nothing I want more than to have you with me, but just not now. This could get dangerous."

"And who's going to be there with you if it gets dangerous? You're sixty-seven years old, Gray. This isn't some damn game."

"It's no game to me, I can assure you of that. I just want this to end. I'm tired of running and hiding."

He squeezes her hand.

"Look, if I can't get some kind or resolution by the end of the week, I promise you I'll try to get the cops involved."

She shakes her head and dabs at a tear.

"You've done more for me than anyone," Gray tells her. "You had every reason in the world to cut your losses when all this crap came out, especially since I hadn't told you about any of it. You're the reason I'm free right now. I will make you glad you did all this, I swear."

He hasn't told her what Corrine Manzi told him about Bobby Wayne Hill. He does now.

"So you see why I think I can settle this, one way or the other?" he says.

She wonders if he will survive the "settling."

"It's going to be OK," Gray tells her, with more conviction than he feels.

"I aim to spend the summer in Richmond," he adds, and Betsy says she hopes so too.

They part like that, with Gray promising to keep her up to speed.

As he waves good-bye to her departing Lexus, he reaches into his left front pocket. He wraps his fingers around his high school class ring, which was wearing a blister on his finger, and goes back to his room to pack.

In his car, he first calls Corrine. Last night he asked her for one more piece of what he thinks could be very important information. This morning, she already has it.

"The *Observer* reporter gave me her number. She got married, then divorced, then married again. Never left Monroe, I guess."

The next stop, before heading west to Annie Lineberger's hometown, is a return visit to Lost Treasures. He parks a block away and walks down the deserted sidewalk. He is pleased to see that the fat man has opened his store on time. At 10:05, he's the only other person there.

"I have a deal to offer you," he tells the owner, who seems less than thrilled to see Gray Melvin in his store again. He goes over and hangs the "Closed" sign on the front door.

"What do you want?" he asks the man whose name he's never known. "I told you what you needed. Leave me the fuck alone."

When Gray explains it all to the fat man, he doesn't want any part of the plan at first, but Gray eventually convinces him that failure to cooperate could lead to some serious jail time.

When they finally come to an agreement, Gray wants to shake on it.

"I'd rather touch a snake," the proprietor says, then turns away.

"Just make sure you do what you're supposed to do," Gray says.

The fat man says yes with his back to him.

THE NEXT day, Isadora Goforth will be surprised to see a pickup come up her driveway with a disheveled, overweight man at the wheel.

He will explain to her that "someone" he'd never seen before brought the belongings now in the truck's bed to his antique shop back in February and wanted to sell them. The man will explain to her that he had no idea that the goods were stolen, but that "an investigator" came to his shop looking for a stolen high school ring and suggested that he should give any other items sold to him at the same time back to their rightful owner.

If he did so, the inspector told him, he wouldn't be prosecuted.

The fat man will apologize profusely to Isadora Goforth, who is astounded for the second time in four days to be reacquainted with items she had given up as gone for good.

Most of what he will return is relatively useless. The only stolen items she will be able to think of that aren't in the truck bed are a couple of silver cups and Bobby Wayne Hill's baseball card collection.

The fat man will assure her that he had never seen the seller before, that he must be from out of town.

She will thank him for his kindness.

"Wait a minute," she'll tell him as he starts to unload Nubby Quick's ill-gotten gains. "I don't have any use for any of this stuff. Why don't you just keep it? Maybe somebody else can get some use out of it."

And so the fat man will drive back to his shop with the same things with which he left. He will shake his head and wonder what the hell just happened. As glad as he was to see the old guy with the ring leave his sight, he will still wish that he'd found out a little more about why he was forced to do what he just did.

The bastard looked familiar, like maybe the fat man had seen his picture somewhere.

Gray, meanwhile, heads west for what he hopes is the residence of Susan Carpenter, née Vanhoy.

The address Corrine gave him seems to be correct. The mailbox in front of the two-story redbrick Colonial reads "the Carpenter's."

He parks across the street and ponders his next move, drawing stares from a couple of women walking their dogs.

Finally he gets out and walks over to the "Carpenter's" house and rings the doorbell.

He rings again and finally hears a noise from within and then the metallic click of a lock being turned.

The woman who answers the door is not recognizable to him at first. Running into acquaintances he hasn't seen in decades is usually a shock, a reminder of how damn old he himself has become. But time has not been kind to the former Susan Vanhoy.

She seems to have shrunk about half a foot, for one thing. The girl he remembers was at least five foot nine. He towers over the woman she has become. She is using a walker.

"Yes, what is it?" she asks from the other side of the half-open door.

Gray doesn't know any easy way to introduce himself.

"You probably don't remember me," he says. She has the hint of a smile on her face at first, trying to figure out what ghost of her past is at her front door, trying to dredge up a name. And then she recognizes him, and the smile fades.

"I remember you, all right," she says and she starts to slam the door.

"Wait. Please," Gray says, sticking his foot in the narrow gap. "Please. I need some information, Susan. I didn't do it, I swear to God. Just let me talk to you."

She glares at him, trying to decide whether to leave the door and grab a phone before he can come inside, a hopeless task for a woman dependent on a walker, or maybe just to scream until one of the dog-walkers hears her.

"Look, I'm just here to get some information. I'll take my foot out of the door, and I'll call you from my cell phone. You can lock the door. Just let me talk to you."

She doesn't say anything. She seems to be equal parts fear and loathing. Gray doesn't know what else to do. He removes his foot, and the door slams. He hears her turn the lock.

Still standing on her front steps, he takes out his cell phone and calls the number Corrine gave him.

The phone rings five, six times, then is picked up.

"Leave me alone," the shaky voice on the other end says. "I'm calling the police."

Gray begs her to give him just one minute to explain what he needs. When he hears nothing but silence on the other end, he starts talking.

He explains about the ring that showed up in a shop in Sykes, how he traced it back to a woman in Red Hill who was once married to a man from Monroe by the name of Bobby Wayne Hill who seems to have gone to the same high school as Annie Lineberger.

"I need to know," he says, "how this Bobby Wayne Hill came to be in possession of my high school ring, when the last time I saw it, Annie Lineberger was trying to give it back to me."

He wonders if she has hung up, or is frantically dialing 911 on her own cell phone.

Finally she speaks.

"Bobby Wayne Hill," she says, almost in a whisper. "I haven't heard that name in a long time."

"Susan, I didn't do it. I didn't kill Annie."

More silence.

"Can I talk to you about it? I just want to know who this guy is."

"Why don't you just call the police?"

He explains, in case Susan Carpenter doesn't read newspapers, that he is not the favorite son of the criminal justice system at the present time.

"I'll tell you what," she says finally, "come back tonight, after seven. My husband will be back by then. And, I warn you, he'll be armed."

Gray sees that this is the best offer he's going to get.

He gets lunch and then checks into the cheapest motel he can find, wondering just how much credit he has left on his VISA card. He calls Corrine Manzi to thank her again for her help.

"Do you need any more of my rusted-out reporting expertise?" she asks him. "This was kind of fun."

"Not right now."

At seven on the dot, he's ringing Susan Carpenter's doorbell again.

This time her husband answers. Jack Carpenter has a pistol in his right hand as he lets Gray in. He seems a little less apprehensive when he realizes that the man he's letting in is an out-of-shape, gray-haired Medicare recipient who seems to not be packing anything except a wallet.

He isn't exactly pleased to have Gray Melvin in his home, but he apparently hasn't called the cops either.

He points Gray toward the couch, perpendicular to the easy chair where his wife reclines uneasily, then sits beside him.

"Say what you have to say," he instructs his guest.

Gray reaches in his pocket, causing Carpenter to point the pistol in his direction. He slowly pulls out the ring.

"Remember this?" he says.

Susan Carpenter takes it and examines it. She seems to choke back a sob.

"Oh, my gosh," she says. "Annie looked so ridiculous, wearing that big old clob-knocker on her finger."

She turns the ring around, even holds it to her nose, as if she could somehow conjure Annie by smelling it.

"It just about killed me, when she disappeared. We'd been friends since we were little girls, and then, not knowing all those years. I went to Chatham because she went there. We were like sisters."

She looks up at Gray. In her shrunken state, she reminds him not so much of an old woman as a strange little girl, still growing.

"We all knew you did it," she says. "We hated you. We wished you could have suffered like she did. And then when they found her body, her bones . . ."

Gray thinks it unwise to tell her that he has suffered too.

She reaches down and moves the recliner forward, lifting herself to an upright position. She grimaces as she does it.

"Osteoporosis," she says. "I've had both hips replaced. Old age isn't for sissies."

Her husband asks her if she needs any help.

She waves him away.

"I'm good. Now what do you need to know?"

He repeats the story of the ring's strange trip.

"I don't know if I can help you much, don't even know if I want to. Bobby Wayne, I haven't seen him since maybe a month or two after we graduated. I think he went into the army or marines or something like that, and if he ever came back here, I never knew it."

She leans forward a little.

"It's funny, because we were all pretty tight in high school. Good lord, it's all coming back to me now."

The former Susan Vanhoy then proceeds to give Gray the lowdown, as best she can remember it, on Bobby Wayne Hill.

When she's through, neither she nor her husband offer Gray a cup of coffee or something stronger. He gets up to leave, thanking them for their time.

He is nearly out the door when he hears Susan speak. She's standing now, leaning on her walker.

"You know, she did love you, there for a while. But Annie was kind of flighty. She was independent. She was young."

She sighs and winces.

"Hell, we all were."

BACK AT the motel, Gray pulls into the only available parking space. At eight thirty on a Wednesday night in Monroe, North Carolina, the place where he's staying seems to be a hub of activity.

He soon sees the reason. There's a lounge attached to the motel, and it's karaoke night.

He walks toward his unit, the sound of an Elvis wannabe butchering "Heartbreak Hotel" fading in the background as he rounds a corner. He is unlocking the door to his room when he hears footsteps behind him.

Gray turns and catches the first blow to his stomach. He crumbles, gasping for breath. He sees the shoes of the two men now facing him as he tries to get up, and then one of them kicks him in the face. He can taste blood, and his nose feels like it's been pushed back into his head.

"Stay the fuck away from here, asshole," a voice above says. When he tries to look up, the other man kicks him in the ribs.

He's in the fetal position now, taking a couple more kicks to his kidneys, then another to the head.

"We ought to kill your ass," he hears the same voice say. "I'm depending on the state to do that, though, even if we do have to wait awhile. But don't ever come snooping around this town again."

Gray can hear a car drive by. "Come on," he hears the other one say. "We better get the hell out of here."

He is sure that his attackers were younger men, and he's almost as sure that he's heard those voices before.

He waits until their footsteps recede, then turns around, the pain in his ribs searing him like fire when he does. All he sees are a couple of heavy-set bodies headed back around the corner he just turned.

He manages to get up and into his room before anyone sees him. In the bathroom mirror, he examines his battered nose and split lip and determines that nothing seems to be broken. He spits into the sink and sees that the cap from a long-ago salvaged tooth has been knocked loose. He catches it before it can fall down the drain and jams it back on.

He isn't so sure about his ribs. The pain doesn't seem to be letting up.

He manages to get himself into his car and finds a doc-in-a-box clinic not three blocks away. His ribs are only bruised, according to the young physician assistant who sees him. She asks him if he's been in a fight. He tells her he ran into a door. She shrugs and prescribes painkillers. He fills the prescription at an all-night drug store and is back at the motel by ten thirty, at which time he is able to get a parking space directly in front of his room.

Even with the drugs, he does not sleep well.

He wonders how the hell Tree Lineberger found out he was in Monroe.

CHAPTER NINETEEN

MAY 26

He hasn't dreamed of Annie for years.

This one seems to go on all night. He will wake up from it, fall back into drug-induced sleep, and then he's in it again.

Annie is talking to him, but the room is crowded, and he can't quite hear her. Not being able to hear people is a common occurrence these days, as his ears go south along with the rest of him, and so the dream doesn't seem so unreal.

She is trying to tell him something, but they're separated by fellow partiers. He's her date, but somebody else is talking to her, and when Gray tries to get closer, he's blocked by others who seem to be laughing at his predicament. Some of them are from his college days, some from high school, some acquaintances over the years.

Even though he has never met the U.Va. student whom Annie was seeing when she broke up with him, he somehow knows that the boy with whom she seems far too comfortable is the villain Winston.

He wakes up for good at six A.M., feeling more tired than when he lay down after his beating. He has learned that he has a very brief time to remember his dreams before they fade away. He tries to remember the one that's been looping through his brain all night long.

One thing sticks with him before it evaporates into the morning air. Annie says something to him that he can finally understand.

While he's trying to reach her, she laughs and says something that jogs his memory back to 1968.

Gray knows, as he rolls over and reaches for the bottle of painkillers beside his bed, that he has heard the words before, but not in a dream.

THE THURSDAY night before she was lost, he called Chatham. Annie seemed distracted, maybe even annoyed. She asked him why he was calling her when he was coming up the next day.

He said he just wanted to hear her voice.

He could hear her sigh.

They talked for a few minutes. Since Gray was on a pay phone in his dorm, feeding precious quarters into it, he couldn't talk long anyhow, but at the end of the conversation, he told her he loved her.

There was a silence on the other end. He couldn't let it go.

"What about you?" he said at last.

"Yeah, me too," she told him.

He said he'd see her the next day.

She said she'd be there. Then, when he was about to hang up, she said, "Gray, you're not gonna freak out, are you? It's been done before, you know."

In all that followed, the breakup and then Annie's disappearance, he never thought much about what she had said.

Now, as he checks his body, assessing the damage from the night before, he remembers her words like someone is playing them back to him on a tape recorder.

CHAPTER TWENTY

Gray plays with the loose cap sitting precariously on his molar, finally conceding that he'll just have to take it off, pack it away, and be careful how he chews until dental treatment rises to the top of his to-do list.

His nose might not be broken, but he won't be breathing much out of it until the swelling goes down. He has a very fat lip, but nothing stitch worthy.

The ribs, though, are going to be a problem. Walking and breathing require some effort. Every step he takes seems to jostle something that doesn't want to be jostled. And, when he goes to the bathroom to relieve himself, he sees that his urine is an alarming pink color.

On a normal day, these symptoms would be cause for a call to his doctor. Right now, though, he decides that physical health can wait.

It takes him more than an hour to shower and get dressed. The shirt in particular causes problems, and he wishes he hadn't spurned Betsy's offer to stay with him.

He goes to the diner attached to the motel and draws concerned looks from the other patrons.

"Looks like you had a rough night," the waitress says as she pours his coffee.

He looks up at her and tries to smile.

"You don't want to know."

She shrugs and tells him to take it easy. It apparently isn't that uncommon, at the cut-rate motel where he's staying, for people to show up for breakfast with their faces rearranged. No one else comments on his appearance.

After a painstakingly slow meal, in which he tries to remember to chew on the left side and definitely keep hot coffee away from the right, he pays his bill and goes back to his room. He has a few calls to make before he leaves town.

He waits until nine to phone Susan Carpenter.

He tells her what happened to him after he left her house.

He asks her the question whose answer he thinks he already knows.

"Did Tree Lineberger know I was here?"

She doesn't talk for a few seconds. Then he hears her say, "Damn! I am so sorry, Gray. I think I know what happened."

As it turns out, Susan called a friend, a woman who had gone to school with her and Annie Lineberger, after Gray left to tell her about the strange visitor from the past she'd just talked with.

"And Carrie Beth, she knows the Linebergers. I have all ideas that she called and told Tree you were here. But I didn't think he'd do something that stupid. Although I did see the picture of him in the paper. He really does hate your guts."

Gray says he's well aware of that, has been for some time.

"To tell you the truth," he says, "I don't really blame him much. If I thought somebody had killed my little sister, I'd hold a grudge for life too."

He tells her that he doesn't think Tree himself did the actual beating, although he suspects his assailants were related to him.

"One of them sounded like one of the goons he had with him up in Byrd County."

"So are you going to press charges?"

Gray says he'd prefer to leave the police out of it for now, especially since he has no way of identifying the men who beat him up.

"Well, if I were you, I think I might want to get out of town."

He assures her that his next move, after he makes two more calls, is to put Monroe in his rearview mirror.

He asks her if she by any chance mentioned anything about Bobby Wayne Hill to her old friend.

"Damn. Yes, I did."

Gray can only hope that the man he wants to talk to won't have prior knowledge of his upcoming visit.

"You know," Susan Carpenter says before they disconnect, "I would have liked to have seen you dead. I think I hated you almost as much as the Linebergers did. And now, with what you told me, I think I've been wrong. That ring, I can't figure out how Bobby Wayne Hill came to have it."

Gray tells her he hopes to answer that question in the near future.

After he hangs up, he calls Marcus Green, whom he hasn't talked with in the last two days. Willie Black has warned him that Green is probably charging him by the minute, so he's keeping his calls to his lawyer to a minimum.

Green's partner, Kate Ellis, answers the phone.

"Oh, you're Willie's friend. You're kind of famous up here right now. Or infamous."

He'd forgotten that Marcus Green's partner is Black's third ex-wife.

She tells him that the local paper had the story about him making bail on A1.

"I guess our local rag still sells some papers down in Portman, where they found the body, so they're playing it up big. Anyhow you'll get un-famous again soon enough. Somebody else will screw up. Always happens. Not that you screwed up."

"Not on purpose."

"You might want to think about maybe getting a haircut or something, though, maybe hit the tanning salon. You aren't exactly photogenic in the picture they ran in the paper."

Gray thanks her for her brutal honesty and tells her that she should see him now that he's had his involuntary makeover.

"They beat you up? Really? You need to get some protection. You have a gun?"

He tells her what he's planning to do.

"My advice? Call the cops now. Amateur detectives have a pretty rough life, as you probably already know."

Maybe he will, he tells her.

"But I think I have to do this alone."

"Your funeral," Kate Ellis says. "Figuratively, I mean."

"I hope so."

She transfers him to Marcus Green, who seems more amused than concerned about his ill-fated evening.

The thing is, Gray explains to his lawyer, it wasn't all that ill-fated. He knows where Bobby Wayne Hill lives, and he knows a couple of other things, too.

"Like what?"

"If I told you," Gray says, "I would have to kill you."

Green's big, booming laugh makes Gray hold the phone away from his ear momentarily.

"Well, don't do that. But stay in touch, and give that Massey guy a call, you know, your 'official' lawyer down there. But my advice? You've got some pretty good information there. Talk to the cops."

"Is that free advice?"

Another laugh. "Never is, man. Never is. But it's pretty good advice all the same."

Gray thanks the man and tells him he has to go.

He knows there is wisdom in what Marcus Green and his partner are saying. But when he talks it out inside his head, he can't see a situation where local police, or Towson Grimes back in Colesville, will jump up, give him a medal, and tell him, "We'll take it from here."

He needs something else.

He makes one more call, to Betsy. He doesn't mention the beating, figuring if he did, she would jump in her car and be at his side within hours, something he doesn't want right now. If he's going to be in harm's way, he'd rather do it solo. He figures he's caused her enough grief for the time being.

She tells him that a couple of reporters have come by, but when they realized that Gray Melvin wasn't going to be back in the state for a while, they went away quietly.

"Quiet is good," he says. He tells her he loves her and hangs up.

HE'S ALMOST to the city limits when he hears the siren and sees the blue light in the rearview mirror.

He is reaching toward his registration card in the glove compartment when he hears the booming, bullhorn-enhanced voice coming from the police car.

"Keep your hands on the steering wheel! Do not move!"

Gray, who hasn't had a speeding ticket in the last twenty years, is so rattled that he almost reaches down again to close the compartment door.

"Hands on the wheel! Now!"

This time he obeys. He realizes his hands are shaking.

He is ordered to get out of the car, which takes him longer than the two cops converging on him seem to think is proper.

"On the ground! Now!" one of them says, pushing him as he tries to get his aching body into a prone position.

He tries to ask them what the problem is, but they advise him to shut up.

Finally, after he is allowed to painfully extract his license from his hip pocket and then walk around and show them his registration, he asks again what the problem is. He's starting to move past the shock and get pissed off.

"Do you know how fast you were going?" the lead cop demands. His hat is off, his reflecting sunglasses and cue-ball head shining in the late-morning sunlight.

"I don't know. Thirty-five, I guess."

The cop shakes his head.

"You were going thirty-nine miles an hour."

"And you give tickets for that?"

The cop moves closer to Gray.

"Don't be a wise-ass, sir. We don't like wise-asses around here. Sometimes they wind up in jail."

Gray shakes his head. The other cop moves up and gets in his face.

"You don't approve of our cracking down on speeders? I guess they just let 'em do whatever the fuck they want up in Virginia."

Gray thinks at first that he says what he said because of the Virginia plates. Then the cop moves a little closer.

"Let me tell you something, asshole," he says as Gray backs away but is pinned against his car. "My momma went to school with Annie Lineberger. You want to protest this ticket, why don't you just take it to traffic court?"

He rips off the ticket he's been writing and shoves it in Gray's right hand.

"You have a nice day," the second cop says as the two of them turn and walk away.

They follow Gray's car the few hundred yards to the city-limit sign, then for half a mile more as he tries to concentrate on both the road ahead of him and the speedometer.

He wonders, as he watches in the rearview mirror as they make a U-turn, if there is anybody in that town who doesn't know who he is and what they think he's done.

THE REST of his trip to Lexington is without incident. He half expects to be "greeted" by every law-enforcement entity en route, but vengeance seems to have stopped at the city line, at least for now.

When he arrives, he pulls in at a convenience store and buys a city map, on which he finds the address he got from Corrine Manzi without much trouble.

It's in an apartment complex close enough to the inter-state that the afternoon traffic is a dull roar from the parking lot where Gray sits and waits. The buildings are three-story, with outdoor stairways for the upper units. Gray sees from checking the mailboxes outside that Bobby Wayne Hill is in one of the ground-level apartments, which are actually slightly below ground. Gray gets a faint whiff of mildew as he approaches the front door. The brick wall outside Hill's

unit has been the victim of graffiti that someone has unsuc-
cessfully tried to clean off.

He has had time, on the hour-plus trip over, to think
about what he should do. The idea of a plan of action seems
laughable right now, when the mere act of getting in and out
of his car causes so much pain.

At first, he thought he'd just confront the son of a bitch
with what he knows, lay the facts out to him, standing in the
door and definitely not going inside the apartment.

By the time he got to Lexington, though, he felt he'd
come up with a plan that had less chance of getting him
hurt even worse than he already is. He's standing in front of
Bobby Wayne Hill's front door right now because he wants
to see where the man lives. He feels that he has, with a lot of
help from his old friend Corrina Corrina, come to the end
of a long and tortuous maze. Everything that has happened
since he got the call from Dot Gaines about his ring seems
to have led him here.

But he won't make his stand here or now. Even under
the influence of painkillers whose presence might have
caused him to be spending the night in jail back in Monroe
if his tormentors had known about them, he has more sense
than that.

He finds a hotel that seems to be a big improvement
over the place he stayed the night before and checks in.
He stopped at a Kmart on the way and bought some clean
underwear, socks, and a cheap shirt. He hadn't counted on
his North Carolina sojourn lasting so long. He figures his
khakis will be good, or good enough, for a couple more days.

Gray can see inside through a crack in the curtains.
Bobby Wayne Hill's apartment appears to be unoccupied at
present. So he goes back to his car and waits.

Sometime after six, a Ford Taurus with rusted fenders and a missing hubcap comes pulling into the lot, parking only three cars down from Gray's. The man who gets out seems too old to be his prey, but then Gray realizes he would be that old now too. He's tall but stooped, thin, and mostly bald. Gray has no idea what Hill looks like, but when the man goes directly to Apartment 3A, he knows he has the right man. The man even gives a brief, curious glance in Gray's direction, as if he's been expecting him, before he turns toward his front door.

Even with his bruised ribs and kidney, a face that hurts and a tooth that's starting to ache, Gray thinks he might be able to take this guy. But he knows he can wait.

After Hill goes inside, Gray leaves. He realizes he hasn't eaten since breakfast. He finds a barbecue place a mile or so down the strip the hotel is on and eats his way through a platter loaded down with hush puppies and french fries, accompanied by sweet tea. On the way back to the hotel, he stops and buys some Zantac. He wonders how much weight he's gained since he left Richmond and tries to remember the last time he ate something green. But in a world pretty much devoid of comfort the last few days, he figures he's entitled to some comfort food.

Back in the room, he gets a call from his sister.

Kaycee says she's been reading all the reports in the paper.

"Gray," she says, "I've got to ask you something. You didn't really do it, did you?"

He assures her, again, that he really, truly did not kill Annie Lineberger.

"But they'll be able to get you off, won't they? I mean, that district attorney, he seems like he thinks he can nail your hide to the wall."

"The district attorney doesn't know what I know."

"What's that supposed to mean."

Gray says he can't tell her right now.

"Soon though," he promises.

"Well," she says, "folks around here, they act like you're some kind of mass murderer or something. A lot of my so-called old friends won't even look me in the eye."

He tells her she ought to get better friends.

"Look," he tells her, "just trust me. This is going to get better."

She starts telling him the latest installment in her long-time war with her daughter. Krystal has married again, for the third time.

"And she calls me, I haven't heard from her in almost six months, and wants me to send money. What it was for, I finally found out, was to get this deadbeat she's married out of jail. I told her I'd think about it, and you know what she said? She said I'd never been there for her. Be glad you never had kids, Gray."

Between Krystal and Little Jimmy, who lives with her now because she can make him take his medication often enough to keep him nominally functional, he knows his little sister has her hands full, and he's sorry that he has somehow made her life a little harder than it already is.

But his head hurts, his ribs hurt, and now his stomach is weighing in as well.

He promises her that he will have good news for her soon.

"I could use some," she says as she hangs up.

Over the years, Gray has tried hard not to think about all that has happened since that night in 1968. It is difficult, though, not to imagine a parallel universe, one in which Annie Lineberger returns to her dorm unharmed, goes out with the snake Winston the next night, and gets on with her life while he mopes around for the requisite time, then loses himself in school and the newspaper. Pretty soon, he finds another girl who makes him get over if not forget Annie. The drunken trip back from Chatham becomes part of his personal history, something to laugh about when he relates it to his kids and then grandkids as his wife smiles indulgently and shakes her head, a tale that shows them Granddad was once young too. He becomes a successful journalist, like Corrine Manzi.

In that parallel universe, he has a life.

He examines the ugly purple bruises on his face and body in the hotel room's mirror. He knows Annie did nothing worse than be young and spirited, and he knows he's an oaf for feeling sorry for himself. He is, after all, living. They didn't dig up his bones while clearing a site for a Food Lion in Portman, Virginia. He has had, despite all that's happened, some good moments, good friends, and especially a good woman who has been willing to go to the wall for him.

Still, though, the darkness gets past his guard sometimes. Easing his way back to the bed after his digestive system's spectacular rejection of his most recent meal, he does feel that he's about ready to set the record straight.

He could make the call right now. Instead, he waits.

CHAPTER TWENTY-ONE

May 27

Gray's back in the parking lot where he spent part of Thursday afternoon. He's a good distance away from the beat-up Taurus he saw then. The sun hasn't been up long. He isn't sure if his prey has a job or not.

The phone rings five times before he hears a croaky voice, full of phlegm and irritation.

"Yeah."

"I'm trying to get in touch with Bobby Wayne Hill."

"Who wants him?"

Gray doesn't give his name. He assumes that it might be familiar to the man he's talking to.

"I've got something of yours, I think. A ring."

There is a pause, long enough that Gray wonders if Hill has hung up on him.

"I'm not missing any ring. Who is this?"

"The initials on it are JGM. I can talk about it with you, or I can talk about it with the police."

"You're crazy, man. I'm goin' to hang up now. Quit bothering me."

"OK. But I'd get a good lawyer, if I was you."

Another pause, and Gray thinks his plan isn't working. Then:

"What do you want?"

"I told you. We need to talk."

"You know where I live?"

"Yeah, I know where you live. But we're not going to talk there."

Gray gives him the name and address of the breakfast joint next to the hotel where he's staying.

"Be there in an hour, or I go to the police."

Bobby Wayne Hill tells him again that he's crazy, but when Gray reiterates the name of the place, he says he'll be there.

"Just let me put on some damn clothes. Jesus."

Gray waits until Hill comes out his front door forty-five minutes later, then follows the Taurus to the Egg Barn. He waits until the man gets out of his car. Hill is just inside the entrance when Gray comes up to his rear.

"Let's go in," he says. The man jumps, but then he follows as Gray leads him to the back of the long, narrow eatery that's just wide enough for an aisle and two sets of booths. Hill doesn't get a good look at his face until they're seated.

If anything, Bobby Wayne Hill looks worse than he did yesterday. Whatever charm he might once have possessed no longer is evident. What hair he has left sticks out in unruly wisps from underneath a greasy red baseball cap. His shirt is missing a button. His pants have no belt.

If Hill recognizes the man whose call brought him here, he doesn't let on.

He looks across the table.

"What happened to your face?" he asks Gray.

"Ran into a door."

"Maybe the door thought you were bein' too damn nosy."

"That's entirely possible."

Hill sets his big, bony hands in front of him on the table and looks at Gray straight on with bloodshot eyes.

"Now suppose you tell me what the fuck this is about?"

Gray takes out the ring and sets it on the table. He explains, line by line, what he knows about its journey since the last time he saw it in Annie Lineberger's possession.

He stops to let the waitress take their orders. When she leaves, he turns back to Hill.

"What the fuck does this have to do with me?" he asks. "I got that ring at a yard sale. Can't remember when, but it didn't mean nothin' to me. Hell, I hadn't even thought about it. Just left it with all the rest of the junk when Isadora and me split up."

"That might all be true," Gray tells him. "But there's this other thing. You remember Susan Vanhoy?"

"Yeah. She was a stuck-up bitch. Probably still is."

"Be that as it may, she told me some things about you."

"And you believed her?"

"She told me about you and Annie Lineberger."

Bobby Wayne Hill is silent.

Gray tells him what Annie's old friend said, about how Bobby Wayne was the good-looking star forward on the high school basketball team and Annie was the head cheerleader. About how they went steady, and everybody thought they'd get married someday.

"But it didn't work out, did it? Annie went on to college, and you stayed behind."

Hill shrugs his shoulders.

"Puppy love. You get over it."

"Well, sometimes you do, and sometimes you don't."

"Well what the hell do you care? What's it to you?"

And then the light goes on in Bobby Wayne Hill's brain.

"I know who you are," he says, pointing a bony finger at Gray. "You're the son of a bitch they say killed her. I recognize you now."

He says it loud enough that the closest patrons, a couple two tables away, look back, then throw some money on the table and leave.

"You're quite the detective," Gray tells him.

Hill lowers his voice a little.

"You got a lot of nerve, coming in here and trying to start some shit, when the whole damn world knows you did it."

"So I guess you've been following the case pretty closely."

Hill looks away.

"Just what's on TV. It took me awhile to figure where I'd seen you. I can't believe your ass isn't locked up. I'm gonna get a lawyer and make sure you don't come nowhere near me again."

They grow quiet while the waitress approaches, a little uneasily, Gray thinks, with their food.

When she leaves, Gray leans forward a little.

"So you want me to believe that you and Annie broke up. Susan says it was Annie who broke it off, and you didn't take it well. And then she disappears. And then the ring she had with her that night, my ring, somehow winds up at a yard sale, and you, of all people, buy it?"

"Man," Hill says, "all that shit's ancient history. You don't know nothing."

He reaches toward the ring that Gray has laid on the table between them.

"Let me see that thing," he says, but Gray snatches it away.

Hill leans closer.

"I'll tell you all about it, if you really want to know. But you'll have to come back to the apartment with me. I'll show you something."

Gray shakes his head.

"Not going to happen."

Hill smiles for the first time, showing a mouth full of dental neglect.

"You think I'm goin' to hurt your pussy ass? Is that it?"

"Yeah. That's about it."

"Tell you what. I can tell you something that might make you change your mind. Look, I don't know nothing about who killed Annie Lineberger. She was a high school crush, didn't mean shit much to me after she left Monroe. Just come out to the car with me."

Gray leaves a twenty-dollar bill on the table.

"OK," he says as he painfully eases his body out of the booth. "Show me."

Gray figures he's safe in the open parking lot. Still he keeps a few feet between them.

Hill goes around to the trunk. He fishes his keys out of his pants pocket and opens it.

"This is gonna change your mind about everything," he says, leaning into the trunk.

When he rises up again, he is holding a big-ass pistol with both hands, like he's used it before.

"Get in," he orders. "We're going for a little ride."

They are no more than a hundred feet from a four-lane highway, and the Egg Barn, half full of customers, is closer than that. It doesn't seem to matter to Bobby Wayne Hill.

Gray knows he can't run. Hell, he can barely walk. But he's damned if he's going to let himself be taken somewhere more private by a man with a gun.

More or less out of options, he falls to the ground and begins hollering for help. He is able to crawl between two trucks, but Hill is right behind him.

"You son of a bitch," Hill says quietly as the sound of the gun going off makes Gray's ears ring. He's sprayed with pieces of asphalt, but he hasn't been hit.

Adrenaline overrules his pain, and he's able to scurry around the back of the delivery truck closest to him. He's half on his feet when the second shot is fired. He feels a burning sensation in his right arm and tumbles head-first to the pavement.

He lies there, waiting for what comes next, pondering the wisdom of going it alone. He hears a click, but he feels nothing. Then he hears the sounds of footsteps, one set running away, others coming toward him. He opens his eyes and sees two younger men in uniforms with "Carpet? You bet!" stitched across the front looking down at him.

"Damn. You OK, buddy?" one of them asks.

The other one looks up and says, "Hey! Hey! Stop!"

He hears a car, no doubt an aged Ford Taurus, squeal away.

"Call 911," the first one says to his partner. Then: "Hey, you're bleeding."

So he is, Gray realizes, but he figures the second shot must have only grazed him. Either that, or he's in shock.

They walk him over to his car while one of them calls the emergency number.

"I'm OK," he tells his rescuers as he opens the driver's side door. "Just let me sit here a minute."

And when they step away from the car and wait for the police, he starts the engine and drives off.

They try to stop him, but he locks the doors and assures them, through the glass, that he's fine, that he's just going to go somewhere and get a bandage. A handful of the breakfast joint's patrons come outside to take in the morning's excitement.

He's a block away, headed out of town, when the first police car, and then the EMT vehicle, go screaming past in the other direction.

He wonders if the two Good Samaritans who saved him had wits enough to get his license number. He hopes they didn't. He promises himself that he'll look them up later and thank them.

He pulls into a Walmart parking lot two miles away and checks his arm. As he thought, he's only nicked, but he has managed to bleed an alarming amount all over the car seat and his shirt and pants. And, yeah, he's in a little additional pain. He has made the discovery that he can only really concentrate on one form of discomfort at a time, so he's not that much worse off than he was before Bobby Wayne Hill shot him.

He figures Hill must have piss-poor aim, his proper stance when firing notwithstanding. He's grateful for small favors. He opens the car trunk, takes out the T-shirt he wore the last two days, and wraps it around his right arm at the elbow, just above the place on his forearm that looks more like a bad scrape than a bullet wound.

He stops once at a convenience store, for a bottled water with which to wash down the painkillers. He draws mercifully little attention from the young female African American clerk.

Then he checks his road map and heads north.

CHAPTER TWENTY-TWO

The trip to Colesville requires several turns, from the interstate to a US highway and then to a couple of two-lane state roads. The combination of painkillers and the pain itself gives the drive a dream-like quality. A couple of times, Gray isn't sure exactly where he is for a few seconds.

His route takes him through Chatham. The girl for whom he stops at a crosswalk on the street separating the college from the town looks so much like Annie Lineberger that he feels compelled to pull his car into a no-parking space to collect his thoughts. When he looks in his rearview mirror, the girl is gone.

He finds his way to the courthouse complex. Still in the car, he looks up the number on his iPhone for Marcus Green.

"You'd better get that North Carolina lawyer of yours over to the courthouse right away," Gray says, and he explains what he's done and what he's planning to do. He doesn't mention the fact that he's been bleeding a lot and generally is a little worse for the wear.

"Shit, man, this can't wait until I can get down there?"

"No, it can't. Now, can you call him, or at least give me the number?"

A sigh.

"I'll call him. I can get his attention. Now stay there. Don't say anything to any damn DA, or especially to that judge, before you have a lawyer present."

Gray laughs.

"If I say something and neither you nor this Flint Massey is there, can you charge me for that?"

"Glad to see you still have your sense of humor."

Marcus Green hangs up.

Gray is out of his car and walking up the brick walkway leading to the main building when he realizes that he doesn't even know the judge's name.

He finds it on the directory inside the building: John Henry Trott. He figures he needs to get to the judge's office as soon as possible. The makeshift bandage seems to have stemmed the bleeding, but his shirt and pants are a mess, as is his battered face. The first deputy who spies him is liable to stop him from going any closer to the judge's quarters than he is now.

Gray makes his way to the third floor, thankful that Friday afternoon at the start of a Memorial Day weekend seems to be a rather sleepy time at the Byrd County courthouse.

He walks through the door. The woman sitting at the desk in front of him looks up and stifles a gasp.

"Are you all right, sir?" she asks him. He can see her already reaching for her phone.

Gray explains as quickly as he can that he is fine, that he is Grayson Melvin, out on bond for the murder of Annie Lineberger, and that he has important information for Judge Trott, information that he needs to convey "right damn now."

She's nervous as a cat. She asks him to please take a seat while she checks to see if the judge has left for the weekend.

She goes into the office behind her desk. He thinks he hears a lock click.

He isn't surprised, half a minute later, to hear somebody or bodies running down the hall toward where he sits. The door flies open, and a couple of deputies walk in, weapons drawn.

They order him to first put his hands up over his head and then get on the floor. They are in the process of hand-cuffing his hands behind his back when he hears the inner door open.

"Easy now, fellas," he hears the judge say. "Don't hurt him. He seems harmless enough."

Gray is staring at the judge's feet and legs. He's wearing sandals and shorts.

"What are you doing, barging in here and trying to screw up my weekend? Sorry about the handcuffs and all, but you scared the hell out of Lucinda here."

John Henry Trott walks over and pulls up a chair in front of Gray.

"Now tell me what this is all about."

Gray asks if he can be allowed to get off the floor. The judge nods, and the deputies help him, somewhat roughly, to his feet. One of them grabs another chair, and now he's sitting facing the judge.

Trott shakes his head as he looks him over.

"Damn," he says, "you look like you took an overdose of whip-ass. Please tell me that police brutality wasn't involved, or at least not from our police."

Gray assures him that, other than an undeserved speed-ing ticket, he has not been harmed by any law-enforcement officials.

"Well, go on. Tell it," the judge says.

So Gray does. He goes back to the call he got eight days ago about his class ring. He takes the judge along the trail that led to Bobby Wayne Hill. He tells Trott about his near-death experience this morning.

Trott asks him why he didn't call the police after he was shot.

"I'm a little leery of law enforcement right now," Gray tells him. He sees one of the deputies scowl. "I'm a little leery about being in Byrd County right now, to tell you the truth, but you're about the only person with any clout who seemed like he might listen to me."

"You didn't think you'd get a fair shake from Towson Grimes?"

The judge seems to almost smile when he says it.

Gray shakes his head.

"Well, where is this ring, anyhow?"

"It's in my right-hand pocket."

The judge tells one of the deputies to fish the ring out. He does, and hands it to the judge.

"Well, it's a ring all right. And I see it has what you say are your initials on it. But right now all we've got is your side of the story. What if you had this ring all along and you're just making up this cock-and-bull tale?"

Gray assures him that he can get corroboration from Dot Gaines and Isadora Goforth and probably from the fat man at the antiques store.

"And there's a guy running around loose in a beat-up Ford Taurus who shot me this morning."

The judge tells the deputies to take off Gray's handcuffs. Then, as they're talking, Flint Massey comes bursting through the door, out of breath. One of the deputies reaches for his gun before he sees who it is.

"Don't say anything," the lawyer says.

"Too late, Flint," the judge tells him. "He's already spilled his guts."

Then Trott laughs and shakes his head.

"Nah, he didn't confess to anything, unless confessing for somebody else counts."

The judge makes a call.

"Hey, Towson. You better get your ass over here. I think your forty-eight-year-old murder case might have run into a little bit of a snag."

He looks at Gray.

"I probably caught him just before he left for the beach. If you're going to mess up my weekend, I am not going down alone."

In the twenty minutes before Towson Grimes joins them in the crowded office, Gray's North Carolina lawyer tries to counsel his client, stopping once to make a call to Marcus Green for advice.

It's obvious that Massey thinks he should keep his mouth shut, but Gray tells him that's not going to happen.

Grimes, whose leisure wear approximates what the judge has on, looks angry and concerned when he joins the party.

"What the hell is going on, John Henry? You're not going to believe this piece of crap, are you?"

Trott looks up at the district attorney.

"It's 'your honor,' or at least 'judge,' if you don't mind. Now I've just been told a rather amazing story. We don't have time to check it out right now, but I can assure you it will be checked out. And if it does check out, you might wind up looking like an asshole. Which is why I'm going to ask the state police to step in and investigate. No offense, but if we're going to try to send this man to the gas chamber, I reckon we ought to make sure we've got the right guy."

He asks the DA if anyone has checked hair samples that might be among Annie Lineberger's bones.

"Why the hell would we do that? We've got the guy that did it, the one they knew did it all along. For forty-eight years they've known it. He's sitting right here."

"That may be so, Towson, but it's not looking so cut-and-dried from where I sit."

The DA looks like he's very close to getting arrested himself. It's hard for Gray to believe that he's the same easygoing, slow-talking character he first met a couple of weeks earlier.

"We can handle the investigation, whatever this son of a bitch claims. We can find out if he's lying."

The judge shakes his head.

"No, Towson. We're turning this one over to the state. If you try to go over my head, I can assure you it won't be pleasant."

Towson Grimes looks at the judge, then looks at Gray. He seems to know that he's fighting a losing battle. He turns without another word and stomps out of the room, slamming the door behind him.

"He always was a hothead," the judge says to Gray as they hear Grimes's footsteps recede. "He was a few years ahead of me in school, and he was like that then. When he made up his mind, he didn't want to hear any back talk about it. That works sometimes."

He turns to Gray.

"Mister, you've totally messed up my weekend. You better not be lying about any of this. If you are, I'll revoke that bail and let you spend the rest of the year as our guest while you wait for your day in court."

He has Lucinda take Gray's information, including the make and model of Bobby Wayne Hill's car.

He looks at Gray's shirt, taking in all the dried blood like he's seeing it for the first time.

"In the meantime, while we're checking all this out, we better get you over to the clinic, if not the county hospital. And we'll get you a room at the Days Inn, so we can stay in touch while we see if you're lying or not. We don't want you leaving town right now."

He tells the deputy to drive him to the clinic, reminding him that Gray is not under arrest and shouldn't be treated as if he were. The deputy nods, grim-faced.

The clinic is only two blocks away. The deputy never says a word to him, then drives off as soon as Gray leaves the car.

The nurse there takes care of the wound to his arm and asks him if he's had his nose looked at.

Gray tells her he has. He doesn't mention the ribs.

He walks the two blocks back to his car. The judge has arranged for him to stay at the motel "compliments of the county" while they vet his story. He drives there and checks in. It's almost dark, and there doesn't seem to be anything open that would serve food in the general area. Gray treats himself to a pack of Nabs, a candy bar, and a Coke from the vending machine down the hall.

He gets a call from Marcus Green as he's about to succumb to the latest round of pain pills.

"My associate says you weren't terribly cooperative today," Green says by way of greeting.

"He and I have a different idea about my defense strategy," Gray tells him. He thinks he might have said "stragedy."

"Well you ought to listen to the experts. That's what you're paying us for."

Gray tells him what he told the judge earlier.

"Damn, man," his lawyer says. "That took a lot of stones, going right to the judge's office. You're lucky they didn't shoot your ass."

Gray reminds him that it wouldn't be the first time his ass has been shot at today, and that he's kind of getting used to it.

Green laughs.

"Well, rest assured, I will be down there tomorrow. Hell, I've got all summer to go to the beach. My tan ain't going to get any better. You're better entertainment than watching the tide roll in."

Gray tells him he's glad to be the source of such apparent revelry.

While he was on the phone with his Richmond lawyer, he sees that he got another call.

He returns it.

"Holy shit," Corrine Manzi says by way of greeting. "You've been a busy boy. I just saw a clip on the news about a shooting over in Lexington. They described the guy who they said got shot and left the scene, and they've managed to get the shooter's name. And I recognized it. That was you, right? The shootee, I mean. Are you OK?"

Corrine tells him that they haven't caught Bobby Wayne Hill yet, but they're pretty sure Bobby Wayne won't be that hard to round up.

"Where the hell are you?"

He tells her where he's staying, and why.

"Damn. I think I'm going to come up there. I think this might be the best story we've had all year."

"What do you mean, 'we'? You're retired, remember?"

She laughs.

"Reporters are like marines," she says. "There's no such thing as former reporters. Not the real ones anyhow."

"So I'm just a story now? Something to hang one last byline on?"

"Aw, it's not like that, Gray. I never thought you did it, and I didn't do enough to help you back when I could've.

"But, I gotta say, this will be one hell of a story."

He makes her promise not to come to Colesville in the middle of the night.

He makes one last call and tells Betsy Fordyce about his interesting morning and afternoon.

"I'm getting in the car in about fifteen minutes," she tells him, "and I don't want to hear any more bullshit about it. You've played Lone Ranger long enough."

He tells her he loves her, something he knows he doesn't do often enough. He asks about Josh, and Betsy tells him the boy is starting at second base for his Little League team.

"Maybe," he tells her, "we ought to get married."

After a short silence, she says, "Wow. Those painkillers must be something. Talk to me when they wear off."

He gives her the name and location of the Days Inn and his room number. He warns her that he probably won't even hear her knocking if she starts out right now and bangs on his door at two in the morning.

"Well, then, I'll get another room and wake you up bright and early tomorrow."

"Betsy."

"What?"

"I'm not worth it."

"I'll be the judge of that."

She hangs up and leaves Gray to a restless sleep.

When his cell phone buzzes again, he is dead to the world, only waking as the phone goes silent.

Blurry-minded, he checks the call. It's a number he doesn't recognize. The clock reads nine forty-five P.M.

Then the phone buzzes again.

"Yeah. Who is this?"

"You know who it is."

Even half asleep, he recognizes the voice.

CHAPTER TWENTY-THREE

MAY 28

The last call spawns a continuous loop of dreams that keeps Gray suspended between sleep and consciousness for much of the night, painkillers notwithstanding. The morning sun is barely streaming in the window whose blinds he neglected to close when the loud rapping on his door wakes him up. The bedside clock says 6:18.

He wonders if Towson Grimes has sent his minions to arrest him again, or if what he half thinks he dreamed last night has borne fruit, but when he peeks through the spy hole, he sees Betsy standing there.

"I couldn't sleep," she explains when he opens the door. "My God. You look like hell."

She got into Colesville at one thirty in the morning and realized there was no one at the motel's front desk after midnight.

"I didn't want to wake you up, so I slept in my car, in the parking lot. Can I use your facilities, by the way?"

He opens the door and lets her in.

"Sorry," she says when she comes out of the bathroom. "I'm not exactly dressed for company right now, am I?"

He tells her she's far and away the best-looking person in the room at present.

"Cold comfort. Jesus, Gray, let me look at you. Somebody really did a number on your face."

He winces when she gives him a hug. She lifts his T-shirt and stifles a gasp when she sees the rainbow of colors along his rib cage.

"And you haven't been to a hospital yet?"

He explains that he has been somewhat preoccupied.

"Well, first thing, we're going to get you to a hospital. A real one. You're too old to be messing with possible broken ribs."

He doesn't mention that he's still pissing blood. His urine seems to be losing some of its blush though.

She asks him if he's running a fever. She goes to retrieve the blood-pressure kit she keeps in the trunk of her car.

She frowns when she checks the numbers.

"One-fifty over one hundred and five. That's not so good."

Gray tells her that he forgot to pack the Lisinopril he takes every day, or is supposed to, to keep his blood pressure in check.

"I'll get back on it when we get home."

"I'm going to get your prescription refilled today, down here. Don't worry. I can take care of that."

He tells her his blood pressure will be just fine if he can finish taking care of a little business with the legal system.

"And I don't think it's going to take much longer."

"You sound pretty optimistic, for a guy who looks like he's got one foot in the grave."

So he tells her about the last phone call he got, the one that disturbed his sleep for the rest of the night.

When he's through, she just sits back in the room's only chair and doesn't say anything for a few seconds.

"Well," she says at last. "I hope you took notes."

He tells her that he didn't really need to, but that he did scribble a summary on the notepad at his bedside, although he's having trouble reading it at present.

"What I need right now," he says, "is for you to come over here and lie down beside me."

"You think you're up for it? No pun intended."

"Not that. Just lie here and let me hold you."

"But don't you need to tell somebody, about that call you got?"

He shakes his head and pulls her to him.

They are still lying there, him spooning against her and sleeping like a baby, when the phone next to the bed rings.

Gray answers it and sees that it's half past nine.

"Mr. Melvin," the voice says. "We need you to come over to the courthouse right away. We're sending a car around to pick you up."

Gray doesn't ask why. He tells the judge he can drive himself. The judge tells him to stay where he is.

ON THE way over, in the back seat of the county car, Betsy asks him, as she has twice already, what exactly they are going to the courthouse for. It took her half an hour to help him get dressed and to "put myself together so I don't look like some whore you spent the night with" while the deputy waited more or less patiently outside. When he says he thinks she looks great, he isn't lying.

Gray tells her again that he has a pretty good idea, but he doesn't want to jinx it.

"It's about that call, isn't it? Did they catch the guy?"

"Let's wait and see."

When they get there, a couple of state police cars are parked next to the brick walkway leading to the courthouse. Next to them, Gray sees a Lexus with Virginia tags and a vanity plate that proclaims "MGBEME." He is impressed that Marcus Green has gotten there already. And, standing next to the car beside the Lexus, is Corrine Manzi.

"We've been waiting for you," she says.

The lawyer meets them at the door. Gray asks him if he knows what's going on.

"Hell, I just got here," Green says. "I was hoping you'd be able to tell me. All I know is, this place is hopping for a Saturday morning. There's some tight assholes around here, I can tell you that."

The North Carolina lawyer shows up five minutes later, and they're sitting there on a bench in the hall outside Judge Trott's office for another ten, watching as a variety of law-enforcement types and what appear to be lawyers dragged from their holiday weekend go inside. Some leave and some stay. The ones who leave glance at the party waiting on the bench, but nobody says anything to them.

Finally the door opens one last time, and John Henry Trott himself steps outside.

"Well," he says, "you all can come on in now. I think we've got things pretty much sussed out."

Inside they join a couple of other lawyers and two state troopers. The judge makes the other lawyers stand so Gray and Betsy can sit. He tells Corrine to wait outside.

"You look like you need to be sitting down," he tells Gray. "I hope you can now appreciate the folly in playing amateur detective.

"So," he continues, turning to the two troopers, "why don't you all tell these people what you found this morning."

THE POLICE in Lexington didn't have too much trouble finding Robert Wayne Hill. His brothers both swore they hadn't
seen him, but one of the brothers' neighbors told the cops
that Bobby Wayne had come by in a somewhat agitated state
an hour earlier, about seven o'clock in the evening.

Faced with charges of harboring a criminal, the brother
who had in fact seen him admitted it and said Bobby Wayne
told him he was going to hole up somewhere for a few days,
maybe stay with his girlfriend.

They finally tracked down the girlfriend who, it turned
out, had a job cleaning toilets and changing sheets at the
Holiday Inn out by the interstate. A visit to her, sometime
after nine, soon revealed the fact that Bobby Wayne had,
with her assistance, moved into an unoccupied room on the
second floor.

By the time the state troopers got involved and had the
place surrounded, it was almost midnight. Because the police
hadn't locked up the girlfriend yet, it was assumed that she
had given Bobby Wayne a heads-up at some point, and they
knew he was armed, or at least were sure as hell he had been
that morning.

They had already emptied the place of paying customers. The guy with the bullhorn tried to get Bobby Wayne to
talk to him. He gave him his cell phone number and asked
him to get in touch.

They didn't hear anything until the gunshot, which
occurred around two thirty in the morning. It took them
another forty-five minutes to reach the point where they
didn't think Bobby Wayne Hill was going to blast anybody
who came through the door. They knocked the door in, to
the manager's dismay. Bobby Wayne was lying on the bed.
His aim was better than it had been in the Egg Barn parking

lot. Part of his skull and what was inside it was splattered on the wall behind the bed.

The manager, creeping in behind the troopers, shook his head and said he didn't guess they would be renting that particular room for a while.

"Now, we don't know for sure that this means anything," Judge Trott says, "but it does look somewhat suspicious."

By this time, Towson Grimes has joined the party. He looks as if he had a poor night's sleep interrupted by a most unwelcome phone call.

"He didn't leave a note or anything," the judge goes on after silently acknowledging Grimes. "This guy wasn't a hardened criminal, best we can tell, and we can't come up with many possible reasons why he would have tried to shoot you yesterday morning, or why he'd want to blow his brains out last night. Other than the reason you gave us here yesterday, of course."

The judge clears his throat.

"However, Mr. Hill did make one phone call. He made it about a quarter to ten, according to the records. He was on the phone for quite some time."

The judge leans forward, close enough that Gray can see he's wearing contact lenses.

"You wouldn't happen to know anything about that call, would you?"

Gray's pretty sure the judge knows the answer already, but he nods anyhow.

CHAPTER TWENTY-FOUR

They figure Bobby Wayne Hill probably phoned Gray just a few minutes after Bobby Wayne's girlfriend called him to inform him his number was up.

Gray said he didn't have a chance to talk much. He wondered how long the man had been waiting to tell somebody about it. Maybe he thought he'd take his story to the grave, until that 1967 East Geddie High School senior class ring changed everything.

"You think you're so fuckin' smart," he'd told Gray. "Well, you don't know shit. Let me tell you how it was, bright boy."

When he was through talking, Gray had to agree with Bobby Wayne. He wasn't so fucking smart. He didn't know everything. He didn't know shit actually.

"I ain't telling you where I am," Bobby Wayne said. "But I can tell you one damn thing, they're not going to get me. By the time they get here, I'll be long gone."

After his caller told him everything and hung up, Gray knew he should have called the police. After he wrote down what he could remember, though, a terrible tiredness overtook him. He felt the way he felt after he finished his one and only marathon, all those years ago. He couldn't go one step farther, not without rest.

"And you didn't call anybody, after he called you?" the judge asks.

Gray shakes his head.

"Hell," Trott says, "they probably had him surrounded by then anyhow. He knew he was a dead man walking."

The judge sits down right in front of Gray, backward in his chair, leaning over the back of it.

"Well," he says, "you might as well tell us. We're all dying to hear what the dying man's confession was, especially Mr. Grimes over here."

Grimes starts to say something, then leans back against the wall and shuts his eyes.

BOBBY WAYNE and Annie broke up in July. It hadn't been Bobby Wayne's idea, and it had not been amicable. They had gone steady for two years, and he assumed that they would be spending the rest of their lives together.

"She just told me she was too young," Hill said. Gray could tell he was slurring his words. He imagined the man buying a couple of six-packs of cheap beer on the way to his hideout.

Bobby Wayne seemed to have been the kind of boy who peaked at eighteen, right after the last high school basketball game. He didn't ever plan to go to college, although he eventually would, after he got out of the army, on the GI Bill.

"Maybe if I'd of gone to some college then, been a damn college boy like you, she might not've dumped me."

Annie tried to ease the pain, but to Bobby Wayne that just made it worse.

"She said we ought to give it some time, maybe not see each other for a couple of months. Hell, I was ready to marry her. I mean, I knew she was planning to go to college and all, but we could have made it work, somehow."

Annie Lineberger went away to Chatham in late August. In the five weeks between the time she gave Bobby Wayne his walking papers and then, he saw her only briefly, now and then.

He said he approached her a couple of times, following her to the local drive-in where they used to go together. After the second time, she told him he needed to stay away, if he ever had any hope of them getting back together.

"She told me to just give it some time," Hill said. "It was like, 'Don't call me, I'll call you.' Except she never did."

He joined the army that December, when he was about to be drafted anyhow. They sent him to Fort Campbell, Kentucky, for his basic training and advanced training "right in the middle of the damn winter."

He had written Annie six times at Chatham before he went to basic and got one letter back. He thought maybe she would think better of him for going into the army, probably headed for Vietnam, where he might get maimed or killed.

"But it didn't make a damn bit of difference. She wrote me twice in Kentucky. I looked at her picture every night."

Gray wonders if it's the same picture he has in the depths of his wallet, and if Bobby Wayne kept his too.

He had some leave after his sixteen weeks at Fort Campbell. The last letter he got from Annie contained a small ray of sunshine in a world that had been overcast for nine months.

"I can still remember what she wrote: 'I hope we can get together when you get back. Long time, no see.' "

Gray can hear the man either laugh or cry.

"That's a hell of a thing to hang your hopes on, ain't it? Long time, no see."

And yet he did.

Hill admitted that he had "seen" a couple of girls in his exile, "but they weren't anything like her. They weren't anything like Annie."

Maybe he had deceived himself, sequestered away in his army outpost with nothing but hope to keep him going. Whatever the reason, when he got a short leave from Fort Campbell in late April, before he was to report to Fort Bragg, he headed straight for Chatham, North Carolina.

Now with spring busting out, seemingly getting more verdant by the mile as he drove his beat-up Ford Fairlane east and south, Bobby Wayne Hill probably thought anything was possible, even Annie.

He knew where she lived. He'd written enough letters to that damn address. When he reached his destination, though, he hesitated. It was late afternoon by the time he found her dorm, and he sat there in his car for an hour at least. He drank the last two beers in the six-pack he'd bought a couple of hours before.

Maybe he thought she would just happen by, and she'd see him and leap into his arms in her cheerleader outfit like it was basketball season his senior year and he'd just hit a jumper at the buzzer to win the big game.

What he saw instead was something a bit less hopeful.

He saw Annie Lineberger come out of her dorm in the company of another boy.

"That was you, right? I figured it must of been. You're the boy from Carolina, the one they thought did it."

Gray figures he doesn't have to say anything.

"Well, I followed you. I bet you didn't know that, did you?"

He waited until they drove off in Gray's car. He parked at the restaurant where they went, which was so close to campus he wondered why they'd even bothered to drive, and he waited in the parking lot, feeling as low as he had ever felt.

"I could see her inside. You all had a booth by the window. I guess I knew she was seeing other boys. I mean, hell, how could she not be? She was like a guy magnet. But this really tore me up, seeing it like that, thrown in my face."

He waited for more than an hour.

"When you all came out, it didn't seem like you all were too happy, which made me happy."

He waited, not a hundred feet away, unaware that Annie Lineberger was telling Gray that they needed a time-out.

"I knew something was wrong when I saw her get out of the car and slam the door and walk off."

He saw her walk to a path that looked like it was leading in the direction of her dorm. He drove off and went back to a place not far from where he had waited earlier, in the parking lot outside the residence hall.

The path from the restaurant to her dorm went through a patch of woods. Bobby Wayne found the place where the path emerged on campus and was walking toward it just as Annie came walking out of the woods.

"It was like it was meant to be," he told Gray. "I mean, if I hadn't seen that path there, and been able to park right where it came out on the other side, none of this might of happened. I might of gone to her dorm, and she might of come down to see me, and she'd have set me down in a nice, well-lit parlor, with some house mother or something watching, and told me it was definitely over.

"Right time, right place. Or wrong time, wrong place, I guess."

He said Annie seemed more than a little surprised to see him.

"She let out a little scream. I reckon I was the last person she expected to see. I could see she'd been crying. From what I read later in the newspapers, you said that you all had just broke up."

When Bobby Wayne tried to take her in his arms, like he had been wanting to do for months, she pushed him away and told him to leave.

"I reckon her idea of 'get together' and mine were a little bit different."

He thought about all the time he'd been hoping for a moment like this, and how it was all turning to shit.

"I don't know what got into me. I just grabbed her, and I took her around to the passenger side, and I pushed her in."

He said she didn't scream, but when he tried to explain why he had driven all the way from Fort Campbell, Kentucky, and why he believed they were meant for each other, she put her hands over her ears.

She didn't try to stop him or jump out of the car when he drove off.

"She just sat there, like she was in a trance."

He didn't know the area, but he had seen a sign coming into town pointing toward a municipal park. That's where he headed.

"She was acting a little more normal by the time we got there, but I knew she wasn't exactly delighted to see me."

"When I told her I wanted to marry her, that I'd do anything to make her happy, she just looked at me, shook her head, and said it was too late."

He told her it was never too late, and she laughed "kind of mean like."

That's when she told him why it wasn't going to work.

"She just said, 'I'm late,' and I thought she was talking about some kind of curfew in her dorm or something. And then she explained it to me."

Suddenly the room must have gotten colder, because Gray realized he had goose bumps on his arms.

Finally, as the silence grew, he asked Bobby Wayne, "How did she know?"

"How the fuck do you think she knew? She said she'd missed two periods already."

It had taken Bobby Wayne a few seconds to get his mind around the fact that the girl he'd mounted on a pedestal had been having sexual relations with someone other than him. The two of them had done it a few times toward the end of their senior year, before the breakup that summer, and she had told him that he had spoiled her for other men.

"Apparently," Bobby Wayne said, "she got over that."

Gray couldn't think of any delicate way to put it.

"Did she say, you know, whose it was?"

His caller started laughing, which led to a coughing fit. When Bobby Wayne finally could talk again, he said, "Nah, man. She didn't say."

Hill said he accused her of being a whore, sleeping around with everybody and his brother. When she tried to get out of the car, he locked the door on her side and grabbed her wrists.

"I told her I would marry her and take care of the kid, whoever the daddy was. And you know what she did? She laughed.

"She said there was no way in hell that she was going to have a baby, and no way she was going back to Monroe. Plus she was pretty sure her parents would disown her and never speak to her again. She said a boy she knew, a boy who was rich and had some connections and such, was going to help her get an abortion."

She said she was going to see him the next day, and that he was going to set it up, that he'd arranged somehow for her to get it done at the big teaching hospital in Richmond the next weekend.

"I think she said he was another college boy like you. From Virginia, I think."

"Winston," Gray said.

"Hell, I don't remember. That was a long time ago. Could have been."

She told Bobby Wayne Hill that she really liked "the boy from Carolina" who she had just broken up with.

"She said, if she was going to let anybody marry her and raise her baby, it would have been him. Meaning you, dumbass. But she said she just wasn't ready for anything like that, and that she knew you weren't ready, and that you sure as hell weren't ready to deal with a girlfriend having an abortion."

Bobby Wayne asked her one last time to let him take care of her.

"She just shook her head and said it was over."

She broke free from his grasp, unlocked the passenger-side door, and started walking off into the woods.

"I don't know where she was going, but I got out and tried to follow her. I caught up with her over by this little creek. I don't know what happened then. I just kind of lost it, I guess. She slapped me, almost knocked me down, and the next thing I know, it's like I blanked out or something, but I'm squeezing her neck, and I can't seem to stop, and then finally she stops kicking and hitting me. She just goes limp, like a rag doll.

"I tried to revive her, used what first aid I'd learned in basic training, but it didn't do any good. She was gone. I swear to God, I never meant to hurt her."

He said he could have left her there, but he felt like he had to get rid of the body. He had a shovel in the back of the car that he'd used to get out of snow drifts in February in Kentucky. So he drove his car as close as he could to where Annie's body was and dragged it into the trunk.

He told Gray he drove several miles before he found a rut road that went off into some woods. He followed it for a couple of hundred yards, then got out and used his flashlight to find a place between two trees about twenty feet off the road. That's where he started digging.

"It seemed like I dug all night. I think I got it down about five feet. Then I threw her body in and covered it up and left. I never looked back."

He said he returned to Monroe the next day after staying overnight at a motel an hour out of town, where he freshened up.

"I don't even know why I took the damn ring. It fell out of a pocket in her skirt when I was lifting her out of the car trunk to put her into that grave. I should have thrown it away, or just buried it with her. But I didn't. It was like all I had left to remember her by.

"I did love her, I swear to God I did. I didn't mean for any of that to happen."

Gray hears what sounds like a beer can being opened.

"Sometime over the years, it must of got mixed in with a bunch of other junk. I should've thrown it away, but I'm kind of a pack rat. Hell, I tried to find it one time, when me and Isadora was breaking up, but I couldn't. I figured it was just lost."

Bobby Wayne Hill's words were getting more slurred.

"I'm sorry it all fell on you. Sorry I had to shoot you. But what the hell was I supposed to do, confess? They never even got around to questioning me about her. Folks back home treated me like I had lost a loved one, after she disappeared."

Bobby Wayne went on after what sounded like a short break to take another swig.

"And what the hell were the chances that someone would steal a bunch of my crap and sell it to that half-ass junk shop, and that some busybody would find the ring in there and start playing Nancy Drew, tracing it back to you?

"When they dug up her bones, I felt like shit all over again. I mean, what are the odds that the place I buried her would turn out to be part of the parking lot for a grocery store some fool's building? It was in the middle of the woods in 1968, or that's what it looked like to me. Maybe I should of gone a little deeper.

"I wondered if somebody was going to come talk to me, even after all those years, but they fixed on you right away, like they knew it was you all along, and I sure as hell wasn't going to step up to the plate."

Gray interrupts at last.

"I never knew. That she was pregnant."

He heard Bobby Wayne Hill laugh.

"Well, ain't that a kick in the nuts. Question is: Would you have done the right thing, if she would have let you?"

"In a heartbeat. But she wouldn't have."

Gray knew that Annie Lineberger was not going to let anyone, no matter how much she liked him, turn her into a mother at nineteen.

"She'd have told me the same thing she told you."

But it's a safe bet, Gray thought as he listened to Bobby Wayne ramble on, that he would not have choked her to death because she rejected him.

Gray was scribbling frantically, hoping he could read what he was writing in the morning.

His caller hung up after sharing a last few thoughts:

"I killed the only girl I ever loved. If I could do it over again, yeah, I'd do it a hell of a lot differently. But you can't go back. All you can do is go to hell."

Those were the last words Gray heard from Bobby Wayne Hill. He supposed the police arrived a short while later, and it all went downhill from there.

CHAPTER TWENTY-FIVE

MONDAY, JUNE 6

The sun breaks through while Gray is watering the tomato plants in Betsy's backyard, checking for the first flowers giving hope that he will indeed be able to eat a homegrown tomato sandwich in the near future.

He's on his knees in the damp soil when he hears the phone ring inside.

He isn't able to get there before the message machine comes on.

"This is a call for Mr. Grayson Melvin from the Byrd County, North Carolina, district attorney's office," the woman's voice begins. "Please call us back at your convenience."

He feels light-headed, at least partly from jumping up from his gardening so quickly. He takes the number and calls back.

"Mr. Melvin," says the voice in the office of District Attorney Towson Grimes, "I believe we have some encouraging news for you."

MUCH HAS happened in the nine days since Gray learned of Bobby Wayne Hill's demise and then related to Judge John

Henry Trott, as best he could, his final conversation with the deceased, leaving out one important part.

Judge Trott thought it was appropriate, considering the circumstances, that Gray be allowed to return to Virginia, noting that there was every possibility that there would not be any trial, nine months later or ever. He added, though, that the charges would stand, and that there would be a more thorough investigation of Annie Lineberger's remains to see if they could find a hair sample to match against Bobby Wayne Hill's.

"It's hard to believe that all that violence took place and he buried her and all and didn't leave at least a strand of hair," the judge said. "I believe due diligence will turn up something."

So Gray went back to Richmond. He wasn't exactly greeted with palm branches when he returned to the city, but he did get a few calls from people he considered friends, some from whom he had not heard since Annie's bones were discovered. There was a certain sheepishness in their tones.

They all knew about it because Willie Black, in cahoots with Corrine Manzi, had written the story in time for the Monday editions two days after Gray's return. It ran in the Charlotte and Richmond papers at the same time and was picked up by the wire services, leading to another round of TV trucks and camera crews tromping all over Betsy Fordyce's Kentucky fescue grass.

Gray had gotten Corrine in touch with Willie after the Saturday morning meeting at the Byrd County courthouse. She wanted to write the story for the Charlotte paper, and Gray said she could but only if she shared it with Willie.

"He seems like a good guy," Corrine told Gray on the night before the story broke. "I can tell he's ingested a lot of whiskey and nicotine. Old school. Old farts like me, we like that."

The headline read:

Suicide puts murder case in limbo

The subhead:

Melvin could be cleared soon

"You're a big deal now," Willie told him the morning the story came out. "You're not 'local man,' anymore. You've got a name."

Gray said he'd had about enough publicity to last a damn lifetime, and that was before the TV types and national press started showing up. But he thanked Willie for helping set the record straight.

"Be assured," Willie said. "There will be some assholes out there who won't remember the punch line. They'll just remember you were arrested for murder."

Gray told him he could live with that.

The story, which took up a third of A1 and most of the turn page, followed the tortuous path of Annie Lineberger's ring, leading back to Bobby Wayne Hill. It drew extensively on Gray's call from Hill. There were a lot of places where Corrine and Willie had to take Gray's word on everything, as he was the only witness to the man's confession. But, as Corrine explained, the dead can't sue. They didn't get much out of the Byrd County district attorney's office.

Gray didn't tell them everything though.

He related what Hill told him about taking her to the park against her will and then chasing after her when she ran away, and then choking her to death.

The part about the pregnancy he kept to himself. Thinking about Annie Lineberger, murdered and buried in an unmarked grave all those years, dying for nothing more than the crime of wanting to be young and free, he knew there was one detail of her sad demise that no one would ever know except him.

Well, him and one other person.

It wasn't hard to track down Winston. Gray couldn't remember his last name, so he called Susan Vanhoy Carpenter, who didn't recall much about the boy who was supposed to go out with her roommate that Saturday. She did think, though, that Annie said he was an engineering student, and that he was a junior.

"I met him once," she told Gray. "He had blond hair, I remember that."

Gray went to Charlottesville, where he was able to look at University of Virginia yearbooks from 1968. Winston wasn't that common a first name. He found one Winston in the engineering school, a junior. It was a black-and-white picture, but his hair was obviously blond. Winston Keppler.

Gray Googled the name and found an amazing number of Winston Kepplers. Only one, though, was sixty-nine years old and living in a suburb of Washington.

Gray called the number that was listed. He told the man who answered what his name was and what he was calling about. He didn't have any great hopes that Winston Keppler would agree to meet with him. It really wouldn't matter much, he figured. Either they would find some trace of hair or other evidence of Bobby Wayne Hill among Annie's bones, or they wouldn't.

But he wanted to know, just for his own sake.

Keppler surprised him though.

"I wondered," the man on the line said, "how long it would take for you or somebody to find me."

On Thursday, Gray drove up to Northern Virginia and eventually found the home he was looking for.

Keppler himself came to the front door. Gray recognized him from the forty-eight-year-old photograph. The man looked to be about six foot three, still looking fit and lean, a man who could pass for ten years younger.

He led Gray into a living room where an ancient Irish setter looked up at him but didn't bother to bark or rise. He poured himself a bourbon on the rocks and offered one to his guest, who declined.

"So," Keppler said as he sat back in an easy chair, facing Gray, "what can I tell you?"

"Everything."

HE MET her through a friend who had grown up in Chatham and convinced Keppler the girls' school there was a great place to pick up smart, attractive, hot-blooded girls. It was before U.Va. admitted women into the general college, and "rolling" to various women's colleges around the state was standard practice.

He met Annie much the way Gray had. He said he was "smitten," but that she made it clear early on that she wasn't ready to get serious about anybody yet, although she was up for the occasional date. So he stayed in touch with her, had her up to Charlottesville once, but by then he had met a girl from Sweet Briar, and he didn't see Annie much after that.

The night Gray met Annie, Winston was supposed to come down, the first time he'd seen her in two months, but he canceled out at the last minute.

"The girl from Sweet Briar, who, I might add, was my wife for twenty-five wonderful years and fifteen shitty ones, found out I was going down to Chatham, and she had a fit. So I had to cancel. I felt like a jerk, which I was, and I figured that was the last I'd see of Annie Lineberger."

She called him in late March and said she was scared, she needed help. Could he come down to Chatham? It was a measure of her hold on him still that he came.

"She knew my father was a doctor, and that I had some medical connections."

She told Keppler that she was sure she was pregnant. She told him she didn't want to wait any longer, that she wanted "to be done with it."

She came up to Charlottesville in mid-April, and the two of them traveled to Richmond, where they met a doctor at the big teaching hospital who, with a word from Winston's father, said he could help her.

"I was supposed to come get her that Saturday, but when I got to her dorm, she wasn't there. Nobody had seen her since the night before."

He was questioned by the police after Annie disappeared, but he could prove he had come down from Charlottesville that afternoon, and his whereabouts the night before.

"I told them what I'm sure Annie told her roommate, that I was taking her up to U.Va. for the weekend. I never mentioned anything about the abortion. My father said it would be better if we just left that part out of it."

His father made a quiet call to Richmond, and "the procedure," with Annie using a pseudonym, was canceled.

"Like everybody else, I assumed you had done it. I really hated you for a long time, because it seemed like you had literally gotten away with murder. And then I just kind of forgot about Annie Lineberger. Oh, I'd think of her once in a while, but it was back pages for me until they found her remains."

Keppler shook his head and took a sip of his bourbon.

"Stupid word, remains. Like anything remains except maybe memories."

Gray asked him if he had ever had the urge to get in touch with him and tell him about the aborted abortion.

Keppler took a sip of his bourbon and reached down to scratch the setter behind the ear.

"I don't think she wanted you to know about it. She just wanted a clean break. She said she needed to have some distance from men for a while.

"And besides, up until Monday, I thought you had murdered her. I wanted nothing to do with you. When I saw that they had arrested you, I was glad."

Gray thanked Keppler for his time and saw himself to the front door.

The man followed him, leaving the now-empty glass on the table.

"I see you didn't mention anything about her being pregnant, at least not in the paper I read."

"There wasn't any reason to."

"Well, that was decent, at least. She deserved some decency, don't you think?"

Gray had to ask one last question.

"Did you sleep with her? I mean, would the baby have been yours?"

Keppler looked at him as if he was crazy.

"We did it one time, and I used a rubber. No, she was sure it was yours. She said so."

As Gray was headed out the door, Keppler asked him to wait a minute. He walked over to the bookshelf that covered one wall of the study and pulled down a book. He opened it and took something out.

"I guess you could say that maybe I didn't forget her all that much," he said, showing Gray the picture and asking him if he wanted to keep it.

Gray, who had the same photo in the deep recesses of his wallet, declined.

On the way back to Richmond, he thought about what might have been. He and Hannah had talked about kids, but they never got around to actually making any. She was still on the pill when they split. Over the years, he had thought from time to time about this missing part of his life, but he put it off, the way he put off marrying again. He wondered, while stuck in traffic on I-95, if he hadn't just decided unconsciously to put life on hold a long time ago. He let himself think, as much as he could bear, on that alternative life, the one where Annie Lineberger tells him she's late and they do something about it, together, either get married far too young or at least share in the anguish she was prepared to go through without him in that Richmond hospital.

He glanced at the SUV in the next lane as traffic crept along. He saw a young girl staring over at him, and he realized that he was crying.

THE WOMAN in the DA's office tells Gray what he expects to hear. There was hair among Annie's bones, and it matched Bobby Wayne Hill's. In the struggle, she might have grabbed some of it in her hands as she tried to fend him off. No one will ever know.

"Mr. Grimes wanted me to tell you that we are dropping all charges against you immediately."

Gray wishes that the DA had had the grace to make the call himself, but he can imagine that he is busy trying to spin what happened into a positive for Byrd County and for him, with reelection looming.

He calls Marcus Green and gives him the good news.

"Next thing," the lawyer says, "is we file the biggest lawsuit in the history of the world. Forty-eight years of being wrongfully suspected of the murder of the girl he loved. You're going to be a rich man, Mr. Melvin."

Gray tells him he doesn't think so. He can't make Green understand that he wants nothing now so much as to never hear about 1968 or Byrd County ever again.

Green says he'll get over it, as soon as he realizes just how much he can shake "that bastard DA and that redneck county" down for.

But Gray can't even work up much bile for Towson Grimes, and he wonders what exactly the man did wrong, other than be a self-serving publicity hound trying to get reelected.

It's just that, well, an apology would have been nice.

"You'll change your mind," Marcus Green says as he hangs up. "At least let me sue 'em for enough to pay your hard-working team of lawyers."

Gray says he'll think about it, just to get him off the phone.

He calls Betsy at work to tell her. She says she can't get away until her shift is over, but that she will be bringing champagne when she comes.

Before he can make another call, Willie Black calls him. The DA didn't waste any time holding a press conference, and Willie, who listened in on the conference call, gives Gray the particulars of it, mostly centering on how the district attorney's office, not willing to accept the obvious answer to who killed Annie Lineberger, kept at it tenaciously until finally the truth emerged.

"Jesus Christ," is Gray's response.

"Yeah, well, anybody who can read knows what a bunch of bullshit that is, and we'll remind 'em of it big time tomorrow. Whoever's running against that guy for DA must be whistling a happy damn tune right now."

Gray thinks that maybe a big-ass lawsuit wouldn't be such a bad idea after all.

CHAPTER TWENTY-SIX

JUNE 11

Betsy nudges me awake, deleting my dream.

She leans down and kisses my cheek.

"Better get up," she says. "They're going to be here in less than an hour."

I rise from my nap and try to shake out the cobwebs. Already the dream has receded almost out of sight. There's no sense telling Betsy what it was about.

Annie Lineberger has long since ceased to be a real person to me. What remains is something I can't quite explain. I don't go to church, but what I feel makes me think there is something out there, something beyond what you can see and touch and rationalize.

I have been more open with Betsy than I ever had been before about Annie. It was so long ago, I told her, when I told her most of the whole story. I lied that I didn't think it was worth mentioning.

But, with my second wedding on the horizon, it seemed like full disclosure was appropriate.

"Well," she said, "just as long as I'm not competing with a ghost. Ghosts are hard things to beat."

I assured her that there was no competition, that she had won the dubious booby prize of James Grayson Melvin.

The dean of the community college from which I was so recently divorced called and said I was welcome to come back for the fall semester. I am forgiven, it seems, for being a murder suspect. I didn't tell my erstwhile friend to go fuck himself, only silently gave him the finger while telling him that I was pursuing other options.

I haven't heard from Hayden Tremain Lineberger III and don't expect to. He is not, in my experience, a man to own up to his mistakes. Plus it has to be hard to get out of the habit of hating me.

Kaycee phoned the day after I got the news from Byrd County. I should have called her, she admonished me. She said her daughter had come home from out west, and we soon were off on the next chapter of her and Krystal's mother-daughter Texas death match. Frankly I was glad to turn the subject away from me.

Before she hung up, she told me that everybody in East Geddie was happy that everything had turned out so well for me, and that they knew I never could have done such a terrible thing.

I told her it was good to know I'd had their confidence all along.

THE BIG event from which Betsy disturbed my afternoon nap is what you might call a homecoming party. I haven't been gone that long, but I guess part of the impetus for this shindig is the knowledge that most of the folks coming today probably thought they might never see me again unless they visited me in prison, which I surmise most of them were unlikely to do.

I guess you'd have to call it a not-going-away party.

The guests start arriving, solo or in couples. They, like most of the people who have conversed with me lately, seem not to know what to say.

"Welcome back." "We're so glad it all worked out." About as far as anybody goes toward acknowledging what just happened is, "We knew you'd be exonerated."

Willie and Cindy Black come, as does Marcus Green. I am surprised that his partner, Kate Ellis, Willie's third wife, accompanies him. She and Cindy seem to get along fine, and when I mention this to Cindy, she whispers, "She's still our landlady. I have to be nice to her."

A gaggle of friends of mine and Betsy come, although a good half of the invitees didn't. I think that half has been marked off Betsy's Christmas card list. Some of the neighbors drop by. One old gentleman, must be in his eighties, takes me aside and says, wheezily conspiratorial, "I heard you're going to make her an honest woman."

I told him I couldn't make her more honest or better than she is already, that maybe she would make me an honest man.

At some point, I am able to slip away into the den, where, mercifully, no one is present except Josh. He's watching a baseball game on Fox. There is nobody within thirty years of his age at this party. He's sitting on the ottoman and scoots over when I drop down beside him.

We watch for a few minutes, and when the inning ends, I ask him if he doesn't think baseball is a little boring.

He looks at me like I'm crazy.

"No!" he says, looking up at me. "Baseball's great. Soccer's boring."

He's at that marvelous age, before he gets too cool, too testosterone-distracted, to think baseball's a drag. I could tell him, but don't, that he probably will abandon baseball for a time, but that he will come back to it later, when he learns patience and starts finding gray hair in his comb, and that baseball will forgive him for his temporary abandonment.

I've been helping coach his Little League team, mostly hitting grounders to the infielders and fly balls to the outfielders and helping pay for the pizza afterward. This is my second year, and although I did have a prolonged absence from the Tigers' bench this season, all the boys seem happy to have me back. Unlike the adults, they don't dance around the big issues.

"My dad said you killed somebody," one red-haired eleven-year-old said to me the first game I came back, "but then he said you didn't."

I tell the kid that's about right.

After a while, I figure I'd better get back to my guests, although I'd be just as happy if they threw a really nice party for me in my absence, like a good Irish wake.

"Come back and watch the rest of it with me," Josh says. I promise that I will, as soon as the guests leave.

The thing is, I've got it good. Unlike Annie, I have had forty-eight good years to walk the Earth, breathe the spring air, smell steaks on the grill, sit and watch a baseball game with a boy who seems to enjoy my company.

I have no legitimate complaints. I have told Marcus Green that he is free to sue the pants, or at least the socks, off Towson Grimes and the county he represents at least until Election Day. But he's only allowed to sue for enough to pay his expenses. I want the same thing Annie got: nothing. And Betsy, to her credit, is not even hinting that she might like to be the recipient of some of the court's largesse.

"We're happy," she told me. "A few million isn't going to make us more happy."

But I do think of Annie. I'm glad they found her sad remains. That dream, the one Betsy woke me from, was about Annie. I didn't tell her, the same way I didn't tell her about the future child Annie was carrying.

I reach in my back pocket as I leave Josh to his game, before heading back to my party. In the rear of one of the compartments of my wallet, I pull out that worn photograph, as ravaged by age as Annie herself would have been by now. I showed it to Betsy in my full-disclosure mode. She said Annie was certainly a pretty girl. She didn't say anything else when I put it back in my wallet.

I should throw it away, dispense with it as cavalierly as Winston Keppler was willing to give up his copy.

Maybe I will.

But not just yet.